The Medici Emerald

THE
MEDICI EMERALD

by

Martin Woodhouse

and

Robert Ross

E. P. Dutton & Co., Inc. · New York

The Medici Emerald was first published in 1976 by
Hodder & Stoughton of London, England.

First American Edition
10 9 8 7 6 5 4 3 2 1

Library of Congress Catalog Card Number: 76-11873

ISBN: 0-525-15458-2

One

From the private diaries of Cardinal Domenico della Palla, Apostolic Chancellor to the Church at Rome, August 1478:

Our Almighty Father in Heaven knows how many years have passed since I gave up the belief that my Office, the most powerful in the world, could by the use of that power bring peace to the Christian world, or even to Italy; and He knows, too, how badly our City-States need such a peace, if only to prepare against the Turks. We shall see no such peace in my lifetime.

Why does Rome herself, for example, pursue her quarrel with the Republic of Florence? Here is futility enough, in all conscience. Our Holy Father Pope Sixtus, together with his nephew Girolamo Riario, Count of Imola and Captain-General of Rome's armies, may believe Florence endangers us. I do not. Lorenzo de' Medici rules Florence, and does so well enough. It is we who provoke Lorenzo, and to what end? For the sake of earthly dominion and Rome's territorial ambitions, I dare say. As Apostolic Chancellor, I do not feel obliged to consider such trifles; are not all men one in Christ, and is not that sufficient?

As for Florence's young artist and engineer, Leonardo da Vinci, history will take better note of him than I can, if he lives long enough to enter history's pages. It seems improbable that he will do so. He is an irritant, and possibly a heretic. He has come to see me twice this summer. I record the fact, as I record also the fact that I was sorry to see him go. If he continues to interfere in the

5

snarling wars between our City-States, then he and the Florentine gunners he has taken as friends will need a greater protection than mine.

*

Rigo Leone, Captain-Gunner to the Medici, cursed furiously as the sword-edge bit deeply into the muscle of his right shoulder. But he had now gained the advantage he had striven for and, stepping inside his assailant's blade, he swung the rock-like fist that gripped his own weapon and clubbed the assassin to the ground. As the man lay there, gasping for breath in the mud, Rigo wasted no time. He sprang into the air and came down with knees bent, dropping his full weight into his adversary's spine, which broke with a dull crack. Gunners were, by nature and training, street-fighters.

He heaved himself to his feet and turned. Three of their ambushers now lay dead on the sodden road, sprawled in the attitudes of violent death. Two remained. They had redoubled their assault, backing Leonardo da Vinci step by step to the trunk of a roadside tree. There, he was holding both of them coolly at bay, a stiletto flickering delicate as a serpent's tongue in his right hand, while in his left his rapier darted and parried.

Rigo covered the intervening ground in a lurching, awkward trot and hacked down the nearer of Leonardo's attackers with a vicious, back-handed slash. At the same moment Leonardo met the other man's last desperate lunge, deflected the blade with his sword, and lifted the stiletto fractionally, centring it. Unable to halt his own momentum, the artist's would-be killer watched in brief horror as eight inches of wrought steel slid smoothly into his chest. He sank to his knees, eyes fixed on the protruding hilt.

Leonardo absorbed the scene with a sweeping glance: four enemies dead, one dying; Rigo Leone, a hand clamped to his shoulder, blood spreading slowly from beneath his palm. He dropped his remaining weapon to kneel by his dying foe, taking the man's weight in the crook of one arm and lowering him carefully to the sodden earth.

'Your wine-flask, Rigo,' he said quietly. The dying man drank,

6

coughing, and nodded in gratitude. His breath bubbling with the effort, he raised a hand towards his chest, touching the pommel of Leonardo's dagger.

'I am sorry,' Leonardo told him. 'If I pull it out, your lungs will but fill with blood the faster.'

'Then I am a dead man.'

Leonardo nodded soberly. 'Why?' he asked. 'We are harmless travellers. Nor are we rich enough to rob. Why did you and your companions set upon us?'

The assassin coughed again, painfully. 'Dead, you were worth a thousand gold florins to each of us, da Vinci. Rome . . . the Count Girolamo Riario . . .'

'What of him?'

'He gave us the first one hundred . . . and promised us nine hundred more when we returned,' the man replied. A bitter and fleeting smile wrenched at his lips. 'He should have told us . . . that you fight as well with either hand. He should . . .' Air rasped in his throat, and a gout of blood welled from the corner of his mouth, dripping down his chin. He died then, staring at the hilt of the knife beside his breastbone.

'Dog,' said Rigo dispassionately. Intercepting Leonardo's glance, he added, 'Not him, poor fool. It is Count Girolamo Riario I mean.'

Leonardo rose and busied himself. There were five bodies to lay by the roadside, and Rigo's arm to be supported by a rough sling about his neck; there were weapons to clean, and their horses—now grazing quietly in a glade some distance away—to be retrieved. Mounted at last, they began to move off through the little copse and past the stretch of dense bush where their ambushers had hidden. The mist turned to rain, chilling the early summer air. Leonardo pulled his mount to a halt after twenty paces, and turned in the saddle to survey the scene once again. His gaze roved slowly across the bodies by the track, and the streaks of blood that caked the trodden mire; took in the grey banners of fog drifting in the breeze, and lifted to the shrouded hills beyond. In his leather-bound notebook, appended as ever to his waist by

7

its light chain, he sketched rapidly, his right hand gliding over the page.

'Messer Artist!' Rigo Leone's voice was thin with irritation. 'I am wet, sir. Also, I bleed, though this is but light matter. More importantly, I confess to a thirst, and—thanks to your peculiar charity—no wine remains in my flask. An hour's ride from here lies a village, and a tavern; will you make your little pictures there, if you please?'

Leonardo smiled and closed his notebook.

'In the tavern, friend Rigo, I can only make pictures of a tavern. I need to remember this, and so may you, one day.' He clucked his horse into movement and Rigo followed, wincing as he slapped the reins.

'I shall need no picture to help my memory,' he pointed out, 'since I shall be carrying Riario's scar. It is one more debt I owe Rome's Captain-General. By God, Leonardo, I had not thought him so persistent: Five thousand florins. Well. It is a fair price, no doubt, for Italy's finest gunner and an artist-engineer who fights with either hand—or with both at once. I wish I had this trick of yours, I confess. If I had, I might not be wounded now.'

'It may be learned,' said Leonardo.

'Say you so? Then you were taught a useful lesson.'

'I was not taught,' Leonardo said. 'I was born with this skill, to my good fortune. Yet . . . it might be taught, for all that. If you are serious in your wish, then tie your right arm to your side—or carry it in a sling, perhaps, as now—and use only your left. Its muscles will then learn to do what those of your right arm do now by habit, since muscles, I believe, have their own kind of memory.'

They rode in silence while Rigo considered this.

'I will do it,' he said finally. 'Although I do not understand this talk of muscles and their memory, which seems to me to belong to the mind. No matter. When we are next attacked it may be that we shall fight with four blades between us.'

Leonardo lifted an eyebrow. 'When?' he said. '*When* we are attacked? Such certainty, Rigo?'

The gunner spat. 'Rome and her Captain-General have placed

8

five thousand florins on your head,' he replied, 'with or without mine as a bonus. Since Girolamo Riario has spent but five hundred thus far, being a prudent man, he has enough still in his purse to buy himself another attempt. The question remains only of when.'

'A sound analysis.'

'And, if it comes to that, of *where*,' added Rigo. 'Can your damned sketches tell you that?'

'No,' said Leonardo equably. 'But if a man knew where he would fall, there would he first place his carpet.'

They came, in good time, to the crest of a low rise where, below and along the curving sides of the road, could be seen the clustered dwellings of the village of Grino. Neither mist nor rain had abated, and dusk was beginning to draw in.

By now in foul temper, Rigo surveyed the lights of the small community ahead of them.

'I would to God I had stayed in Florence,' he said, 'where I might even now be dry-clad and with wine in my belly. I have much to thank you for, Leonardo!'

'I did not ask you to come with me,' the artist pointed out, 'though I am glad of your company. Your wound hurts still?'

'Only with each movement of my horse,' the gunner replied acidly, urging his mount downhill. 'The wound I can bear, I thank you. It is the thought of riding to Rome, and thus directly into the arms of Riario, that troubles me. Why do we ride for Rome, in any case? In Florence, before we left, did you not say to Lorenzo de' Medici that you were bound for Milan?'

'So I did.'

'Then here is folly. Look you, artist, Milan is the most comfortable of cities. I have lived there. I learned my gunner's trade there. Milan is pleasant, entertaining and safe.'

'All of that,' said Leonardo agreeably.

'Then why, in the name of heaven, are we riding south to Rome rather than northward to Milan?' Rigo demanded. 'I have lost a piece of my arm in Rome's countryside; what am I likely to lose in the city?'

9

'And, more than that, how will you explain matters to Lorenzo de' Medici?' asked Leonardo in the blandest of tones.

'How indeed? Though,' Rigo added hastily, 'I do not know what you may mean by that.'

'Rigo, Rigo,' laughed the artist, 'we have fought through the campaign for Castelmonte together, you and I. Together we defeated Rome. Therefore who should know better than I that it is not the idea of a fight or two that sticks in your throat? Did not Lorenzo order you to keep track of me? Confess it, Rigo. The plain truth is that you are unfitted by temperament for spying, and that you enjoy being Lorenzo's leash no more that I enjoy— or intend to endure—being his dog. Well?'

Rigo made no reply to this, but turned his mount to follow Leonardo into the modest yard that fronted Grino's solitary tavern. A young lad came out to hold their horses' heads and to bid them both a cheerful welcome. Dismounting swiftly, Leonardo reached up to support Rigo as the latter slid, gasping, from his saddle.

'Come, my friend,' Leonardo said. 'You have lost some blood, and if the woman of this house has a serviceable needle and some thread, we will close up this cut of yours so that you lose no more.'

'First,' said Rigo firmly, 'a bottle of wine.'

'Oh, by all means. First things first.'

Holding the eye of the long needle between his fingertips, Leonardo da Vinci rotated its point slowly in the candle's flame while it grew red. It hissed briefly as he dipped it into one of the two small cups of wine that stood on the table. Rigo Leone watched these preparations warily.

'Hot needles?' he said. 'I like not the look of this. And why your wine?'

'I cannot say, my friend,' said Leonardo. 'A surgeon taught me so: one cup for the needle, the other for the threads.' He fished one out with the needle's tip and threaded it deftly. 'But he could not tell me why, though I asked him, even as you have asked. He was a Turk; a pleasant and learned man.'

'A Turk? I like it less and less,' announced Rigo. His eyes fixed on the needle, he tilted his wine-bottle and took several deep swallows. 'Do it, then,' he said. 'Though I would rather fight than watch your surgery.'

'You have no need to watch.' Leonardo moved behind his patient and gently but firmly pressed the lips of the wound together, slipping the needle and thread deep under the cut and forcing it out through the skin at the other side. Rigo, his head averted, affected not to notice this procedure. He lifted the leather bottle to drink again, and hiccupped.

'God bless wine,' he intoned. 'Six or eight more flasks of it, and I may even survive our stay in Rome.'

Leonardo tightened a knot. 'We shall be in Rome only briefly,' he said. 'In fact, our visit will be both short and secret.' He paused, thrusting the needle yet again through skin and flesh. 'We are bound for Malta,' he said.

Rigo set the wine bottle down cautiously.

'Malta?' he said. 'Malta is the end of the earth. What of the lady Bianca Visconti?'

'What of her?'

'She is in Florence, which is a long way from Malta,' Rigo said. 'That is what.'

'Well?' asked Leonardo.

'When a man is in love . . .' Rigo said.

Leonardo's fingers hesitated. 'I?' he said. 'In love?'

'Why, man, it hangs on your face like the sign on this tavern,' said Rigo with an air of triumph. He drank once more, and belched loudly. 'Furthermore,' he asserted, 'there are worse things to Malta than its distance from the lady Bianca. It is full of men burned black by the heat of the sun, who eat one another. Did you know that? I had it from a sailor in Livorno. They are called by a long and tongue-wrenching name, which I cannot recall for the moment.'

'Anthropophagi,' said Leonardo.

'That was it. Or something like it. Therefore——'

'And they dwell in Africa, not Malta,' continued Leonardo, 'if

11

they dwell anywhere at all.' He tied off the final knot and inspected his handiwork closely. 'It will heal cleanly,' he said. 'I have a silk in my saddle-bag to cover it, and another to serve as a sling. Oblige me by refraining from moving your arm too violently, my friend, or the stitches will tear out.'

From the depths of his bag Leonardo extracted the two squares of cloth and, after a long moment, a neatly folded letter which he laid upon the table. Seating himself on a footstool facing the gunner, he wrapped one of the silks tightly around the wound and pleated the other diagonally, a thoughtful look upon his face. Then he picked up the letter and tapped it slowly against the tips of his fingers.

'Listen,' he said at last. 'It is true that I did not leave the lady Bianca happily; when you say that I love her, you have the right of it. Yet, when this letter came to me in Florence some weeks ago ... we have shared much, Rigo, you and I, and it seems likely that we shall share more. Let me, then, whet the edge of your curiosity, at least.' He unfolded the letter and read it aloud, slowly:

'To Leonardo da Vinci from his friend, Felippo Mendoza, also of Vinci, Greetings: From my ship *Pyramus* at anchor in Malta I write; come quickly for I am in danger and need your help. Venice seeks my secret and, it may be, my life. Only remember the day we talked in Beppo's orchard at Anchiano when we were twelve; and make haste to see your friend Felippo who is called *Il Fortunato*.'

Rigo was leaning forward. 'And is that all?' he demanded. He pointed with his left forefinger to the very foot of the sheet of parchment. 'What are these words here?'

The phrase he indicated was written in bold characters, set apart from the body of the letter itself. It read: **PEREVNT ET IMPVTANTVR.**

'It is but a tag in dog Latin,' said Leonardo carelessly.

'Indeed. With what meaning?'

'All in good time, Rigo. I promised only to whet your curiosity, not to satisfy it.'

'By which I take it,' said Rigo shrewdly, 'that you do not understand its import yourself.'

'Perhaps not altogether,' agreed Leonardo, smiling faintly. 'However, I shall find out what it means in Malta; and so will you, if you decide to stay with me.'

The voice of Pope Sixtus IV shook with pious outrage.

'These Florentine dogs! They have hanged our archbishop designate by the neck like a common thief!'

'True, Your Holiness,' agreed Girolamo Riario. 'Rome talks of little else. And yet it was a small loss, surely? Francesco Salviati was a poor creature, when all is said, and unworthy of your favour. Calm yourself, I pray you. Your Holiness is not without power of your own.'

'Quite so,' said Sixtus IV, recovering some semblance of poise. 'These Medici attacked and seized our fortress at Castelmonte; they have murdered our archbishop; they protect our foes, detain our convoys, humiliate our emissaries, thwart our purpose at every turn. Well, we shall see. We will declare Lorenzo de' Medici excommunicate, and if Florence will not deliver him into our hands for judgment, then I shall extend our interdict to his entire city.'

Rome's Supreme Pontiff and her Captain-General were sitting together in one of the new small reading rooms of the Papal Palace, the *Bibliotheca Secreta*, which flanked the great gallery of the library itself. By unspoken consent they often met here, since high windows and thick stone walls provided a secrecy rare in Rome. Wainscoting of finest English oak lined the sides of the room; cabinets picked out in gilt preserved the ancient documents which it had been built to house. In the free spaces above these, Melozzo had painted stately frescoes in *chiaroscuro*. It was a room which, expressing both wealth and a discreet power, gave Pope Sixtus considerable pleasure.

'Very well,' said Count Girolamo Riario. 'A few ornate words of damnation, and your Papal Bull may serve our designs. I approve.'

Sixtus lifted his head slowly, his jowled face reddening.

13

'We seek none of your approval,' he said, staring at the Count with open distaste. 'I suffer your insolence from time to time, Girolamo, since I have need of you. Yet I advise you to grow less free with it.'

'I apologise to Your Holiness, naturally,' Riario said, his voice still negligent. 'And where have you need of my services now?'

'In Venice. Our negotiations for alliance with Ferrante of Naples are almost complete. You are Captain-General of Rome's armies. It is your task, therefore, to set Venice at the Medici's backs while Ferrante groups his forces for an assault from the south. These are diplomatic matters, nephew. I trust you feel able to handle them.'

' "Nephew?" I think,' said Girolamo, 'that I prefer to be addressed as your son, though it is but a custom and therefore,' he grinned bitterly, 'a trifle.'

Sixtus shifted uneasily in his ebony chair. I have accepted and shaped a weapon for Rome, he thought, and my grasp upon it fails; and what now? He glanced upwards, involuntarily. The Melozzo painting had been a mistake; the paternal resemblance between the Pope and his four 'nephews' was already too notorious to confirm by having the panel destroyed. He rallied firmly.

'You interrupt me, nephew. I was about to add that since you failed to distinguish yourself at Castelmonte'—here Girolamo's countenance darkened angrily—'you might approach Venice with your overbearing conceit less in evidence. One dare not hope for humility, but perhaps you will exercise a decent restraint. Is that clear?'

Girolamo Riario looked the Supreme Pontiff in the eyes.

'As Your Holiness commands,' he said. 'For so long as Your Holiness lives, I exist but to serve you, and Rome. In connection with the unfortunate Castelmonte affair, it may interest Your Holiness to know that your balance sheet shows one small item of profit. I have trimmed a weed for you.'

'Speak plainly,' said Sixtus.

'The painter who turned Medici engineer,' said Girolamo. 'Leonardo da Vinci. He, at least, will interfere with Rome's designs—and your own—no further. He crossed me at Castelmonte; he will not do so again. He is dead.'

'It would have been better,' said Sixtus, 'had he been persuaded to enter our service.'

'No,' said the Count flatly. His gaze was withdrawn and baleful.

The Pontiff rose abruptly, ending the audience. 'Go with God, my son,' he said. 'Serve us in Venice. And learn obedience.'

'Who will teach it to me, I wonder?' Girolamo Riario bent his narrow head swiftly to the papal ring, turned, and left the room.

A mile or so away, Rigo stifled the father of all yawns. Circumspectly, he scratched at his healing wound. The stitches were out at last and—as Leonardo had accurately prophesied—it itched like the very devil. Idly, his mind afloat as he stood by the doorway, he followed the sound of the Cardinal's voice questioning, the soft tones of Leonardo in answer.

A most impressive man, this Cardinal Domenico della Palla, Rigo mused. There were good lines in his face, though it was somewhat stern and ascetic. No plump churchman here. The Cardinal looked lean and hard. Fifteen years younger and he would have made a useful gunner. The thought startled Rigo and he straightened, almost guiltily. The discourse, he realised, had suddenly taken a more practical turn.

'This Office has laws, my son,' the Cardinal was saying, 'since without laws there can be no discipline, and through lack of discipline souls are lost. Do you understand me?' Wisdom, of a sort, thought Rigo; I could not captain my gunners without discipline.

Leonardo, however, was shaking his head.

'My laws, your Eminence, are solely those which are presented to me by the facts,' he said, 'since without facts there can be no truth, and without truth souls are liable to be lost just as surely.'

'No doubt,' replied della Palla with some asperity. 'Let us, therefore, consider duty. The Apostolic Chancery acknowledges duties, if you do not. And as Chancellor, my duty here and now should be to summon my Swiss guards. Your presence here, Messer Leonardo, may compromise me; be sure that it endangers you.'

'Just so,' Rigo put in. 'Rome is dangerous. So I warned him. But he is stubborn, Eminence.'

The greying Cardinal smiled fleetingly. 'You have no need to tell me,' he said. 'Do I not know it well, from personal experience?' He turned back to Leonardo. 'Speak, then, my son. My guards can wait awhile.'

From a pocket in his tunic Leonardo took out a small notebook, which he placed on the desk. 'There rests the fulfilment of my pledge to Rome, and to yourself, your Eminence,' he said.

'What pledge is this?' demanded Rigo from the doorway.

'A promise made before the siege of Castelmonte,' Leonardo replied. 'Your Eminence recalls it, no doubt?' Cardinal della Palla nodded, and Leonardo pointed at the notebook. 'There lies all I have discovered of guns and gunnery,' he went on. 'My designs for the Medici Gun in every particular; notes of nine recipes for gunpowder, a system for the burnishing of cannon balls, the drawings for my range-finding and sighting inventions, the calculations for each experiment I have performed.' He swung round to face Rigo Leone, whose jaw had fallen in outraged shock. 'Peace, good Rigo,' he said. 'We are not here to become gunners to Rome, however it may appear.'

'Lorenzo de' Medici will be glad to hear it,' said Rigo shortly.

'Lorenzo has his end of the bargain,' replied Leonardo. 'I promised him the citadel of Castelmonte. We took it from Rome, you and I, and gave it to him. I could not have devised the means to do so without the help of Rome's own Apostolic Chancery and its archives, and therefore I must pay my debts, as must all men. We came here to do so.'

'And also to bargain?' said the Cardinal.

'And perhaps, to bargain.'

'Very well,' said Cardinal della Palla. 'Your pledge stands redeemed. You are in no danger from me.'

'Why, as to that,' responded Leonardo, 'I never supposed that we were. Did you really intend to call your guards, Eminence? Not for an instant. There is more bargaining yet to come.'

Rigo Leone had by this time recomposed his features. 'Forgive him, Eminence,' he said wearily. 'If he will not thank you, then let me do so—for both of us.'

'We bear a like burden, it seems, Captain Leone,' said della Palla dryly, 'which is the preservation of Messer Leonardo from the consequences of his own rashness. It may yet prove a profitless task.' He picked up the notebook. 'What is the remainder of your price?' he asked the artist.

'I should like,' Leonardo said, 'to study the *Ephemerides* of Archbishop Regiomontanus.'

'The movements of celestial bodies?' Cardinal della Palla's eyebrows lifted minutely. 'A large leap here, surely; from guns to stars?'

'Perhaps,' agreed Leonardo. 'And yet, the leap is not so great as you might suppose.'

Some three quarters of an hour later, Rigo stood in front of a folding table, set against the outside of the wall surrounding the Lateran Palace.

'*I write in code, Magnifico,*' he dictated, '*to confuse unfriendly eyes. We go not north to M ... but first to R ... where we now lie ... and later southward to M ... Il F sent a letter to L from M which is why we go there. The Roman pig Girolamo has tried yet again for our lives, Magnifico. Praise be to God that we are safe ... yet islands are safer still, I think, for which also I give thanks. In your service, as always, I remain ... RL.*'

The gunner heaved a sigh of relief. 'Done,' he said. 'You have it all?'

'Yes, sir.' From his first copy the young scrivener read the message back to Rigo, word by word, letter by incomprehensible letter. Rigo was vastly pleased.

'Excellent work, fellow,' he said. 'Now make me your fair copy and tell me what I owe you. It may surprise you to learn that this has been my first business conducted in writing. What do you think of that?'

'You amaze me indeed, sir.'

'It seems simple enough, I admit.'

'You have no small talent for it, sir,' the clerk said with quite unperceived irony. Pocketing his fee, he thoughtfully studied the gunner's broad and retreating back until the latter was out of sight.

By private messenger from the Medici bank in Rome, Rigo's letter arrived safely at its destination, seven days later. It was delivered—as Rigo ordered—to none other than Lorenzo de' Medici himself, in his secluded courtyard-garden.

At twenty-nine, the ruler of the proud and free Republic of Florence was already widely loved. Seeming in his appearance both ageless and changeless, he guided the fortunes of the Republic as he guided his network of potent banking houses; in modesty, with common sense, and through the exercise of an utterly realistic mind. Never, said his people, was he seen to lose his serene composure nor heard to raise his voice in boast or anger. Lorenzo's grief upon the recent death of his younger brother Giuliano, murdered by Rome and the Pazzi family, had been expressed in private. His rage upon the battlefield at Castelmonte, if terrible, had been deadly in its restraint. His justice had been swift, and he had emerged from the tragedy and the triumph with a scarred neck and a temperament as clear as before. Florentines loved him for his habit of walking through their narrow streets, pausing here and there to talk easily with them. What other ruler, they asked each other, came down to play with their children at the first snowfall, as Lorenzo did?

He sat, now, upon a stone bench beside a pond wherein golden fishes swam languidly. Beside him was his ward and favourite, the lady Bianca Maria Visconti, her young head bent close to his own as, together, they struggled to make sense of Rigo Leone's attempts at code.

' "*North to M*," ' read Lorenzo, 'will signify Milan, whither our Leonardo was to have travelled and—impertinently—did not.'

His ward nodded her agreement. 'And since your courier came from Rome, it follows that this "*R*",' she pointed, 'means that they are also in Rome. And from Rome they are going to travel to . . . where does he write it? "*South to M*." Another "*M*"?'

'Not Modena or Mantova, then,' Lorenzo said, 'they being to Rome's north. Malfi, perhaps? Pest! There is half Italy and more to the south of Rome. I am beginning to think Captain Leone a trifle over-subtle.'

'Yet see,' Bianca pointed out. ' "*Islands are safer*," he writes.'

Lorenzo considered for a moment.

'Malta,' he said. 'But why? And furthermore, who in the devil's name is this "*Il F*"?'

'I know not, sir, and neither do I care. No more should you. What matter it, so long as they are safe?'

'It matters to me, since I have Florence in my care,' said Lorenzo de' Medici, tapping the letter on her knee. 'Consider: your Leonardo and my Captain-Gunner saved Florence for me at Castelmonte. Florence may need them both—and soon—to save her again. While my alliances melt away, be sure that Sixtus is making new ones against us. Because I made so bold as to defend myself when the Pazzi sought my life not six weeks since, I am excommunicated. So my agents tell me, and I believe them. It is but a shot in a long war. I must rely on men who are tested. My engineer, Leonardo da Vinci, for one. Rigo Leone, for another. In Milan they would have been near at hand; but in Malta? Malta is very far, Bianca. Will I find them there when Florence needs them?'

'Yes, sire, you will.'

Lorenzo studied her shining face for a long moment and smiled ruefully. 'I wish I had your confidence,' he said. 'Find them? I think I have already lost Leonardo, at least. To you, child, as I have lost you to him.'

'What nonsense is this from Florence's most wise ruler?' Bianca responded. 'You have lost neither of us. I love you both, and dearly.'

'Though not in the same fashion, I will venture,' said Lorenzo dryly. Bianca coloured, but upon seeing that he still smiled at her, she kissed him soundly on the cheek before going to kneel beside the pool.

Girolamo Riario, Count and Protector of Bosco and Imola and Rome's Captain-General, sat behind his desk of varnished pine and listened attentively to the youth—a distant kinsman—who was twisting his soft cap nervously between his fingers as he told his story. Before the count lay a single piece of paper; he glanced at this now and again, his face neutral.

The young man was by trade a scrivener.

Riario heard him out.

'You have done well, cousin,' he said finally, 'save that you have been over-long in bringing this matter to my attention. Why?'

'Noble sir,' began the youth hesitantly, 'I ask pardon. I . . . that is, I spent many hours in thought before . . . to be plain, sire, there is a most offensive reference to yourself—if it be yourself, as I believe—contained in what I have set before you, and . . .'

Since he needed information, Riario set himself to be charming.

'You feared my wrath?' he said. 'Come, come. Rest easy, cousin. A man in my position makes enemies. They are sometimes offensive. What of it? Your assessment is undoubtedly correct. He was from Florence? You feel sure of this?'

'Sire, I would swear to it. A Florentine by his accent, and a soldier from his bearing. The letter is clearly meant for Lorenzo de' Medici.'

'Quite so. Describe him again.'

'Below middling height, my lord, and broad as a bear. Forty years of age, at a venture. Dark-haired, and with gunpowder stains at his wrists and his neck.'

'Good,' said the Count. 'And he was alone?'

'While he dictated his letter to me, sire, yes. Before that I noticed him talking with a companion, a younger and taller man of slim address, handsome, fair-skinned, with hair between brown and gold; well dressed, though serviceably, and cheerful of demeanour.'

'Very good indeed. Nothing else?'

'He had a book at his waist, on a chain, sire.'

'Excellent! It was well observed, cousin. Would you know both of them again?'

'Beyond doubt.'

The Count of Imola surveyed his young informant with the benevolent grin of a sated wolf. 'Your eyes have served me well,' he said, 'and have thereby earned you ten ducats. They may earn you forty more, if you follow my instructions.'

'Brief, and secret!' said Rigo the following day. 'In Grino you told me so, nor shall you deny it. And what is the result? For a week and more we march to and fro across Rome for all the world to see. Pah!'

'We are in little danger,' said Leonardo.

'We are in constant danger, so spare me your bravado. And for the sake of a book filled with figures? It passes belief.'

'Why, then,' Leonardo said, 'engineering is a hazardous pursuit, as you were the first to point out to me at Castelmonte last year.'

'But I am not an engineer,' Rigo argued.

'You are. Gunnery is engineering; therefore bear the trials of science with patience and fortitude,' advised Leonardo. More seriously, he added, 'I must study the *Ephemerides*, Rigo, before we go to Malta, and the figures and conclusions they hold cannot be grasped in a day. But we are almost done, I promise you.'

They began to mount the steps that led to the entrance gates of the Apostolic Chancery. Absorbed in argument, they did not look about them, or they might have seen a young scrivener, his folded table and chair clamped awkwardly under either arm, staring at them as they passed between the high portals.

'And what the devil are these *Ephemerides*, in any case?' Rigo demanded.

'They are tables of stars and planets, for navigators.'

'Who are likewise engineers, I make no doubt.'

'Very true,' Leonardo agreed.

The scrivener watched them until he had satisfied himself which of the buildings they were about to enter, and then scurried across the square to the headquarters of the Swiss Guard.

'I come on the orders of the Captain-General,' he announced to the nearest man-at-arms. 'Summon me your commander, and make haste! There are murderers at large in the Chancery itself!'

The corridors and chambers of the Apostolic Chancery, at once Rome's repository of learning and the seat of Cardinal Domenico della Palla's power, were—it must be said—a most unseemly refuge for murderers. The generously-vaulted hall which occupied the greater part of its ground floor housed row upon row of shelves and cabinets wherein were contained the archives of Holy Mother Church in all her recorded wisdom, or such at least of her wisdom as might be considered acceptable for study by the commonalty of clerics. To this hall, accordingly, came students, priests, and approved members of the laity, as to a library. It was a place for whispered discourse, the soft brushing of dust from parchment and leather, and the occasional crackle of a turned page.

Rigo Leone felt for it all the enthusiasm of a cornered fox for the canyon walls which confine him at bay.

Running down one side of the great hall and some fifteen feet above the level of its floor was a long gallery, reached by a series of narrow spiral staircases spaced at intervals along a supporting colonnade. Ascent of any one of these stairways brought one to the bookshelves of the gallery, and behind its carved rail one might proceed along it past the doors of several reading rooms reserved for visitors of privilege.

It was in one of these rooms that Leonardo da Vinci presently sat, the *Ephemerides* of Regiomontanus open in front of him and several other weighty volumes at either hand. He was writing placidly and with concentration.

A few paces away from him Rigo, as he had done every day for the past week, stood at the barely open door that gave onto the gallery and ranged a vigilant eye back and forth over the hall below him. His own interest in astronomy being non-existent, the fact that his companion had developed a passion for stars was, to the gunner, merely irritating. We are in a bottle, he thought for the hundredth time; let them cork it by closing the main doorway yonder at our left, and we are done.

And, even as he watched thus, and thought, it happened. He stiffened suddenly and turned his head, calling a low and urgent warning.

'Hssst! Leonardo! We have visitors. Seven of them . . . no, eight; Swiss guards, Messer Artist! Did I not tell you so ?'

He crossed the reading room and pulled at the handle of its opposite door, which was behind Leonardo and led to an interior corridor of the Chancery's upper floor. Opening it the smallest crack, he was in time to see a tall figure in officer's uniform knocking for admission to Cardinal della Palla's office, and to observe that the head of the main stairway was now held by three more Switzers.

The Swiss commander, for his part, did not catch sight of Rigo. He waved aside the ancient cleric who ushered him into the presence of the Apostolic Chancellor and strode forward, sword in hand.

'Your pardon, Eminence,' he said brusquely, 'but an urgent matter presses, and I must speak with you at once.'

Marking a line of text with his finger, the Cardinal inclined his head serenely. 'Then speak, my son.'

'Two men, Eminence, have been seen to enter the Chancery below; dangerous men and proscribed agents of Florence. With your consent, my men wait upon my orders to search this building.'

Cardinal della Palla looked at his drawn sword.

'And if you find them ?' he asked.

'Sir,' said the captain evasively, 'they are assassins, and Rome's enemies.'

'Nevertheless,' the Cardinal suggested, 'you will not, I trust, shed their blood here, or you will risk my extreme displeasure. Well. Since I see that you wear the badge of Rome's Captain-General, and your men are already here, let us consider that my consent has been sought and granted, good Captain.'

His irony was not lost upon the commander.

'My thanks, Eminence. I do but follow my orders.'

'Then proceed,' said Cardinal della Palla.

Rigo Leone, having returned to his original post overlooking the hall, watched the dispositions being made below him and reported them in hoarsely whispered alarm—an alarm which, so it appeared, he was having the greatest difficulty in communicating to Leonardo da Vinci.

'They wait for orders,' he said. He turned to find the artist still deep in study, writing industriously in one of his notebooks. 'Pikes,' he added. 'And here is their captain now. They are forming a rank across the hall, their halberds butt-to-point. Aha! I perceive their purpose ... they are making a barrier across the width of the room, and all must pass through it, one by one ...' He turned again. 'Sweet Jesus, man!' he said. '*Will you move?* These are Riario's guards, I doubt not!'

Leonardo rose slowly, in the manner of one who is loath to relinquish what he is doing, his eyes still scanning the columns of figures before him. He completed a line of writing while half standing. Then: 'What are their positions?' he enquired.

'Two men at the main doorway itself,' said Rigo. 'And four who make a fence with their weapons, some six paces within the hall. Bones of God!' he added, 'but yonder stands my little scrivener, conversing with their captain, which makes me the greater fool.'

A murmurous buzz of query and protest was beginning to arise from below.

'We have but one chance that I can see,' said Rigo, 'and a slim one at best. We can descend from this gallery by the farthest stairway and thus bypass their barrier of pikes—but what then?'

'Well concluded,' said Leonardo. He snapped his notebook shut and fastened it at his waist. Pulling a large and weighty tome from a shelf, he offered it to the gunner, who took it with the initial air of one humouring a lunatic. The artist selected one of equal size for himself, and thrust the *Ephemerides*—a smaller volume, though thick—inside his doublet.

24

'Onward, then,' he said. 'Slowly, but not furtively, my friend. We are innocent scholars, until fate decides otherwise.'

Rigo hesitated, and Leonardo pulled the gallery door open gently. Turning to his left, he began to walk the length of the gallery, ignoring the humming crescendo of clerical outrage from beneath them. As they passed directly above the line of halberdiers, he paused to tear a piece of flysheet from the massive book he held and to scribble on this, leaning it against the gallery wall for support.

No eye was as yet lifted to observe their passage overhead. Leonardo reached the head of the spiral staircase nearest to the hall doors, with Rigo at his heels. He buried his head behind his uplifted book in deep concentration, and began to descend as though oblivious to his surroundings.

He had reached the floor of the hall before one of the two guards at the door called him—and the gunner behind him—to halt.

'*Now*, Rigo!'

At once Leonardo sprang into motion, sprinting full tilt towards them. The remaining pikemen, their backs towards the doorway as they held their barrier against the press of scholars beyond, began to swing in confusion, but any intervention they might have made came too late. The scrivener, at the far side of the room, bleated recognition. The two men in the doorway lowered their points to meet Leonardo's charge, driving them deeply into the stout leather cover of the onrushing book. As they struggled vainly and in fury to release their weapons from this unlikely shield, Rigo slammed into the nearer of them, knocking him five paces to land winded and gasping like a gaffed fish upon the flagstones of the porch. Raising his own volume high, the gunner smashed it down on the helmeted head of the other, and the man's legs crumpled.

Leonardo stopped only to wrench the fallen soldier's pike free of his improvised breastplate and to skewer his last, hastily-written note upon its tip; he then dashed through the doorway behind Rigo. They emerged into the open air of the Chancery courtyard and gained the safety of the crowded *piazza* beyond its gateway a moment later, their sole discomfort being the laughter that threatened to crack their ribs.

Some twenty minutes later, Girolamo Riario was shaking with fury in front of Cardinal della Palla's desk.

'Conspiracy, your Eminence!' he said between clenched teeth. 'They were here, with your permission and under your protection!'

The Cardinal made no reply to this; he appeared, indeed, not to have heard it. The only sound in the pause which followed—the industrious scratching of della Palla's quill pen on paper—provoked Riario still further. 'That you have long been partial to this Medici spy is well known to me,' he said, white with anger. 'But that you conspire to bring him to Rome itself, conspire to warn him, and finally conspire to allow him to escape, is beyond partiality. It is treason!'

The Apostolic Chancellor, in measured calm, completed the final lines of his composition and signed the parchment carefully. He sanded it lightly, brushed free the grains, and rolled it into a neat cylinder before tying it with a purple ribbon.

'An important matter, I trust, Eminence,' said Riario with raging sarcasm.

'Sufficiently important,' said della Palla. 'Count, you appear to me to have taken leave of your senses. Do you forget who I am? I hold the highest legal office in the Church; and words such as "treason" and "conspiracy" are shots fired upon a battlefield which I control and you do not. Have a care, Count! I have noted your appetite for spilling blood in God's holy church and, here today, in Rome's own Chancery. I do not take such things lightly. I have accordingly written,' he raised the document in his hand, 'to the Holy Father, advising him to curb such tendencies in you.' He rose from his seat, seeming to tower over the other. 'Be thankful that I do no more. And now, if you will excuse me . . . ?'

'And what,' asked Rigo, 'was that scrap of paper you left as a memento upon a pike-end?' Now safe in their room at the *taverna*,

26

they were packing their saddle-bags in preparation for their departure—at long last—from Rome.

'Ah, that,' said Leonardo, tossing a book into the air and catching it deftly. 'I was forced, as you see, to borrow this copy of the *Ephemerides*; and courtesy demanded that I leave a note so saying to his Eminence, the Apostolic Chancellor.'

Two

THE SECRET ARCHIVES of the Most Serene Republic of Venice, wherein are contained all facts both great and small, duly recorded the arrival on June 14, 1478, of Count Girolamo Riario, Rome's Captain-General and Emissary Plenipotentiary of His Holiness Pope Sixtus IV.

Yet his welcome, be it said, was one of carefully measured warmth; Venice guarded jealously its independence from Roman influence in all things.

'A small gathering this evening, my dear Count,' said Nicodemo da Parenzo, half apologetically, 'it being our impression that your mission here might prove to be of some delicacy.'

Riario nodded politely as he allowed the young Venetian diplomat to refill his crystal goblet. A very small gathering indeed, he thought in sour approval. Two sombre merchants and their wives who, well instructed, spoke only when spoken to; this young functionary, and himself. 'I am, in fact, well pleased that we meet in this more private setting, Messer Nicodemo,' he said, sipping slowly of his wine. 'An estimable vintage, by the way. From the Bergamo region, is it not?'

'You reveal a taste for our diplomacy as well as a taste for our wines, my dear Count. Bergamo it is indeed, from the Val Brembana region.'

The Venetian's expression displayed no more than the faintest curiosity.

'Wine,' murmured Riario reflectively. 'I suppose it may be said that I come to Venice on behalf of a greater prosperity in her growing trade of wine.'

'Rome's interest is—flattering indeed, sir.'

'Yes,' said Riario, lingering over the word, 'this wine of Bergamo is most pleasant. Then why not add the wines of—Mantua? Modena? Of—Ferrara, even? If Bergamo's wines are pleasant, here are three regions whose wines are, shall we admit it, superb.'

'Our Governing Council will be pleased to hear of your interest in the wines of Venice,' said Nicodemo da Parenzo drily. 'However, they may choose to remind both of us that these three regions remain, for the present, outside the boundaries of our vineyards.'

'So they may,' said Riario. 'And yet, my mission here is to explore certain ways wherein Rome's Holy Father might persuade these cities to—join their vineyards to your own.'

Da Parenzo's eyes gleamed; he seemed, suddenly, not quite so young, not quite so much the functionary. 'His Holiness presents us with a most intriguing thought,' he said. 'He has others, perchance?'

'He does, sir.' Riario leaned forward to take the decanter, so bringing his face closer to the Venetian's. 'An alliance,' he whispered. 'What of that? Rome, Naples, Venice. In league against the heretic Lorenzo de' Medici and, it may be, his Milanese friends. Join us, and Mantua, Modena and Ferrara shall go to Venice; that is our offer.'

'Much as I predicted,' da Parenzo nodded. 'My lord, I am instructed to say this. Venice will consider such an alliance so long as His Holiness privately continues to renounce all churchly claims here. I add one thing more, my dear Count; Rome may reach for her horizons in Italy, if she wishes. Our horizons are elsewhere; Trebizond, Constantinople, Crete and Cyprus, Rhodes and Malta, London and Bruges. I hope we understand each other?'

'Of course. Venice has interests in Malta, you say?' Riario's eyes narrowed suddenly.

'A most conveniently placed island, dear Count. Our arrangements with Spain there yield much profit to us both. May one be permitted to wonder at your unexpected interest, my friend?'

'An enemy to Rome has fled there, Messer Nicodemo. I seek his death; that is all.'

'From such matters may great alliances spring,' said da Parenzo easily. 'Please allow us to assist you in this, as a matter of business.' For the first time, Nicodemo da Parenzo smiled. 'His name?'

'Da Vinci. Leonardo da Vinci. An artist and engineer, and a spy for the Medici.'

'Ah yes. The architect of Rome's loss at Castelmonte, was he not? Our embassy in Florence reported the matter in full, of course. Well, then. We have . . . a certain man in Malta even now, as it happens; in Mdina itself. He is, I will say only, the very man we would ourselves assign to such a task. I will provide you with orders for him, bearing the seal of Venice, if you like, so that he may know that he is authorised to assist you. You will of course reward him yourself. Ten thousand florins, shall we say? If this be agreeable, we are delighted to send him official orders to this effect.'

'Done—and I thank you,' said Riario. 'I shall need to know his name, this man of yours.'

'Naturally. His name is Uberto Neri.'

'And what sort of man is he, this Uberto Neri?'

'Why, my lord,' said Nicodemo da Parenzo, 'he is in some respects rather like yourself—though perhaps not in all things.'

A convenient island, Malta, so Nicodemo da Parenzo had said, and so it was. Others called it the crossroads of the Mediterranean, with equal truth. It was well placed indeed to serve the six galley-fleets of Venice. Africa and Tripoli lay an easy sail to its south, while to the west sat Spain and the narrow straits that formed the gateway to London and the ports of northern Europe. To the east were Byzantium, the rich cities of Aleppo, Acre, Damascus and Alexandria, and beyond these the fabulous caravan routes to Persia and Cathay.

From harbours at all points of the compass the roads of the sea gathered like invisible threads and led to Venetian wharves in Malta, to Venetian warehouses for loading, unloading and trans-shipping, to repair yards for fitting out the endless stream of vessels that called at Birgu and Senglea. Trade commanded all, and Venice was the queen of maritime trade. What mattered it to Venice that Malta this summer was—as ever—sweltering under a relentless sun and parched by the desert winds that swept unimpeded across from the burning sands of Africa?

In his room behind the ramparts of Mdina, Malta's capital city, Uberto Neri stirred and woke, satiated, from his light half doze. His body hair, blond and fine, lay damply upon his flesh; perspiration dewed his face. Only his feral eyes remained, as always, cold and hard as new ice.

His latest plaything, standing at the mirror, called again, petulant, flirtatious and insistent.

'Uberto! *Look!* There are teeth-marks here; yours, Uberto, upon my neck near to the shoulder!' He turned, long raven hair swinging, his voice seductive. 'Kiss them away, Uberto.'

Neri swung to a sitting position and reached for a cloth to dry his face and body. 'No more, Lemmo, no more,' he said. 'There is a time for pleasure, and another for work; and we must talk, for it is in my mind that you have disappointed me in the one small task I have set for you. Well?'

'Bah! Felippo again? The cabin on board the *Pyramus* is ever locked, or else the crew stand about. He drinks little wine—and that mixed with water—and so he is never drunk. So what am I to do, dear Uberto?'

'A harder problem than I had considered, perhaps,' Neri admitted. 'It may be... it may be that if we cannot have *Il Fortunato*'s secret, then we had better have his life. It is one way of solving the problem.' He stood up, slipping his arms into the sleeves of a silken robe. 'What do you say, Lemmo? Can you use a knife on him?'

'For you, dearest Uberto? Why not? What is Felippo to me? A dirty sea captain, full of ugly smells, that is all. And I *hate* the sea! Yes, if you ask it of me, I will do it. Although...'

31

'What, boy?'

'I am thinking of the boatswain, Tommaso. He is a thief, and I know that he has his eye on the cabin door. A dozen gold pieces, Uberto, and I might persuade Tommaso to serve you better in this.'

'What troubles you, Tommaso?' the girl asked.

He stood with his back to her, staring out of the single small window through a slit between the drawn curtains. A whore's room needs but little light. Decima sighed and rolled from the bed, drawing a shawl about her body as she rose to stand at the boatswain's side. 'What is it, man?' she repeated. 'Surely you can tell me?'

'I have much on my mind,' Tommaso said at last.

'And so? Look you,' she said quietly, 'these things can happen even to men with the hottest blood. I do not count it strange that you feel no urge for loving, nor does it offend me. I know that something troubles you; tell me, and things may go better. What is it?'

'You are a good woman,' the boatswain said slowly. 'One that a man might gladly marry, if it came to that.'

'Foh!' she replied. 'Is that all? And perhaps you could make a good husband, Tommaso, and what of it? Let us have no more of this idle talk of marriage.'

'Hold your chatter, girl. There is more to it than that.'

'Of course there is. Where is the money, for one thing? I am not to be satisfied with a hovel in some village full of peasants, let me tell you.'

Tommaso raised his hand. 'Will you listen, Decima?' he pleaded. 'The means for marriage I now possess; and if you would know what troubles me, then see for yourself.' From the simple pouch at his belt he drew a small packet, cloth-wrapped, and unfolded it. There, set into a crescent of ivory which was crowned with a crest of curiously notched design, was an emerald as large as a plover's egg. Even in the room's dim light it shimmered as though lit by some magical inner fire of its own; faceted, oval, and flawless.

32

Decima's hand flew to her mouth. 'Sweet Mother of God! How came you by this, Tommaso?' she asked him.

The sailor's eyes shifted uneasily. 'I stole it from Felippo's cabin,' he replied. 'See; land, a house, fine furniture and clothing, a shop perhaps—here it is, all of it, Decima.' He placed the gleaming treasure in her hand, closing her numb fingers around it. 'Now listen carefully,' he went on. 'I am in danger so long as I carry this where Felippo's first search will find it. I would have you keep it for me while I plan how I may leave both his service and the *Pyramus*. I must find us passage in a ship, not to mention purchasing you from that fat cow who owns you. Can you hide it for me . . . for us?'

'Of course.' She thrust back her dark hair impatiently, and then returned to her study of the emerald and of the pale crescent that framed it. 'Look here,' she said, 'at these letters cut into the ivory and filled with gold. What do they mean, Tommaso?'

There were three words, carved in an arc that followed the crescent's outer curve. They read: PEREVNT ET IMPVTANTVR.

The boatswain shrugged. 'Who knows?' he said. 'All men call him *Il Fortunato*. It may be that these are the magic words that bring him his good fortune. His ship is the fastest in the whole Mediterranean. But what matters it? Let him keep his magic, if we hold this jewel.'

'They separate, I think,' said Decima, examining the crescent more closely still. 'See? At these four points? It is held so.' She pressed her finger against the side of the stone and, with a tiny click, it dropped from its ivory mounting and fell into her palm. 'So,' she repeated. 'Have no fear, Tommaso *mio*. None will find it. Which being so, Tommaso . . . come to bed.'

Rigo Leone came to Malta, and was conquered. Of no part of it would he allow the slightest criticism; the island's spare and rocky hillsides were majestic in his eyes, its stony fields gentle and pleasing. For three days he had followed Leonardo through the small fishing villages and the wharves scattered about the natural harbours of Birgu and Senglea, in a fruitless—but, to him, none the less pleasant—search for Felippo *Il Fortunato* and his ship the *Pyramus*. He sampled the famed honey from which Malta drew her name, and found it sweeter than nectar; drank deeply of Malta's wine, vowing that it spoiled all other wines for him for ever. His cheerfulness was almost oppressive.

At last, on the morning of the fourth day after their arrival, they were rewarded. An old fisherman, a section of torn net hooked to his great toe and held by his ancient teeth, paused in his mending to tell them that *Il Fortunato* never anchored in these waters.

'He puts off his cargoes near here, messires, then ups anchor and sails east along the coast and moors there; perhaps in one of the coves by Marsasirocco. I know not.' His accent and language were all but incomprehensible. He gestured with his head. 'Climb to the headlands, messires. From there you can see far down the shore. You will find him.' The old man accepted Leonardo's coin with a small nod of thanks, waved his gnarled brown hand, and returned to his work.

The climb to the heights was a long one, up and along narrow dirt roads that twisted around jutting rocks. Three hours later, they stood upon the topmost slab of a great escarpment to scan the coast that lay below them to the east. Coves in plenty there were, as the old man had said, and in one of them the barely visible tip of one tall and painted mast swayed back and forth to the Mediterranean's gentle swell.

'Felippo,' said Leonardo, as though in greeting. 'Come, let us sit and break our fast. Yonder cove is a full hour's walk, and there are things you should know about Felippo *Il Fortunato*.'

Rigo sat down on a nearby rock and drew some bread, cheese and fruit from his wallet. Unslinging his wine-bottle, from his shoulder, he rested this upon a patch of scorched grass. '*Il Fortunato*,' he said. 'A name to tempt the Fates, one might think. How did he earn it?'

Leonardo da Vinci began to peel an orange. 'Think back upon these last few days,' he invited. 'What have we seen in Malta?

Ships, Rigo. Ships in their dozens, from the world over, which put in here. For Malta sits at the very crossing of all the roads of the sea.'

'Very well. What has this to do with your fortunate friend?'

'Listen, then. A ship leaves Constantinople, let us imagine, with a fine cargo of silks and rare dyes. Yet it leaves with something far more important; knowledge. Knowledge that there is a heavy demand for—what? Lace from Bruges. English oak. Tin, it may be, or alum. Woollen fabrics from Florence. Thus, a ship that bears this knowledge carries with it the prospect of great profit for its owner.' Leonardo paused to chew thoughtfully. 'Now, then,' he went on, 'such knowledge is rarely secret. Many captains will hear it from many different agents. All know that the sooner they make their destination, the sooner—and the more profitably—they may use this knowledge for the voyage back. Therefore, Rigo, *all ships race to be home first.*'

Rigo nodded.

'And one ship,' said Leonardo, 'always wins these races. The *Pyramus,* owned by Felippo Mendoza. He wins by a week, or two weeks; or three days, or one only. It is enough. Thus is he known as *Il Fortunato.* More than this; he who arrives first in port makes the market. His cargo—whatever it may be—will command on a Tuesday five times what others will get for an identical cargo on Friday. Do you see?'

'I do indeed,' said Rigo. 'And how does he explain this good fortune?'

'In part, that is why we are here, my good Rigo; and it may turn out to be a matter that might interest you. For sea captains, Rigo, aim their vessels from this port to that, much as you aim your cannon; and, as I invented an aiming device for the Medici Guns last year, so do sailors have their means of aiming. These means are, for the most part, crude; and a small error——'

'As with a gun,' interrupted Rigo. 'Tilt it a hair'sbreadth too high, and it may throw the ball forty paces out at the target.'

'Just so. As with guns, so with ships. Aim for Alexandria and let the wind push you off course by even a single degree, and you may miss your mark by fifty or a hundred miles; and then you will be forced to crawl along the coast until you find it. Whereas a better-aimed ship will reach Alexandria directly—and days before you.'

'As Felippo does?' said Rigo.

'Always. Voyage after voyage, his is the first sail to be seen from the dock, bearing the first news, the earliest goods, and the most useful knowledge of what cargo to take on for a quick return.'

'And?' Rigo prompted.

'And what I would like to know,' said Leonardo, 'is exactly how he does it.'

A long march from the uplands brought them to the fishing wharf at Marsasirocco just as dusk was falling. There, from among several that were offered to them, they were able to hire a small skiff for a few coins.

With Leonardo at the oars, the little boat edged its way in the gathering twilight towards the tip of the promontory that protected the cove in which the *Pyramus* lay at anchor. They rounded this, and at once saw the vessel before them and barely a hundred paces distant, a dark shape in the gloom. Leonardo began to pull towards her with a will.

It was Rigo who first noticed that all was not well.

'Ship your blades,' he said.

Leonardo, who had his back to the *Pyramus*, complied. They drifted broadside to her, both men peering across the soft intervening swells. No lights showed aboard the silent hull. As they watched, the *Pyramus* veered at the end of her chain until her stern was towards them, and it became obvious that she was listing badly.

'Hurry, Leonardo,' whispered Rigo. 'She founders!'

A minute later, two final mighty heaves at the oars brought the skiff alongside the ship's ladder. In a clatter of ropes and rungs they clambered aboard. As though disturbed by their added weight the big vessel tilted, her timbers groaning as her mast swayed farther to one side.

36

Leonardo shouted in questioning alarm and raced along the slanting deck to the main cabin, Rigo at his side. They pulled the door wide, and stopped, transfixed by the scene of horror that met their eyes.

There, under a single smoking lantern that hung crazily askew, *Il Fortunato* lay in the arms of a lad who sobbed and strove to comfort him. He was, as could be seen at once, beyond all comfort. Beneath his chin glinted the haft of a dagger, whose blade was buried deep in his throat. His tortured breath whistled past the obstructing steel; he was dying hard, and had lived yet harder in the hour that preceded his death. He was shirtless, and his chest and arms were pocked by a myriad small burns and ugly, irregular gouges. An eye had been stabbed in its socket and had dripped dark blood across the cuts that patterned his cheeks; his upper lip, half severed from the muscles that surrounded it, disclosed the ragged stumps of what had been his teeth.

The boy at his shoulder lifted a tear-stained face towards them.

'Oh God, help him please! Sirs ... I beg of you ...' He lapsed into incoherent sobbing again.

Rigo, alert and practical, was looking about him.

'Where are they?' he asked.

Leonardo shook his head at once. 'His enemies are no longer here,' he said, 'or else we should have seen their boat.' Turning to the distraught boy he continued gently, 'How long since, lad?'

'I ... I cannot tell, sir.' He was, Leonardo decided, perhaps fourteen years of age; after a few seconds he seemed to calm somewhat. 'They ... locked me in the hold,' he said. 'I heard my master screaming. The water—the sea began to come into the ship, and I broke down the door. I came here and found ...' he stopped.

'Take him, Rigo,' Leonardo said, as he knelt beside the dying mariner. 'Felippo?'

At the sound of his name *Il Fortunato*'s remaining eye fluttered open, and his ruined features set into something that might have been recognition.

'Soft, Felippo, my old friend. We will take out this blade and let you draw breath. So.' Leonardo withdrew the dagger carefully, pressing the edges of the wound between his fingers as he did so in a vain attempt to stop the immediate pulsing of blood. Felippo struggled weakly, raising his arm to point a crushed finger at the cabin sole beneath the rough chart table. A square tablet lay there, a desk weight, perhaps.

Leonardo reached for it with his free hand, and Felippo turned his head to follow the movement, opening his mouth once and then again. He was still trying to speak when death overtook him.

As though determined to perish with her master, the *Pyramus* rolled heavily. Rigo, at the cabin doorway, staggered as she settled with her starboard gunwhale awash. Gusts of trapped air bubbled up from her hull and burst the planking at the opposite side of her deck, spraying upward the salt fountains of her death throes.

'Quickly,' the gunner said. He held the shuddering boy tightly in the crook of one arm. 'We have but moments, man!'

'You cannot leave him here!' the boy cried.

'Hush, lad. He dies with his ship, as I hope to die with my guns one day. No man can do better.' Rigo urged him out of the cabin and supported him across the after-deck to the rail, now barely inches above the water. Leonardo, with the plaque he had retrieved from beneath the cabin table clutched tightly in his hand, followed. All three of them slipped into the sea as the deck, tilting further, loomed above them like a menacing wall. After swimming a dozen powerful strokes, Leonardo turned.

'She will roll, Rigo!' he shouted. 'To me, and hasten!'

The gunner and his young companion emerged from the surrounding darkness. Leonardo linked arms with both of them, and they kicked out in unison. Over their heads and seeming as though she must inevitably crush them, the great ship made her final swing. Her mast pounded the surface hard by them, and the outflung wave of her capsizing thrust them away as her timbers tore apart, hissing and booming. She sank almost at once, dragged down by her iron keel, and took the moored skiff to the bottom with her.

Rigo trod water, coughing. 'What now?' he asked, when he had expelled some of the sea from his lungs.

'We swim,' replied Leonardo, 'unless you had something else in mind. Come. The exercise will do you nothing but good.'

They rolled on to their backs, and began the long haul towards the distant shore.

History does not record the birth of the citadel town of Mdina—Citta Notabile, as the Spanish called it—nor of its suburb, Rabat. Their roots go deep into Malta's past, beyond the Phoenicians and the Greeks, beyond the surges of Vandal invasion and Islamic reprisal, beyond even the fallen temples of men who left neither name nor language.

If, for the present, Spain was her indifferent landlord, it was Venice who dominated Mdina and controlled—delicately, as was ever the policy of the Most Serene Republic—all that mattered most in Malta; banks, agencies, docks, warehouses. Spanish officialdom came corrupt, and stayed to enrich itself through bribes. Those who were foolish enough to seek proper accounting were soon transferred—or silenced.

Uberto Neri had but recently arrived at Venice's Mediterranean outpost. Now, as he strolled towards the villa reserved for her visiting dignitaries, he was reminded again of the Republic's potency. The villa was an architectural gem of pink and white marble, its roof mortised at the rear into the slope of a hillside. A high wall surrounded its gardens; the single gate was guarded night and day. Of this Uberto Neri approved. He tapped at the iron bars for admission, and was saluted.

Once inside the grounds he saw, coming towards him from the villa itself, the mountainous form of Achmet the Turk, his robe of blue Gaza cloth swelling behind him like a wave.

A magnificent body, thought Neri; a man and a half tall, and two men in breadth. Some would say he was too gross. It was rumoured that Achmet had been a wrestler at the time of his capture by Venice. Chained to a galley's sweep, he had attracted the attention of a travelling diplomat shrewd enough to perceive that he might serve Venice in better ways. He had accepted baptism and a posting to Malta as major-domo to his sponsor, First Secretary Orso Contarini.

As major-domo, and as other things besides.

The First Secretary being absent from the island, Achmet was for the time being assisting Uberto Neri in sundry tasks of a specialised nature. It was in connection with these that he now addressed the Venetian, bowing low before he spoke.

'Ill news, lord of Venice,' he said. 'The man Tommaso is dead.'

Neri stifled his immediate rage, and answered smoothly enough. 'That is ill news indeed, Achmet,' he said. 'I depended upon your skills, for we needed to know what this Tommaso held in his head.'

'What he knew, he would have revealed,' said the Turk, 'since all men, lord, break sooner or later. This one was weaker than I knew, dying early.'

'And what of his whore?'

'She lives, lord.'

'Then let us take care not to lose her too. *Il Fortunato* is lost to us, and now his boatswain; and it is far from certain that we can find the rest of his crew, even if they knew anything that would help us. We need his charts, Achmet; a simple enough matter, in all conscience, or so one would have thought.'

The huge Turk made an obeisance once more. 'Lord, in this I believe you are mistaken,' he said.

'Mistaken, fellow?'

'I am your dog, lord, and the dog of a mighty house, and I live but to do your bidding. But this talk of charts is folly. It is not things of this nature that we should seek, but his talisman; have I not heard it on every lip? For, lord, this captain was known also in my country, in Smyrna, Nicomedia, Trebizond. All men knew that he had a djinn to serve him, and a great charm to summon this djinn.'

'Take care, fool,' replied Neri with annoyance, 'to whom you speak of djinns, since you are now a Christian. Men have burned for less. Felippo was no conjuror, but a man with secrets of navigation possessed by nobody else; knowledge of hidden channels, Achmet, of currents and shallows, the which are contained in charts. And these charts we must have. What of the boatswain? Did he say nothing?'

'To myself, lord, very little. To the harlot . . . perhaps.'

'Then, good Achmet, let us speak with the harlot. But with care.'

Leonardo's pouch having yielded stone and steel, both dry in their wrappings of oiled silk, a fire of driftwood was now burning upon the beach they had gained. Rigo sat close to it, turning this way and that the better to dry his clothing. The night was still; over the empty cove a new moon hung, thin and pale. The boy, his back to the blaze, stood gazing out to sea.

'What is your name?' Rigo called to him softly.

'Lemmo, sir.' He turned, shivering.

'Only that, boy?'

'Sir, I have none other. Captain Mendoza took me from the monastery of the Pauline brothers at Brindisi when I was eleven, and cared for me thereafter.'

'And what of your own father and mother?'

'I knew them not, sir.'

'No more did I know mine, boy,' said Rigo gruffly, brushing sand from his tunic as he rose. 'Well, Lemmo, I am Roderigo Leone, master-gunner; and this is my friend Leonardo da Vinci, a painter and dreamer of dreams.'

The lad bowed to each of them in turn, smiling crookedly.

'What say you, Leonardo?' continued Rigo. 'He is an orphan again, it seems. Shall he stay with us for the while?'

'An excellent idea,' replied Leonardo.

'I need no protection, sirs,' said Lemmo with stiff dignity. 'I am old enough to find work and a place to sleep, in Birgu or . . . somewhere.'

'Indeed?' said Leonardo. 'And have you money?' He pointed to the leather bag which dangled at the boy's waist.

'No, sir,' said Lemmo. He appeared confused. 'That is, sir, a coin or two; sufficient until tomorrow, perhaps.'

'Then do not talk nonsense,' said Rigo. 'You were cabin boy to Felippo, I dare say?'

'I was.'

'Then we have work for you. As, perhaps . . .'

'Our valet and steward?' prompted Leonardo.

'My very thought,' Rigo said. 'At small pay, lad, though 'twill serve until you find better; and you may sleep at our door. Agreed?'

'Agreed, sirs, and I thank you both.'

'Well spoken. And now, since Captain Felippo Mendoza was your guardian and we his friends,' Rigo said, 'let us seek his revenge together. Who could have done this terrible thing to him, Lemmo? Had he enemies?'

'None that I know of, sir. Though many envied him.'

'His crew?' Leonardo asked.

'No. All of us prospered under him,' Lemmo said. 'Why should we seek his death?'

'Where might we look for them? One of them could know something that might help us.'

Lemmo remained silent for awhile. Then: 'Sirs,' he said earnestly, 'unless you were to find them tomorrow, I believe you will be wasting your labour. When they hear of . . . of what has happened, they will seek other berths, and find them easily enough.'

'Shrewdly spoken,' said Leonardo. 'All shipmasters will welcome them aboard, hoping to find out from them some part of Captain Felippo Mendoza's secret. Is that your meaning?'

'You know, then?' Lemmo said.

'Do not all men know he had a secret?' said Leonardo. Seeing a sudden look of wariness upon the boy's face, he added hastily, 'You have nothing to fear from us. We came to this island at his request—as I can prove to you, if need be.'

After another silence, Lemmo spoke again. 'There is Tommaso, perhaps,' he suggested.

'Tommaso?'

'The boatswain. Captain Mendoza spoke to few except for him. If any man could help you, it would be Tommaso.'

'And where should we seek him?' Rigo asked.

'Sirs, he can often be found in Rabat, at a place called the House of Ten Pearls. A place of sin and of wicked women, so the captain often told me, and made me swear that I would never go there.'

Rigo threw a swift glance at Leonardo. 'A wise man,' he said. 'Enough for now, Lemmo. We need food, wine, and'—he stretched—'sleep. Tomorrow, lad, you may point us the way to this House of Ten Pearls.'

The bamboo switch Achmet held was narrow, and its tip had been frayed by use into a thousand separate and razor-sharp strands. It whistled as the Turk brought it down viciously, its impact spattering droplets of bright blood from Decima's back and wrenching one more gasp of pain from her tortured throat.

She lay face downward and naked on a table, her wrists and ankles roped to its legs. She could neither remember nor imagine how long she had been there. In a corner, its chest, arms and face hacked and charred beyond recognition, was the mutilated corpse of Tommaso the boatswain, once her lover; she had only to open her eyes to see it. She kept them closed.

Uberto Neri pushed himself languidly upright from the doorpost and walked across to the girl's side. He lifted her head by a handful of black hair, and then let it drop again with a thud.

'The maps, whore,' he said. 'The charts from the *Pyramus*. Where are they hidden?'

Decima rolled her cheek against the stained planking, and stayed silent.

'She has naught to tell us, lord,' said Achmet.

Neri sighed and moved away. 'Release her, then,' he instructed.

The giant Turk took up a wooden bucket from the floor. It was filled to the brim with salt water, and he threw its contents across the tattered flesh of Decima's back. She screamed, her eyes opening wide in agony. Achmet began to slice through the ropes that held her, one by one, while Neri addressed her with soft menace.

'Listen to me, whore,' he said, 'and listen well. It is our pleasure that you now go free, and at our pleasure we may bring you here again when we choose. This time your skin may heal; next time, be sure that it will not. If you value it, therefore, find yourself another man from *Il Fortunato's* crew, and talk with him as you talked with Tommaso. If you learn aught of secret maps and charts, send us word. Do you understand me?'

Decima moaned and stirred.

'Very well,' Neri said. 'Clean her up somewhat, Achmet, and return her to the House of Ten Pearls. She will not be hard to find.'

Three

LEMMO'S DIRECTIONS FOR finding the House of Ten Pearls were a model of clarity. 'I would guide you there myself, sirs,' he said, 'were it not for the promise I made to my poor master. He is dead, but does not my promise still stand?'

'It does, boy,' said Rigo approvingly. Lemmo lowered his lashes modestly, his brown cheeks colouring faintly. The gunner turned to Leonardo. 'We shall find the place, no doubt,' he went on, 'yet I have never visited a bawdy-house in broad daylight. Is it likely that this Tommaso will be there at this hour? I doubt it.'

'He may and he may not,' replied Leonardo. 'But in any case, we have first to discover the name of the woman he visited.'

'Decima,' put in Lemmo at once. 'At least, so he calls her when he is boasting of her to the others from the ship.'

'Good lad,' said Rigo. 'Your ears are excellently sharp, it seems. Wait here until we return.'

Lemmo stood in the doorway and watched the two men until they were out of sight. Then he leaped nimbly down the three steps to the street and walked briskly away from the tavern, in the opposite direction.

Arrived at the wall which Lemmo had described to them, Rigo and Leonardo found that the small ornamented door in its centre swung open at a touch. Rigo peered inside and gave a low whistle of surprise.

'The women will be costly here, artist,' he said. 'Gardens and

45

fountains, statues and bright birds in cages; and see—there is even a wine shop back there in the corner!'

From behind the counter, her arm lifted in welcome, a large woman hailed them cheerfully. 'Enter, sirs, and welcome! You honour my house!' She had a bold voice, warm with the accent of Greece. Tall, like so many of her countrywomen, big of bone and body, Madame Olympia came forward to greet them, an amberfilled bottle in her hand. 'Come, sirs. Some enjoy women by night, some by day. Why not? We will talk of my Pearls while you try my wine.'

Leonardo swept her a low and courteous bow. 'Alas, madam,' he said, 'we are not here as clients for your pearls or your wine this day.'

Madame Olympia lowered the bottle, her features clouding. 'Indeed?' she said, coldly. 'Then what is it you seek?'

'Your gracious permission, madam, to speak briefly with the girl Decima, if you will grant it,' Leonardo replied.

'She is indisposed,' said Madame Olympia promptly, 'and will speak to nobody.'

'It is a matter of some importance, madam. And since we must perforce occupy a little of her time, we are prepared to pay for the privilege of doing so—generously.'

'One hundred soldi?'

'By all means,' said Leonardo.

Barely a quarter of a mile away, Uberto Neri received disturbing news with his customary coolness.

'I came to you as soon as they left, Uberto!' said his informant. 'No more than minutes ago at most. I swear it! They are the very men you seek—Leonardo da Vinci and his companion, Captain Roderigo Leone!'

'You have done well, I think, Lemmo. Though,' mused Neri aloud, 'my orders from Venice said nothing of a second man. No matter. Someone will pay the more for two birds. Summon Achmet and Antonio to me, boy. Off with you, and quickly.'

46

It had taken nearly an hour to find and lift away each blood-soaked sliver of bamboo from Decima's torn flesh. Madame Olympia, suspicious, had come once to the room, only to depart immediately—her face pale with fear, since she had not until then seen the damage to her charge's back—closing the door firmly behind her.

'I need a jar of clean water, Rigo, and some plain cloth to be torn into strips,' said Leonardo at last. Rigo nodded and left.

When he had gone, Decima looked up at her benefactor, catching her breath in pain as she did so. 'Save that he calls you Leonardo and you call him Rigo, I know no more about you than that you have tried to help me,' she said. 'Who are you, and why came you here?'

'Patience, Decima. We will talk soon. But if I allow your wounds to heal with these splinters remaining in them, they will become poisoned. See; here is another.' Leonardo resumed his search.

Rigo returned after awhile, wearing a bemused expression. 'Each girl here bears a name which is no name, but rather a number, Leonardo,' he said. 'Did you know that? The water I obtained in room One, by courtesy of a pleasant creature called Una. The cloth comes from Dua, next door to her.'

'A conceit of the house, I have no doubt,' observed Leonardo.

He turned his attention to the square of linen, ripping it across to form rough dressings and soaking each strip in water. Decima studied him.

'You are from Venice?' she probed.

'From Florence.'

'And you came to Malta to find ... what? Not me, assuredly.'

'Nay,' said Leonardo, 'we came to find a friend of mine, who had asked our help. He is now dead, Decima. His name was Felippo Mendoza, sometimes called *Il Fortunato*, and now we seek his former boatswain, one Tommaso.'

'Tommaso?' The girl's eyes narrowed in suspicion.

'The same. You know him?'

'Tommaso is dead too,' said Decima bleakly. 'Your errand begins to stink of danger.'

47

'So it does,' answered Leonardo, pausing in his ministrations to ponder. 'Did Tommaso, then, tell you anything that concerned *Il Fortunato* or his ship?'

Decima's mind raced. This man comes too close to Tommaso's emerald, she told herself silently. The others had beaten her for its sake; now this Florentine was trying to heal her. From kindness, or as a strategy? Or both? It was impossible to tell; and how much, then, did he know? She must go carefully.

'Turn over your stool, Leonardo of Florence,' she said at last, reaching a decision. 'Look beneath its seat. There you will find something which Tommaso gave me to hold for him.'

Leonardo obeyed her.

The object he discovered, wedged into a turned seam of the fabric, was of ivory and very old; a hand-span across and crescent-shaped, a sort of plaque or medallion, possibly. Designs of intricately-carved leaves and gold-filled flowers wove around an oval aperture at its centre, and these decorations were interspersed with inscriptions in Latin, Greek, and some Eastern language. He read aloud the words of its brief inscription.

' "*Pereunt et imputantur*." Yes, this is what I seek, Decima,' he said, 'and what Felippo Mendoza wanted me to have. May I keep it for the present?'

'You may.'

'I thank you.'

'You were looking only for this? Nothing more?'

'Only this,' Leonardo replied. He studied the object more closely and smiled. The oval opening—was it mere decoration? From the top and bottom small pegs of ivory protruded towards the centre, each peg cupped minutely at its end.

Leonardo looked about the room.

A niche in the far wall held an image of the Madonna, one arm raised in benediction. It was a trumpery thing in glazed and painted clay, around which Decima had fastened a garland of paper flowers. At its foot was a loose tumble of glass beads and coloured chips of crystal. He crossed to the statuette, aware that Decima's eyes were following him as he did so. Picking among the baubles that lay scattered around its base, he held something up between his fingers; an ellipse of green fire, that winked and glowed alternately as he twisted it this way and that.

'A magnificent stone,' he said. 'It should, I think, fit into this hole just . . . so.' He slipped it between the ivory pegs, clicking it gently into place in the ivory crescent, and then took it from its mounting again. 'A good hiding-place, Decima,' he added. 'And yet I think that you will need a better one. It was this that Tommaso gave you to hold for him, was it not? Here.' He tossed the emerald to the bed beside her.

'You . . . you will not take it from me, then?' Decima's face was a study in amazed confusion.

'Not I. It was never mine, nor yet Tommaso's. It belonged to *Il Fortunato*, and he is dead.'

'But——' Decima began. She still seemed astonished.

A sudden sound at the door interrupted her. Rigo Leone turned in alarm, closing the door softly.

'There are men below,' he whispered. 'Eight men. Armed, Leonardo—and preparing a search. For us, or I am no judge.'

Decima sat up at once, catching her breath painfully as she did so. She rose and crossed to the door, opened it a crack, and peered out. 'Mother of God,' she whispered, 'those are the men who beat me!' She began to tremble, turning on them in angry panic. 'You led them here! You are with them!' Tears sprang to her eyes, and she threw off Leonardo's restraining hand. She made her way back to the bed, to collapse there in sobs of misery.

From the courtyard below, however, a shout could be heard.

'Do we question this Madame Olympia, excellency?'

Neri's voice replied at once, clear and cold. 'No, Antonio. God's breath, it is simple enough. We seek two men, one tall and fair, the other short. Who should be here at this hour, save for them? Search, fools, and make haste about it!'

Decima lifted a bewildered face from her pillow. 'It is not me they are looking for, but you, then?' she said.

'It appears so,' Leonardo replied, 'though who they may be I don't know.'

'Take back the emerald,' said Decima, 'for I must trust some-body, and it may as well be you. If they ill-treat me again, I shall surrender it to them, I know it. Take it, quickly!'

She held the jewel out to Leonardo, who slipped both the emerald and its ivory crescent into his pouch.

'Go to Sixta's room,' continued Decima, 'and tell her that I bid her use her window-trick to save you. She will know what you mean. As for the stone, since you did not seize it from me when you could have done so, I entrust it to you freely. Hold it or sell it, I care not. If there is any profit to it, send my portion to my cousin Selina in the village of Zejtun. Now go!'

Without more ado, Leonardo and Rigo burst out of the room onto the balcony that overlooked the central courtyard. They were seen at once by two men who, with swords drawn, were climbing the steps at their right. Rigo kicked the nearer of them in the chest, hurling him backwards into the arms of his fellow, and both fell down the stairway in a welter of outflung limbs and clattering steel. Four others, including the Turk Achmet, were already ascending the stairs at the far side of the courtyard. Rigo raced after Leonardo; they gained the door of Sixta's room several seconds before their pursuers, against whom they were thus able to bolt the door's stout oaken timbers. Pounding fists beat on these from the outside, and angry voices shouted for entrance.

On the bed Sixta grunted sleepily, and stirred.

Rigo's mouth dropped open in awe as he contemplated the rolling vista she displayed before him in doing so. Three hundred pounds of scantily-clad and shining black Nubian flesh, Sixta's body curved and billowed in mound after mound of thigh and belly, of majestic breast and titanic shoulders, each portion quivering as she heaved herself to a sitting position. She showed no surprise whatever as Leonardo, somewhat overawed himself, repeated Decima's message.

'Easy, sirs,' she said, pointing placidly. 'Sit upon the sill there, and I will hold you by the wrists and lower you. At full stretch it is a drop to the alley of no more than half your height.'

Rigo, who was already at the window, turned with a scowl.

50

'Well and good,' he said, 'but the alley opens only into the street beside the door, and they are fools if they have nobody waiting there. It's a nice trap, this one.'

Leonardo joined him and leaned out of the window, looking not downward at the cobbles of the alley but, instead, towards the sky overhead.

'Can you lift us to the roof?' he asked Sixta.

'If you wish it,' answered the vast Nubian, waddling across to them. 'But——'

'Say no more, then, I beg you, but do so,' Leonardo said.

Sixta's teeth gleamed in a wide and golden-studded grin. She thrust between them, displacing the gunner as though he were a toy, and made a stirrup with her interlocked hands outside the sill. Leonardo slid awkwardly through what opening remained unblocked by her body, and rested his foot between her palms. He turned to face the outer side of the wall, and stretched upward as she boosted him with an enormous and muscular heave. His fingers caught at the edge of the rooftop, and he swung himself nimbly up and over. Rolling, he had only an instant in which to perceive his minor tactical error; the roof edge concealed a large cistern, into whose tepid water he fell at once with a heavy splash.

He surfaced, stood up, and reached his arms down over its wall to grasp Rigo's wrists. It was as well that he did so, since Sixta, in the room below, turned in alarm at a redoubled pounding on the door behind her and withdrew her supporting hands from the sole of the gunner's shoe. Had Leonardo not been holding him securely, he would undoubtedly have fallen into the alley.

Sixta lumbered across the bedroom and set her back against the door. She was confident that no power on earth could move her as she watched Rigo's dangling feet ascend, kicking, until they were no longer visible. Her confidence was thereupon shattered by the arrival outside the door of Achmet. Pushing the rest of Neri's men aside, the mammoth Turk hurtled into the planks, sweeping Sixta forward onto her hands and knees as he exploded into the room.

She at once wrapped herself round his legs, screeching in

51

baritone outrage, and it was several seconds before Achmet could detach himself from her grip. By the time he had slapped her twice with all his might—an action which seemed to have little or no effect on her—and had then fought his way to the window, he found the alleyway deserted and no sign of his quarry anywhere.

'How they slipped by the guards in the street I cannot tell, excellency,' he said to Neri later.

'Fool,' rejoined Neri. 'They went over the alley wall and into some private house, I dare say.' He accepted a goblet of wine from the Turk and drank deeply. 'Well, what is done is done, and they cannot escape me in the end. Malta is an island, and do I not control its wharves? Moreover, Lemmo is with them. We can bide our time.'

In an upstairs room at the tavern, Lemmo lifted his head from his task and listened in sudden alarm. They were alive! He could hear Rigo calling for wine below, and Leonardo's voice adding something in a lower tone.

He darted to the head of the stairs and looked down at them. His employers were dripping wet, and standing at the front door.

Quickly, he ran back into the bedroom and replaced the belongings he had been rifling. He selected such dry apparel as might be chosen by any good valet, and whipped two blankets from the bed, draping these over his arm. As he approached the stair-head once more, he strove to put an anxious expression upon his innocent young face.

'I bring you fresh clothing, masters,' he called down to them, concern oozing from every word, and began to descend.

Four

HER PLAN—admirable in every way, if untruthful—had cost Bianca
Visconti weeks of reflection. To leave Florence and join Leonardo
in Malta she would need the weightiest of reasons in order to
persuade her guardian, Lorenzo de' Medici. If she provided
the one she favoured he might bluster and scold her, but would—
so she thought—melt as always under a few sweet blandishments.
She had therefore come to him buoyant with confidence.

Sadly, however, things were not going as she had planned. She
sat, hollow with unfamiliar fear, as Lorenzo lashed her with a
cutting tongue.

'You spawn a bastard under my roof, madam? How pleased
your uncle, the Regent of Milan, will be when he hears of it!' He
struck the desk sharply with the flat of his hand, making her start.
'You young fool! *I hold Milan by a single thread.* Would you cut
it asunder?'

'I am sorry, sir.' Bianca's voice trembled. 'I had not
thought——'

'So much is obvious. This child you carry—when will it be
born?'

She considered rapidly and uneasily. Already the road back to
the truth seemed rockier than the path ahead.

'In . . . in February, sire.'

'Then we may have time enough. And the bastard's father,
madam? Or may I assume that I already know your answer?'

'Leonardo da Vinci,' she replied faintly.

'Yes,' said Lorenzo. 'In God's name, here is presumption! Does he imagine, this engineer, that because he has rendered Florence and myself the service of winning the battle of Castelmonte, I shall accept his seduction of my ward? Well, madam, your dowry will be a wedding ring and no more, and my gift to Leonardo da Vinci may be his life. Let him think himself fortunate! I will have him here, in Florence, by November. A private ceremony, and banishment—for both of you.'

'Banishment?' Bianca was appalled.

'Did you suppose that you could stay in Florence?' Lorenzo regarded her bleakly. 'Milan's ambassadors are here, and I cannot afford to have you seen. You will leave the city now, and return only to marry. And since I can no longer trust you to constrain your appetites, I will put you where you can be watched.' His eyes strayed to a map on the wall. 'Pisa,' he continued. 'The Medici support a convent there; a severe establishment, madam, where strict vows of silence may give you time to reflect upon how basely you have repaid Florence her hospitality.'

Unreasoning anger brought her to her feet, eyes blazing.

'Is it murder I have done, sir? Have I broken any sworn vow to you? Done wilful treason to Florence? I am with child, sir, only that! There are bastards of your own in Florence, so men say.'

'Enough!' Lorenzo rose and walked slowly to the window, his back stiff with anger and resolve. 'You have my leave to go, madam. Remove yourself from Florence and from my sight. Pack your necessaries. You leave this morning, and under escort.'

As Lorenzo had ordered, she rode out of the city a little before noon. It was a magnificent summer day, brilliant with sunshine. Bianca Visconti said little, however, her mind spinning with the collapse of the plan she had once believed so admirable and now perceived in ruins about her.

Not, it must be observed, that her guard and guide seemed to mind her silence. He, bedecked in a shimmering cloak of rose-pink that set off a green silk doublet, filled the first three hours of their journey with an endless discussion of fashions and fabrics, cuffs and collars, boots and belts. For Cipriano di Ser Giacomo Giachetti di Lucca, gunner to Florence and lieutenant to Rigo Leone himself, had more than a flair for fashion; he loved above all things to talk about it.

'Hose, note you, my lady, of simple wools in grey or brown,' he announced, 'may serve us well, admitted. But the French gave us hose in particolour, one leg in this hue, the other in that; a pleasing notion, thought I. Now proceeding from this I have created a design with tiny red roses embroidered on the one leg upon a ground of russet; my other leg—imagine it if you will—festooned with seed-pearls in a pattern much like ivy and upon a field of palest orange!'

'A triumph, doubtless, Master Cipriano,' said Bianca, breaking her silence at last. 'And costly, too.'

He laughed in delight. 'So said my hosier, Bonini, my lady! An excellent fellow. They will harm my purse not a whit. He is fashioning them for me already as a tribute to my brilliance and his own craft, if I will in return give him more of my ideas.'

'And you agreed, of course,' said Bianca.

'But of course.'

Bianca studied her escort with care. Her guilt and anger, now long cooled, had been succeeded by further calculation. I must not be trapped in this Medici convent, she thought.

'Know you why Lorenzo sends me to Pisa, Master Cipriano?' she asked him pleasantly.

'Alas, my lady. The Medici do not yet confide in me,' he grinned. 'It is foolish of them, but there.'

'And would you like to know?'

'Only if you choose to tell me, madonna.'

'The point precisely, Master Cipriano. I must tell somebody, and you seem like a man of . . . discretion.'

'I hope so, madonna.'

'Then . . .' she paused before taking the plunge. 'I have told Lorenzo that I am with child.'

'I am happy for you.'

55

'It was a lie.'

'It was?'

'I am not pregnant at all.'

'I see. You chose to lie to Il Magnifico? A risky course to take, my lady. May a man of discretion know why?'

'I thought that he would let me go to Leonardo.'

'You told him Leonardo da Vinci was the father? He cannot have been pleased.'

'He was not.'

Cipriano di Lucca stared at her, a smile spreading across his sharp features. 'Well, you have a gunner's nerve, madonna, I grant you,' he said. 'My orders, however, are clear. They are to see you safely to—'

'I know your orders. Carry them out, and I shall be over the wall of that convent in a day. I shall go alone to Malta, and join Leonardo there.'

Cipriano pulled his horse to a stop. 'Malta?' he said. 'Is that where he's got to?'

'Yes,' replied Bianca. 'And Rigo is there with him.'

Cipriano stroked his broken nose. It was a flaw in his otherwise handsome countenance, having been damaged in a brawl with his fellow gunners over the question of whether an interest in clothing and cleanliness should be considered effeminate. Smiling still more broadly, he said, 'Why, then, madonna, you have no need to travel there alone. Lorenzo de' Medici would hardly forgive me if I allowed you to undertake so perilous a journey by yourself. Moreover in Malta, I am told, they have the finest laces and the newest of the cotton fabrics from Ghaza. I have even heard that there is a certain velvet from Aleppo, finer than satin, to be had there and there only. On top of which, if there is a gathering of gunners in Malta, then I smell adventure.'

'There are only two of them,' Bianca observed.

'Two gunners is a gathering.'

'I have very little money, Cipriano.'

'Do not trouble yourself, my lady. I have a satchel fat with Lorenzo's florins. Prize money earned for us by Leonardo at

56

Castelmonte, in point of fact, which appeals to me as ironic. Well, madonna, let us make haste. We will need to find a ship in Pisa, and perhaps another in Livorno, in order to buy passage for Malta.'

'Florence,' said Rigo, his brow furrowed. 'I say we should now return to Florence. You came here to help Felippo, who is dead. Add to this the emerald, which is worth enough to make you a man of substance when sold in Florence, but worth very little here. We have survived three attacks by Riario and his agents. Our supply of good fortune may be gone. And Bianca Visconti waits for you, Leonardo my friend; therefore let us leave Malta. Agreed?'

'The hours pass and are accounted to us,' said Leonardo softly.

'The hours do what?'

'*Pereunt et Imputantur*: they pass and are accounted to us.' Leonardo tossed the ivory crescent onto the bed beside the gunner. 'You see, Rigo? The same words written by Felippo in his letter to me, and here they are, engraved above the jewel.'

'And what of it? That was Felippo's message to you, doubtless,' said Rigo confidently. 'He wanted you to have the emerald, yet feared to say directly. Take it, and let us be gone.'

'And what of this, then?' Leonardo held out the square tablet he had retrieved from the sinking *Pyramus*. Rigo took it.

'Here are more words, I see. What do they say?'

Leonardo glanced at the tablet in Rigo's hand.

'Upon the side you see, they read as follows,' he replied. ' "I RUN MY RACE. I GAIN OR FALL BEHIND."

Rigo turned the object over. 'And on the other?' he enquired.

' "SO SHALL YOU KNOW YOUR PLACE WHEN ALL ARE BLIND",' said Leonardo.

'More mystification,' Rigo said. 'What does it mean? Nothing.'

'Or everything, Rigo. Felippo did not call me to Malta to give me a bauble he might have hidden in any one of a thousand safe places. No; these two pieces of ivory, taken together, hold a key

57

to some other puzzle, a puzzle so important that Felippo died for it. Are you not curious? We stay here, Rigo.'

'And I start to practise left-handed sword-play again,' said Rigo tartly. He would have complained further, but they were interrupted by the arrival of Lemmo, breathless from the climb up the stairway of the inn.

'They had only almonds in the market, sirs,' he said. 'Will they serve?'

'By all means,' said Rigo, accepting the knotted cloth the boy was carrying. 'You are the best of valets and stewards, lad.'

'I am here but to obey you, my masters,' said Lemmo smoothly. He bowed, and made to leave, but was stopped by Leonardo.

'Hold awhile, Lemmo,' said the artist. 'There are questions I need to ask you. It may be that you can assist me.'

'Questions, sir?'

'About your adoptive father and my friend, Captain Felippo *Il Fortunato*.' Leonardo waved him to a chair. 'Sit down, boy. I want you to tell me something of the ways in which Felippo sailed his ship.'

'Sailing? I know little of sailing, master.'

'Yet you sailed with *Il Fortunato*.'

'Many times. But as cabin boy only.'

'It matters not. I need merely to know what you saw and remember. For instance, at what hour of the day would your father change the course of the *Pyramus*?'

'Ah. I know that well enough,' said Lemmo. 'Each day at noon, and sometimes at night.'

'At noon? Good. And how did he proceed?'

Lemmo stared at the floor, frowning. 'Let me see. Not long before noon he would go into his cabin and lock the door. Then he would come out with his quadrant, and shoot the sun—as he called it.'

'Shoot the sun?' said Rigo. 'What is this quadrant, then?'

'It is a thing,' said Lemmo, gesturing, 'with two arms, one of which you point at the sun and the other at the sea. So much he taught me, though I could never grasp why.'

'It measures the sun's altitude above the horizon,' said Leonardo. 'You are doing very well, Lemmo. And then?'

'Little more, good Master Leonardo. He would return to his cabin, locking the door once more. After a short while we would hear the bolts slide again and he would come out and gave Tommaso a little change in the course, this way or that.'

'A *little* change?' said Leonardo. 'Always?'

'Why yes. Sometimes none at all.'

'And always at noon?'

'At noon for the sun,' replied Lemmo, 'though at night he would often do the same thing for the North Star. Or perhaps it was not the same thing. I cannot be sure.'

'But at noon,' persisted Leonardo, 'he never ordered a big swing in the heading of the ship, as it might be from due north to due east? Never so large as that?'

'Never.'

Rigo broke in. 'Then here is how he aimed his ship more exactly, as you told me,' he said. 'Is this his secret, think you?'

'Part of it, certainly,' said Leonardo. 'Yet I begin so see something more, and greater, buried here. If I am right, then Felippo indeed had a secret beyond price!'

'From so little you conclude so much?' asked Rigo.

'If I am right, Felippo knew a means by which to change for ever the way in which men see the world and travel across its face,' said Leonardo. 'No less.'

'How can this be?' asked Rigo.

The artist rose and began to pace the room, his hands clasped behind his back.

'Attend, then,' he said finally. 'Firstly, as I told you, most shipmasters sail coastwise, from landmark to landmark, aided by charts and their memories. It is a slow business, as you may imagine. And so there are times when a bold captain must leave the shore he knows and set sail across open waters, beyond sight of land. For this he needs wind-rose and portolan.'

'So I remember your saying,' said Rigo. 'And here winds and

currents may push his ship off course, spoiling the captain's aim.'

'Exactly so, my friend. Yet if such a captain should, through accident or error, lose himself far from shore, there is a means by which he may come safe to port, albeit a cumbersome one. For if his ship sails north towards the Pole Star, then the angle between that star and the horizon changes as he does so. When this angle is, for example, forty-four degrees, we say that his ship is at the forty-fourth latitude. And since all charts show what ports lie exactly on this latitude—or any other—it follows that our captain need only turn due east or west when he reaches his chosen latitude, and by running along it he must infallibly reach his port sooner or later; and he can do this simply by keeping the Pole Star at a constant angle above the horizon.'

'But this,' objected Rigo, 'may be well and good at night, when he can see the stars. What about the daytime?'

'An excellent question,' replied Leonardo, 'for the altitude of the North Star remains constant, whereas the height of the sun at noon varies with the seasons. None the less a mariner with some skill at mathematics, and aided by almanacks and tables of numbers—such as the *Almanach Perpetuum* by the Jew astronomer Abraham Zacuto—may calculate his latitude from the sun's height, correcting this by a figure which he finds in his tables and which is different for each day in the year.'

'Well?' said Rigo. 'Where is the mystery? I do not see where this leads us.'

'Then you have not attended to me well enough. For I have described a captain who makes a sudden and large change in the heading of his ship, as it might be from due north to due east, have I not?' said Leonardo. 'And yet Lemmo, here, assures us that Felippo made no such large swings, but instead corrected his course only slightly each noon. Therefore, when he ordered his changes in course, it cannot have been merely in order to sail down a latitude. Do you follow me? It was something different, and much more precise.'

'And what was it, then?'

'That,' said Leonardo, 'is what Venice really seeks. For I tell you, Rigo, that sailors know of no way—no way at all—in which a captain might be able to correct his course by a small amount, *once he is beyond sight of land.* But Felippo did, and it made him the fastest mariner in the Mediterranean. He knew, Rigo. And he was killed for it.'

Five

Of Uberto Neri it was said—among other things—that he feared few men in Venice and none outside it. Yet, as he greeted Venice's envoy, he cleared his throat nervously, there being something in the manner and bearing of spidery, elegant Orso Contarini which proclaimed him to be a dangerous man.

For was he not First Secretary to the Cinque Savi Agli Ordini, that committee of five all-powerful maritime directors of the Most Serene Republic? To Orso Contarini were brought all problems affecting ships and trade; from Orso Contarini went forth the cold and sometimes lethal decisions which solved those problems and kept the commercial heart of Venice beating.

Neri, who had upon his arrival commandeered the best suite of rooms in the villa outside Rabat, had been mildly surprised when he did not find himself evicted from them by Contarini. Instead, the little envoy chose a modest apartment at the very back of the house. He now conducted his visitor across the bedroom of this, halting at a silken tapestry adorning the wall beside the bed. This Contarini drew aside, to reveal an iron door which was presently ajar.

Neri's pulse quickened.

The Chart Room. Venice, he knew, had one like this in every port under her sway, and always its location was a closely held secret. Did it, he wondered, augur well or badly that this particular secret was being opened to him? He followed Contarini through the doorway.

They entered a long, deep room, clearly part of some ancient cavern. Ducts and passages, cunningly hidden among the rocks of the hillside above, brought in an abundance of fresh air. Cabinets lined the rock walls, their dozens of glass-fronted drawers holding the maps that were the cement of the Venetian maritime empire. Candelabra cast a steady, golden glow over all, save where some draught made shadows dance in the corners. Globes stood around in profusion: astrolabes, quadrants, portolans in rosewood and wrought silver. But it was the vast table of ebony that dominated the room, inlaid with mother-of-pearl and lapis lazuli and long enough to seat six men in comfort at either side. Ten gleaming black chairs, ranged about it, displayed legs tipped with solid gold; on the back of each chair was painted a half unfurled scroll depicting a heeled carrack or a sea battle.

'Sit down, Uberto,' said Orso Contarini. 'It is time, I think, that we had a private talk, you and I. Venice has need of your peculiar talents.'

'I am honoured, First Secretary,' said Uberto Neri, and did as he was bidden.

'Let us leave this business for a while,' said Leonardo. 'Tell me, instead, what happened when your father brought his ship into Malta.'

'All of it?' asked Lemmo.

Leonardo smiled. 'If you please.'

'It was always a busy time, sir. The sails had to come down while we were yet under way. Lines would be cast to the dock and made fast, the gangplank run out. Then the Spaniards would come aboard to inspect our cargo and give us papers to sign, and after that we would unload the ship.'

'Go on, Lemmo. You are doing well.'

'Then, later, my father would cast off once more and hoist sail to go to his own small cove by Marsasirocco. You know the place. We would anchor there and the men would row to shore.'

'And on shore?'

'Old Marco would meet us with his dray-cart and mules. The men would heave their bags and chests into the cart, jump in after them, and Marco would take them all to Rabat for a few *soldi* apiece.'

'With your father?'

'My father, sir, did not approve of drinking and women, as I think I have told you before. No, he never came here to Rabat with the crew.'

'What did he do?'

'He would walk with me along the quay at Marsasirocco', Lemmo said. "He'd give me a coin or two, and tell me to get some hot food into my belly. Then he would leave me, and go up the Street of Olives with his sea-bag over his shoulder.'

'And then?' prompted Leonardo.

'That is all, sir.'

'So you would eat, and await his return.'

'Yes.'

'For how long?'

'It is hard to recall, sir. Four hours, or five.'

'And why the Street of Olives, do you suppose?'

'Who can tell?' replied Lemmo, now thoroughly bored. 'It is the district where they press the oil. The street leads nowhere—that is to say, merely to the countryside.' He smirked. 'Perhaps he went to pick flowers.'

Orso Contarini rolled up a chart, tied it with ribbon, and replaced it in one of the cabinets before addressing Uberto Neri once more. He spoke slowly, as though choosing each word for precision, so that the effect was as though he were reading aloud from some arid, official document.

'The Committee of Five first learned of your assignment here when it met for its regular monthly convocation,' he said. 'They were, you should know, much displeased at your having been ordered to Malta by our Military Security Committee on a matter which affects Venice's maritime interests. I am instructed to convey to you our highest regard for your past services to the Republic. I am also to advise you that, with immediate effect, you are no longer to consider yourself under the direction of the

64

military people, who have flagrantly exceeded their authority. Is that clear?'

Neri stirred restlessly in his chair. 'With respect, First Secretary,' he pointed out, 'the committee politics of our Republic are no concern of mine. I was sent here by those with the authority to send me, my orders correctly signed. Those orders were clear: to search out and dispose of one Felippo Mendoza, known as *Il Fortunato*. This, I may say, has been accomplished.'

Contarini shut the cabinet door with unnecessary violence.

'Accomplished?' he said. 'How?'

'He is dead, sir, and his ship is sunk.'

The envoy controlled himself with an effort.

'Then I come too late,' he said. 'It was not the man's life we sought, Uberto, but his secrets. That is why I am here. Evidently the military minds that issued your orders think only in one way: murder. In this case, a very great pity.'

'But not my fault, First Secretary.'

'I accept that.'

'In any case,' added Neri, 'here was but one man and a single ship. A mere inconvenience, surely?'

'Please, Messer Uberto, do not try to instruct me. We command six fleets, true. We control the Mediterranean from end to end. Yet—and mark this well—that one captain and his single ship weighed equally in the balance with a hundred of our own!'

'How so sir?'

'How indeed? In report after report, voyage after voyage, our captains would record that the *Pyramus* had come first to harbour, selling its cargo at the highest price, taking on valuable goods at the lowest. I personally recall a certain casket of rare pink pearls, and a shipment of white ermine skins from Trebizond. We dispatched our fastest galley to acquire these. They were gone when we arrived in Aleppo—sold to *Il Fortunato*. Ivory tusks we lost to him, barrels of indigo, pepper and spices beyond measure, a thousand blades of Damascene steel. Do you understand?'

'*Il Fortunato* with reason, then,' said Neri.

'And *mal fortunato* for Venice,' replied Contarini. 'Our

bottoms, heavy with timber and lead, move slowly from port to port, forced to trade in thin milk while Felippo Mendoza skimmed the richest cream. Our charts were the best and most recent. By galley we should have been the faster. How, then, did this one man vanquish us? With better charts still? Secret ones? His trading pattern did not tell us. But the man himself—Felippo— might have done so. Had he been allowed to live, that is.'

'We searched for maps,' said Uberto Neri. 'We found nothing.'

'It was, at least, sensible of you to try,' admitted the envoy.

'And yet,' Neri went on, rubbing the table's gleaming surface with the palm of his hand, 'my work in Malta has taken a curious turn. It may be well that I should report it to you now.'

'Do so. If Venice salvages any of the hidden gold in this affair, you will reap a great reward, Uberto.'

'Then the circumstances are quickly told, sir. A short while ago there came here, from Venice and by special ship, a message from my superiors, instructing me to do a small favour for the Count Girolamo Riario, Captain-General to the Armies of Rome.'

'I heard no word of this,' said Contarini.

'My orders were, as ever, marked "secret". Yet very clear. I was given an official military order to kill an enemy of Rome—the artist and engineer Leonardo da Vinci.'

'Da Vinci?' Contarini's obsidian eyes flickered. 'I have heard of this da Vinci . . . what have I heard? Let me see. Did he not take Castelmonte, in the Apennines, from Rome? I think so. Yes. This is interesting news indeed, Uberto. Venice assists Rome? I wonder why.'

Neri rose from the table.

'Here is something of greater interest, First Secretary,' he said. 'For this Leonardo da Vinci keeps surfacing, like a dolphin, in the wake of Felippo Mendoza.'

'Continue.'

'He was in Felippo's cabin when the *Pyramus* sank. We found him in a Rabat whorehouse, speaking with the woman favoured by Felippo's boatswain.' Neri raised a quadrant to one eye, sighting along it at a chandelier. 'Coincidence?' he went on 'Perhaps. And yet one wonders. Does one not?'

'Well done, Uberto. Well done indeed. Your conversation suggests that you have not performed this favour for Rome yet. Delay it. Let us find the man and—reason with him. At all costs, Uberto.'

'As to that,' said Neri, 'I have made a start. My own spy serves da Vinci as valet; he is Felippo Mendoza's adopted son. I expect word from him soon.'

His prediction was confirmed by Lemmo's arrival at the villa, out of breath, half an hour later. The boy's answers to Contarini's insistent questioning gave the latter—and Neri himself—great satisfaction, as did the object which he placed on a balcony table before them.

'I took it from their room,' said Lemmo simply.

Uberto Neri took up the ivory crescent, adorned with its single huge emerald. Sunlight drew sea glints from the depths of the stone as he passed it to the Venetian envoy, who studied the curved inscription with care.

'*Pereunt et Imputantur*,' said Contarini.

'It was my step-father's, sire,' interrupted Lemmo. 'Tommaso, the boatswain, stole it from his cabin. I heard them say so at the tavern.'

'What do the words mean?' asked Neri.

'Very little,' the envoy replied. 'It is an old saying, Uberto, found on sundials. It means . . . it means merely that the sundial counts the passing of the hours. Whether this is of import to us I cannot say. Boy, you have served us well. Return this to your master, taking care not to let him know that you have—borrowed it. And listen to them when they speak of it. You understand?' And when Lemmo had gone, he added to Neri, 'As for Master Leonardo himself, Uberto, I think you should bring him here. Soon. We might, perhaps, enlist him . . . for a time, of course. Later we must not forget the request of Rome's Captain-General.'

The cobblestones of the Street of Olives gave way to a worn

dirt path. Climbing this track, Leonardo and Rigo found themselves in a bare and sultry landscape of terraced fields, scattered
with rocks, that rose steadily to a series of ridges behind the port
of Marsasirocco. A mile or so beyond the town they paused and
looked about them.

'Not even a monastery,' said Leonardo. 'No crofts, no fences.
Nothing. If Felippo came this way, it would have taken him only
to Rabat, it seems, and we have travelled thence by a far better
road than this ourselves.'

'Nor could he have walked to Rabat and back in four hours,'
added Rigo testily, 'which is the time young Lemmo told us he
was absent. Unless he had as little sense as you, Leonardo, it is
obvious that he stayed in Marsasirocco itself.'

'No,' said the artist. 'He came this way, and with his sea-bag.
I am sure of it. To meet somebody, perhaps, or to hide something?
I wonder. Or to recover something already hidden.'

Rigo leaned against a convenient outcrop of limestone, and spat.

'And you propose to find it,' he said. 'I am becoming familiar
with your tone of voice. Allow me to point out that if we are to
turn over every stone I see from here—let alone those I cannot
see—we shall die of old age before we are a quarter done.'

'Which makes it all the more likely that I am right,' Leonardo
rejoined. 'For a man might do many things, unobserved, between
here and Rabat.' He waved his arm panoramically. 'Think, my
friend. What was it that Felippo *Il Fortunato* did in the middle of
the dry land, and which had something to do with his speed and
skill as a navigator in the middle of the ocean? Well? Does your
curiosity not quicken, Rigo?'

'No,' said the gunner.

'I knew you had no soul,' said Leonardo. 'Now my own curiosity
is so great that I intend, this evening, to accept the hospitality of
Venice. The invitation comes from Uberto Neri.'

'And who the devil is he?'

'A man who employs a large Turk as a bodyguard, or so I am
told. But something also tells me that Venice stands behind his
shoulder.'

'Indeed,' said Rigo. 'Then I suggest you keep yours firmly against the wall. Is this the same Turk who interrupted our conversation at the whorehouse?'

'The same.'

'And would no doubt have killed us, had we given him the chance? I think you'd better let me come with you.'

'I thank you, Rigo, but no. Venice can just as easily try again for my life—or yours—in a back alley as in her own headquarters at Rabat, if that is what she intends. I will follow your advice and keep my back to the wall, but that's as far as it goes for the moment.'

'Or so you believe,' said Rigo, 'but one of these fine evenings, my philosophical friend, you are going to be wrong.'

'He bears no arms,' Achmet announced.

Seeing that the artist was indeed burdened only by his notebook and a small pouch, the guard beneath the arched gateway nodded silently and lifted aside his pike to admit them to the grounds of the Venetian headquarters. At the far end of the garden, the soft limestone façade of the villa glowed in the light of a dozen torches. The Turk led the way indoors and escorted Leonardo up a wide and curving stairway to the upper floor. He knocked once at a pair of imposing doors, which immediately swung open to reveal Uberto Neri himself, resplendent in black velvet tunic and hose adorned with patterns of silver thread. He bowed with a trace of mockery.

'Enter, Master Leonardo,' he said. 'We have, I think, met before.'

'Very nearly, sir,' agreed Leonardo. 'But not quite.' He walked past Neri into the room, surveying it with an appreciative eye. It was a salon of generous proportions, stretching across the entire width of the building. Its floor was of rose-pink marble, and a full-length window of stained glass opened from it on to a balcony overlooking the gardens. To his left, a breathtaking Madonna and Child by Lorenzo Lotto dominated a panelled wall—the very masterpiece, so Leonardo recognised, that had so mysteriously disappeared from the Convent of the Holy Spirit in Bergamo.

Around three sides of the room were ranged forty or more chairs in gilded wood with crimson damask cushions. Two more of these stood in a far corner, beside a small table. Here, awaiting their approach, was a short man of slender build, with dark hair and a neatly curled beard. Neri urged Leonardo towards this personage, and bowed again.

'Your Excellency,' he said, 'may I present to you Master Leonardo da Vinci, the Florentine painter?' Turning, he added, 'This is His Excellency Signor Orso Contarini, Legate-General and First Secretary to the Committee of Five in Venice.'

'I am honoured, sir,' Leonardo said.

'Ah, but no.' The envoy's voice was softly flattering. 'The honour is ours, I believe. I thank you for coming here, for I have travelled far—and fast—to meet you.'

'We are indeed a long way from Venice, sir.'

'Yet with good reason, as I hope to persuade you,' said Contarini. 'To which end, may I first of all offer you Venice's apologies? My friend Uberto tends towards the impetuous, as you have some cause to know. Had I been aware that plans were afoot to attack you, it would have been forbidden. You are, I believe, a man who uses force only as a function of reason, as am I myself.' He waved a hand at Uberto Neri, who moved a few paces aside from them. 'Come, Master Leonardo,' he went on. 'Sit with me, and let us confer.'

'By all means,' replied Leonardo, taking his seat. 'I do see force as the servant of reason, it is true. That you know it of me, I find surprising.'

'You are too modest. Does not every court in Italy buzz with your exploits, and those of the Medici cannon? They are already famous, as you are. The Medici guns? Their design is a triumph of reason which led, at the siege of Castelmonte, to a triumph of force. Let me speak plainly. I have come to Malta, Master Leonardo, to invite you to enlist in the service of our most Serene Republic of Venice.'

'A flattering invitation,' replied Leonardo, 'and one which I might be tempted to consider, if I knew to what end I am sought.'

'Why, sir, for your mind. What else? In Venice we do more than praise this quality; we pay those who possess it, and pay them well.'

'More precisely, however,' pursued Leonardo, 'does Venice also seek cannon?'

Orso Contarini laughed. 'Cannon?' he said. 'No. Cannon may serve Lorenzo de' Medici well enough, since he conducts his campaigns across a mile or two of earth. We are seafarers, sir, and have little use for guns to roll hither and yon upon wheels. Listen: Venice is an ancient city, Master Leonardo. For a thousand years the waters of the Brenta, the Piave, the Tagliamento and the Livenza have poured into the Mare Adriatica to form the lagoons and marshes upon which our ancestors built our city—not upon the dry land to be taken, nor upon the sea to founder, but where sea and land mix and marry. Venice has never been conquered. Can Lorenzo de' Medici say as much of Florence?'

'I dare say he cannot, sir.'

'Then Venice is safer than Florence. Nor does Venice pay any tithe to Rome, as others do. We appoint our own bishops, and when we converse with Rome she speaks softly and with respect. Again, can Lorenzo de' Medici make such a claim?'

'Well,' answered Leonardo diplomatically, 'Florence has been holding her own of late in discourse with Rome, or so it seems to me. But perhaps you are right.'

'Just so. Venice, Master Leonardo, can offer you both safety and freedom. Freedom of the mind. Look about you, if you will. Each painting in this room was created in Venice, by men like yourself, expressing their own vision without interference—and living well while they do so. Consider that also, if you please. We are a rich republic, and grow richer every day. Fools praise Venice for her churches, her palaces, her pretty ceremonials; but we who rule Venice are realists. We know that it is trade which supports our city, not mere wooden pilings. Gold flows to Venice, Master Leonardo, in a river so deep, so full, so broad, that a man need but dip a bucket into its tide to be richer than any princeling of Tuscany. Here, then is your equation. Safety, freedom, and riches. Venice offers you all these if you will perform her a small—nay, a trifling—task.'

'And what task is that?'

'Think of it, perhaps, as a demonstration of good faith. No more. The maps belonging to Captain Felippo Mendoza, which you seek—' the envoy raised his hand to forestall interruption '—Venice seeks also. Therefore, let us find them together. Serve us in this matter, and we will pay you ten thousand florins, as a token on our behalf of future earnings. What do you say?'

'A glimpse of Venice's golden river?'

'Let us call it that.'

'It sounds a large reward for so small a task, sir.' The banter vanished from Leonardo's voice. 'Your Excellency, you have spoken plainly indeed, and I can in justice do no less. I left my father's house many years ago to follow my own road. Not this, nor that of Lorenzo de' Medici, nor Rome's, but my own. I have found my own safety, and as for freedom, I have never known what it is to be without it. Riches? I am happiest when I can hang all I own upon one nail. I thank you for Venice's offer, but I must decline it. Felippo Mendoza was my friend. I do not know his secret, and may never do so. But if, by circumstance, it is revealed to me, be assured that I shall not barter it.'

Orso Contarini rose, and gazed down at the artist.

'Not even for your life?' he suggested quietly. 'Captain Mendoza, were he with us in this room, might tell you what can happen to those who refuse the hand of Venice. I ask you again, Master Leonardo; is that your final word?'

'Why, in such matters, sir,' Leonardo replied, 'my last word, and my first seldom differ.'

Six

TEN DAYS LATER, on a terrace overlooking the village of Zejtun, Rigo Leone looked up from his morning meal and stopped as though in a seizure, his knife halfway to his open mouth.

In the doorway opposite stood the grinning and fashionably garbed figure of Cipriano di Lucca.

'Cipriano? In God's name, it is!' Rigo rose, kicking over the bench upon which he had been seated and strode to meet the advancing lieutenant-gunner. They clasped each other's arms, and Rigo swung a boisterous fist to Cipriano's shoulder, almost paralysing him. 'What brings you to Malta?' he demanded. 'Is it war? Orders from Lorenzo? Or have you left his service? Do not just stand there rubbing your arm, man. *I want news!*'

Cipriano backed fastidiously away, still patting his rumpled tunic. 'Pray contain yourself, Captain,' he said. 'You have all but torn the stitching here with your greetings . . . wait!' He raised a hand against Rigo's warning fist. 'All is well,' Cipriano went on hastily. 'There is no war, though rumours are as thick as always. Nor am I under Lorenzo's orders—at least, I do not think so.'

'Then what——?'

'If you will hold your tongue and look into the adjoining room, Captain, you will find your explanation,' said his lieutenant.

Rigo pushed past him.

'A very persuasive young lady, that one,' Cipriano continued. Rigo stopped at the door that gave onto the living room.

'Do you say so?' he said. 'By the blood of Christ, it is the lady Bianca Visconti! You brought her here?'

'Say rather that she brought me. She wished to be near Leonardo, or so she said.'

'Then she has her wish,' Rigo observed, peering around the half-open door, 'being at this moment as close to him as a maid can get.'

A few paces away, Bianca stirred in Leonardo's embrace. 'Set me down,' she whispered. 'I can scarcely breathe—and besides, they are watching us!' At this Leonardo kissed her soundly again, then allowed her foot to touch the ground.

'My lady,' announced Rigo in an unnecessarily loud and embarrassed tone from the doorway, 'we have food and drink. Will you not eat?'

'Indeed, I will. I am starving,' replied Bianca. 'And how do we find you, Captain Leone?'

'Very well—and the better for seeing you. What do you say, Leonardo?'

Holding her by the hand, Leonardo ushered Bianca onto the terrace. 'Why, that Cipriano here has brought me the best of all possible gifts,' he said, 'and therefore we had better feed him as well.'

'Not I,' put in Cipriano, a curious look on his face. 'That is to say ... perhaps not this morning, at all events.'

'He was seasick all the way from Pisa,' explained Bianca, 'though the cook offered to cure him with a piece of fat bacon.'

'And if you please, my lady,' said Cipriano with dignity, 'I wish to hear nothing of bacon. I am no sailor. In fact I here and now make a vow never to set foot on the deck of any vessel again, so long as I live.'

'Well spoken,' said Rigo. 'A gunner's resolve, indeed. We shall drink with sorrow at your burial, Cipriano.'

'What burial?' enquired his subordinate suspiciously.

'He means,' said Leonardo, 'that Malta is an island, so that unless you mean to end your days here ...'

'By God, I had forgotten,' Cipriano said. 'Well, and why not? It seems a pleasant enough place, and the warehouses at the harbour are amply supplied with lace and silk. What of the women,

Rigo? Are they willing, would you say? Your pardon, my lady,' he added to Bianca. 'I am somewhat unbalanced. It must be the swaying of this floor, I think.'

He averted his face, a handkerchief to his mouth, while his three companions sat down to their meal.

Leonardo turned to Bianca.

'Well, madonna?' he asked her.

His mistress regarded him with an impish eye.

'Lorenzo is furious with you,' she said, somewhat obliquely.

'That does not surprise me,' said Leonardo.

'He is also furious with me.'

'Nor does that exactly fill me with amazement, since you must annoy him even more frequently than I do. Has he banished you, by any chance?'

'In a way.'

Leonardo's amusement turned to alarm.

'You are not teasing?' he asked. 'Lorenzo sent you here, to Malta?'

'No. He sent me to Pisa,' Bianca told him, breaking a piece of bread.

'Why?'

'Because I told him I was pregnant,' said Bianca calmly, 'and that you were the father.'

'What!'

'I was beginning to think that *nothing* amazed you,' said Bianca. 'Surely you don't find the idea impossible? And, by the way, the proper response is to sweep me into your arms—not to sit there with your mouth agape like an oaf. Remember it for the future. For the present, I am not pregnant, you are not a father-to-be, and I have a gunner's nerve, according to Cipriano.'

'Cipriano says that?'

'So he says,' laughed Bianca. She leaned across and kissed him. 'It was the best way I could think of to be with you,' she said. 'Except that Lorenzo seemed to think I should be shut up in a convent for my sins, under a vow of silence. And so I had to ask Cipriano to help me escape.'

At this point Cipriano removed the handkerchief from his mouth and turned it neatly into the front of his shirt. 'True,' he declared. 'Though I have been basely deceived by her, I am official escort to the lady Bianca. Who, I am bound to say, is quite right.'

'In what respect?' demanded Leonardo, recovering something of his usual poise and taking Bianca's hand once more.

'Why, in that a few moments ago you did, indeed, look remarkably like a goldfish,' said Cipriano. 'And now, since you know what brought us hither, may we ask in turn exactly what you are doing in a place like this, five leagues from anywhere and in Malta rather than Milan?'

Leonardo recounted most of what had happened to Rigo and himself so far, a tale which took some little time. 'And therefore, madonna,' he concluded, 'though your presence here makes my heart joyful beyond words, I must beg you to stay always within these walls. We could not remain at our lodgings in Rabat, since in the city our opponents had us at a disadvantage. Out here in this villa they do not. But since we have not yet found what we seek, neither can we be sure what may befall us in our search. Do you understand?'

'Of course,' Bianca replied. 'And for the present, if you will forgive me, all I want to do in any case is to sleep.'

'And I', agreed Cipriano fervently. 'I have not slept for weeks, or so it seems.'

Summoned at once by Rigo's shout, Lemmo appeared from the kitchen and was told to find beds and blankets. Shortly thereafter, Bianca and Cipriano retired, while Leonardo and Rigo made ready for their daily foray into the countryside west of Zejtun.

Half an hour later beneath a broiling sun they stood in a shallow and rock-strewn depression a mile away from the house.

'Our Lemmo is a devoted boy,' said Rigo. 'He came close to weeping I thought, when we told him he could not accompany us this morning.'

'So he did,' Leonardo replied. 'A pleasant and attentive lad

76

indeed—if somewhat over-given to tears. Would you have preferred him to come with us?'

'No. Though an extra pair of eyes might serve us well. Leonardo, we have quartered these damned fields and ridges for days on end. Have you the smallest idea of what you are doing?'

Leonardo looked around. 'Today,' he suggested, 'I thought we might once again try those caves over there.'

One side of the valley was formed from a low escarpment, on whose face a dozen or more openings could be seen from where they stood. On previous visits to this same valley they had already examined the small caverns behind each of these dark mouths, discovering little in them apart from earth and bats. Rigo pointed out this fact.

'I know,' Leonardo said. 'And yet . . . look, Rigo, at the path yonder.' He pointed towards the foot of the rock face, where a narrow track, worn by the hooves of the goats that grazed the dry and spiny vegetation, meandered across the valley's floor.

'What about it?' asked Rigo.

'Follow its course up the slant of the cliff. See how it bends suddenly towards us, there, and then resumes its course? I noticed it the day before yesterday. It passes close in front of the mouths of all those caves except one, as though the animals who made it have been avoiding something. I conclude . . . well, I do not know exactly what I conclude. Wait here for me.'

Rigo at once sat down and unslung the wineskin from his shoulder. Leaving him occupied, Leonardo walked in the direction of the valley's lower slope; he scaled the escarpment and made his way back along the top of the cliff. Arrived at the point immediately above the bend in the goat-path, and acknowledging Rigo's casual wave from below him, he turned away from the edge and began a careful search among the flattened boulders of the ridge. Soon he stopped. At his feet he had found what he was looking for; a small hole in the limestone, bored vertically downwards by some torrent of bygone centuries, now long dried up.

He knelt and rubbed a finger around the margin of this hole.

77

Then, satisfied, he descended circuitously again to the valley, and Rigo.

'As I thought,' he said. 'Come on.'

'What did you find up there?' asked the gunner.

'Soot.'

'A camp fire?'

'By no means. A chimney. One of those caves is inhabited.'

'Leonardo, we have already looked in all of them.'

'Then we did not look far enough. Follow me.'

Rigo rose and dusted off his breeches, sighing. Leonardo was already striding towards the hole in the cliff-face that lay where the goat-trail curved; by the time the gunner caught up with him he had scrambled a few feet up to the ledge immediately beneath it. He extended a hand to help Rigo, and within moments they were in the cool darkness of the cavern. As their eyes recovered from the glare of the outside sun, they were able to make their way to the back of the narrow tube of rock, where they found their way barred by a large boulder that had, apparently, fallen from the roof. There seemed no way of progressing further. Leonardo turned and paced out the distance from the boulder's face to the cave's entrance, returning at once to Rigo, who was leaning against the side wall with his arms folded.

'Well?'

'It goes deeper,' Leonardo said.

'Possibly. We, however, cannot.'

'Somebody does,' rejoined Leonardo, 'at least, according to my measurements outside.'

'God blast and damn your measurements,' said Rigo. He might have pressed his argument beyond this, but instead paused in surprise as the great rock that barred their way began to move. He recoiled, grasping Leonardo's arm; but the latter stood his ground as the mass of stone rotated slowly before them, revealing a narrow cleft beyond it. Into this Leonardo at once marched forward.

After fifteen paces the tunnel widened into a limestone chamber of considerable size, whose walls were lit by candles in iron brackets. Here there sat an ancient hermit, who appeared so—Rigo immediately concluded to be completely mad.

Clad in the crudest of rags and barefoot, the old man was solemnly sucking his thumb, regarding his visitors as blandly as any new-born babe. His hair and beard were untrimmed and of a deep grey hue; only his eyebrows were black, being bushy and curling at either side of his forehead. His eyes seemed never to fix upon them for more than an instant, but slid this way and that, blinking.

Rigo tugged urgently at Leonardo's sleeve.

'Leave him alone,' he whispered. 'They say that madmen such as this one are like a barrel of gunpowder—harmless until some spark sets them off.'

'I think not,' said Leonardo, bowing gracefully in the direction of the hermit. 'He is no madder than you or I, if I judge aright.' He walked to the middle of the chamber. 'Consider his fireplace. It has a perfectly designed flue, the upper end of which I have already found concealed in the ridge above us. Then, consider also the valuable Turkish rugs upon which we are standing; and, yonder, those rows of books, that inkwell, the table and chair which would do credit to any joiner. Here lives, by his own rational choice, a man who reads and writes, who is capable of building a secret doorway to his home—with a mechanism admirably contrived to keep curious peasants from disturbing him; and who, before admitting us'—Leonardo here advanced towards the old man—'takes care to cover his fine clothing with these quite convincing tatters.'

Gently, he reached out a hand and drew aside the patchwork cloak, to reveal a shirt of embroidered linen. Then, stepping back a pace, he bowed again.

'My name, sir, is Leonardo da Vinci,' he said, 'and this is my friend and companion, Rigo Leone. We mean you no harm, as I think you must know. We should feel honoured to talk with you awhile, if you will permit it.'

At that their host rose to his feet, pulling thoughtfully at his lower lip, his eyes now glinting with a sharp intelligence. He stood for a moment, and then pulled the torn and filthy robe from his shoulders, throwing it casually to one side.

'As you have observed, sirs,' he said, 'I am in fair possession of my faculties, being mad only in so far as all men are mad. I bid you welcome. I am Zeser Ibn Hasim.'

'Then we are the more honoured,' said Leonardo. 'For, sir, I have already made your acquaintance, in Rome.'

'Is that so? But of course,' the old man said. 'How foolish of me. I had the strange belief that I had never been to Rome, but perhaps I am madder than I like to think.'

'If you have not, sir, your mind has,' Leonardo replied. 'It was your mind I met there—your *De Rotatio Orbis Mundi*, to be exact. A finer work than the preface to the *Ephemerides* of Regiomontanus, or so it seemed to me at the time.'

Ibn Hasim nodded, absently rather than with complacency. 'Sit down,' he said, indicating two low stools. Leonardo and Rigo complied. 'You are kind to say so, Master Leonardo,' Ibn Hasim went on. 'But have you come so far in order to flatter me? I think not. You are a friend of Captain Felippo Mendoza, known in these regions as *Il Fortunato*, are you not?'

'I was.'

'Ah. I feared that something had happened to him. He has not been to see me for . . . well, no matter. He spoke of you often, you see. And now he is dead, I take it.'

'Murdered.'

'It was inevitable,' said Ibn Hasim softly. 'And do you seek vengeance for him?'

'Nothing so purposeless,' responded Leonardo.

'I am glad to hear it.'

'I seek to make certain that his secret does not die with him. That is all.'

'Captain Mendoza had a secret?' The old man smiled crookedly. 'Sirs, I am inhospitable. I do not, naturally, drink wine myself, but I have water, if you wish it?'

'I thank you,' said Leonardo, 'but we have our own sustenance, and water is more precious than wine hereabouts. Let me not beat about the bush. Sir, we were led hither by chance and reason, in one proportion or another. You are an astronomer—perhaps the greatest of all astronomers, though the world believes you dead. And Felippo was a navigator; by the reckoning of others, the greatest of all navigators. I should have suspected long before this that his greatness stemmed from contact with a man such as yourself. You gave him knowledge. You passed on to him your computations on eclipses and planetary conjunctions. Is that true?'

'It may be.' Ibn Hasim's hand was, almost unconsciously, rearranging his hair and beard, and the image of the ancient madman was dissolving as though it had never existed.

'And yet I still find it strange,' pursued Leonardo. 'For there is more to it even than that. All other captains sail north and south to find their latitude, and then turn their ships through ninety degrees to follow it. Felippo did no such thing.'

'No?'

'No. Were it not incredible, I would almost dare to say that Felippo could find his position—his exact position upon an empty ocean, mark you—each and every day, as though by wizardry.'

'Most marvellous,' said Ibn Hasim sardonically. Of a sudden he cackled shrilly, and raised his hands, spreading them wide. 'Truly you have discovered his secret, my son. I see that. The Seventh Circle within the Nine! The Alpha and Omega! The Holy Kabbala!' Leonardo here made as though to speak, but the old man stopped him through sheer weight of words. 'Hear me, then, strangers,' he pronounced. 'To me came Felippo Mendoza, called *Il Fortunato*; it is true. I cannot conceal it from you. From me he received the mystic signs, the symbols that Neptune reveals only to the true and living Priest of the Sea! Winds were his to command, for I gave them to him! The waves were subject to his rule! For him alone was the ocean made safe and to him alone its paths revealed!'

'Yes, indeed,' observed Leonardo calmly at the end of this oration. 'And besides all these signs and wonders—and other mysterious nonsense—he used certain scientific devices and made certain calculations.'

Ibn Hasim peered darkly at the artist, for a long time.

'Do not speak to me of devices and calculations,' he commanded finally. 'Good day to you, and to your friend.' He turned his back on them.

'Then we take our leave of you, sir,' said Leonardo. 'And when you have thought over all that has been said here, remember this. I grew up with Felippo Mendoza. He was my friend, and when we were boys together we lay in a meadow below old Beppo's orchard and shared our dreams; we watched the clouds sail past above our heads, and Felippo told me that he wanted to sail, like them, around the world. He wanted to see every land, every ocean, so he said. And I promised I would help him, if ever I could. He cannot sail the world now, Ibn Hasim, but others may—and if they need Neptune's smile, they will have need of other things besides. Felippo wrote to me in Florence because he needed me here; it was for that reason alone that I came to Malta. Reflect on it, sir, until we meet again.'

But the old man stood motionless, appearing not to listen. After a moment or two Leonardo turned and left, with Rigo following him. As they reached the sunlit entrance to the cavern and shielded their eyes against the glare of the valley outside, they heard the soft rumble of the boulder behind them, sealing the passage that led to Zeser Ibn Hasim's retreat.

Bianca stood beneath the keystone of the arched window, naked, and watched the waning moon glide into and between the clouds. Cooled by the tendrils of night breeze that caressed her flesh, she savoured her own completeness.

'It is changed, Leonardo,' she said, without turning. 'Or perhaps it is we who have changed, do you suppose? In Florence I knew nothing of love, save what I had heard of it in the sad and foolish songs of minstrels who sang of separated lovers. But here, just now, I felt myself but one half of a single spirit, and wondered why their songs had not told me of this also. Am I foolish?'

Leonardo lay upon his back, his arms cradled behind his head.

'No,' he answered. 'Why should it be?'

'I do not believe you are listening to me, Leonardo. I can tell from your voice.'

'If I am not, it is through no fault of mine. I must paint a picture of you, Bianca, as you stand there, part child, part woman, and all mysterious.'

She turned towards him then, smiling, a smile not for him but for herself. 'And who will commission such a work from you?' she asked. 'Will you say, "Here, my Lord Lorenzo: a portrait of your ward, Bianca Maria Visconti, by moonlight?" ' She laughed at the thought. 'And, besides, which one will you paint, my artist-lover? The child, or the woman? You had best make haste while you can still choose. The child will soon be no more.'

'I will make haste, then. For that itself is the mystery, Bianca. I look at your face, and see the woman. It is your body which seems the child's. Before, it was the other way about; the face of a child and a woman's form. Why should this be? I cannot tell. Yet I must capture them all together.'

'And have you not already done so?' She walked across the room and sat beside him on the bed. She smelled sweetly of love, and between her breasts the cold radiance from the window struck an answering reflection from her skin, still moist with sweat. 'After all,' she continued, 'since I have seen Verrocchio's statue of your body, I suppose it is only fair to allow you to paint mine.' She ran a finger along the white line of a scar on his arm. 'And this is a slip of the sculptor's chisel, no doubt.'

'The record of a memory. No more.'

She bent and kissed him swiftly. 'But I have the man here and not the statue,' she said, 'and there are pleasanter ways of making memories, are there not?'

He pulled her towards him and, as passion touched them both again, it did so slowly and with tenderness. Each moment seemed to slip languorously by as though they rested on the surface of a broad, quiet river. Throughout all the mingled rhythms of love they looked into one another's eyes, finding no words, and needing none.

In the small hours of the morning the sound of footsteps on the stairs woke Bianca and she shook Leonardo gently.

'It is Rigo again,' she whispered. 'He comes home from his woman, Decima, in Zejtun.'

'Bianca, my heart,' said Leonardo, 'why waken me to tell me what I already know? Go back to sleep.'

Insistently, she nudged him again. 'But he goes there nearly every night, does he not?' she asked.

Leonardo sighed and opened his eyes.

'I dare say he does,' he replied. 'He is, after all, a grown man and able to account for himself. What is the matter?'

'Like a man you think first and always of men. It is Decima who concerns me. Is there not danger for her, alone in Zejtun? They took her once. May they not take her again?'

'What do you propose?'

'Bring her here, Leonardo. She could live here with us. It would be safer if she did so.'

'So it would.' Leonardo raised himself onto one elbow and regarded her provokingly. 'Ask her, then, Bianca. However improper it may be,' he added.

'Improper?'

'She is, after all, a whore.'

'And what of that?' said Bianca. 'They have called the Visconti worse than that before now—and what will my confessor call me, do you think?'

'Go to sleep,' said Leonardo. 'In the morning you shall bring her here.'

Orso Contarini walked slowly down the steps of the Venetian headquarters in Rabat with Uberto Neri at his side. At the gate stood a small coach, ready to carry the envoy to his ship at the docks at Birgu. As the guard stood aside to let them pass, Contarini addressed his companion with silken menace.

'Well, Uberto. We want him alive, unharmed, and in Venice. I trust this to be understood.'

'It is, First Secretary.'

'Good. Then, for the present, do nothing.'

'Sir,' Uberto remonstrated, 'this is no great matter. If you will delay your departure until dawn tomorrow, I can take my men and capture him for you tonight. Why waste time?'

The envoy paused by the coach, drawing a glove over his narrow hand.

'Because, my dear Uberto, your pretty boy and your Turk have yet to inspire me with confidence. As for your men, I have seen them; three down-at-heel Spaniards and a brace of petty Maltese ruffians. I think Venice can do better than that, Uberto. Tell me again who his companions are?'

'Da Vinci? He has with him two Florentine gunners,' Neri replied. 'One is a frivolous dandy, concerned only with the cut of his doublet, and the other a brainless and bull-headed lout. If his friends are all that is worrying you, sir——'

Contarini looked at him coldly.

'And the girl?' he asked.

'According to Lemmo, sir, she is a Visconti, originally from Milan. She is an orphan. Her guardian, Lodovico Sforza, entrusted her to the safe-keeping of Lorenzo de' Medici in Florence.'

'Precisely,' said Contarini. 'The provocation of Florence and Milan may be no concern of yours, Uberto. But it concerns me.'

'With respect, First Secretary, I see no difficulty,' said Neri. 'My information is, firstly, that nobody in Florence knows she is in Malta, and secondly that in any case she has disobeyed Lorenzo de' Medici in coming here to be with Leonardo da Vinci. They are, it goes without saying, lovers. If any . . . accident should befall her, therefore, it seems to me that you need only offer Florence an apology for a minor and unfortunate incident, the blame for which can hardly be laid at Venice's door. Would you not agree?'

'Perhaps. None the less, Uberto, and with the greatest regard for your skill in handling these matters, you will oblige me by waiting until I can provide you with six men of my own. They will be responsible only to Venice—which should relieve you of some anxiety—and they will be the best that the Committee can find. Meanwhile, you will have time to set your plans with care. And be sure that Leonardo da Vinci does not leave the island before they arrive.'

Seven

BEHIND THE HOUSE, an olive grove marched gently up the slope of the hill. Between its trees, the ground was carpeted with grass, warm in the afternoon sun and scattered with flowers, above which butterflies haphazardly drifted.

Bianca sat leaning against a tree trunk with Leonardo's head in her lap. Her eyes were half closed as she stroked a lock of his auburn hair. The day was hot and still; even the crickets were silent in their crevices.

'And now?' she asked him. 'What will you do now?'

Leonardo removed a grass stalk from his mouth and twirled it idly.

'Collect Felippo's secret, I hope,' he said, 'which may prove somewhat difficult, since it lies in the cabin of the *Pyramus*.'

'Oh, does it?' Bianca said. 'You've never told any of us that you knew what you were looking for.'

'I was unsure of my ground,' replied Leonardo. 'But I can tell you now.'

'And what is it?'

'A clock,' Leonardo said.

'A *clock*?'

'Yes. It was a matter of solving a riddle, you see.'

Bianca moved her knees beneath him impatiently. 'What riddle is this?' she asked.

'One with many clues, each waiting to be linked with the others,' Leonardo said. 'For, let us consider: what does a clock do? It counts the hours as they pass, does it not?'

'Aha. "*Pereunt et Imputantur,*" I suppose.'

'Just so. "The hours pass and are accounted to us." An inscription commonly found on sundials, which are a form of clock. And then there is the emerald.'

'What has the emerald to do with it?'

'Tommaso, the boatswain, stole it from Felippo's cabin. It is set in an ivory crescent, which—according to Decima—was a key. Tommaso asked the captain what it opened, but Felippo wouldn't tell him. It opened nothing. *It was used to wind a clock.* Remember, too, the second inscription, on the tablet I found in Felippo's cabin myself, and which I now think was the baseplate of that same clock. "I run my race: I gain or fall behind; so shall you know your place when all are blind." That was the hardest riddle of all, because although it seems nonsense, it means exactly what it says, no more and no less. For it was a clock that gained, or fell behind; and in doing so it told Felippo Mendoza exactly where he was. He carried it in the cabin of the *Pyramus,* you see.'

Bianca looked down at him doubtfully.

'It would have to be a very small clock, then, surely?' she said. 'I have seen the workings of the clock in the tower of Santa Angelica in Florence; it is driven by huge weights which are raised with a handle . . . so big.' She extended her arms. 'But a small clock? I have never seen one.'

'Nor have I,' said Leonardo. 'But I will show you one, soon.'

'You seem very certain of all this. What has made you so?'

'An old man who lives in a cave.'

'The man you came across yesterday?' Bianca asked. 'Rigo says he is mad.'

'He is far from mad.'

'And he told you of this clock?'

'By no means. Nor had he any need to. All he needed to tell me was his name: Zeser Ibn Hasim.'

Leonardo replaced the stalk of grass between his teeth and chewed on it thoughtfully. After a moment, Bianca pushed his head away from her lap, allowing it to fall back against the turf beside her.

'Well?' she asked, infuriated. 'Is that all? Do you imagine you need explain things no further?'

Leonardo sat up.

'Does it interest you, then?' he asked.

'Of course it does!'

'Why, then,' Leonardo replied, brushing at his hair, 'I will tell you a story. A legend, or so it was thought until now. Many years ago, it is said, there lived in Persia a certain ruler called the Caliph Abd-al-Rahman, a wise, rich and powerful man whose interests included—among other things—mathematics. At his order, so the tale goes, his court astronomer made a clock. It was a fabulous instrument, fashioned out of Damascene steel and bronze alloys whose composition nobody knew save for its maker, and it was more accurate than any clock ever imagined. It took seven years to build. When it was finished, the Caliph kept it hidden in his private apartments where none could see it. Its case was encrusted with rare jewels, and the emerald which adorned its key—so it is said—came from the very peak of the Caliph's crown. And his astronomer, having built it, used this clock to calculate planetary tables, and charts of the heavens, and other such things, as is the habit of astronomers, and this he went on doing until the Caliph's death.'

'And what then?'

'The Caliph Abd-al-Rahman was murdered by one of his sons. When this happened, the story continues, his court astronomer became fearful that the clock would fall into unscrupulous hands, and he stole it and fled to Accra. There he took ship, and was never heard of again. And the name of that astronomer,' Leonardo concluded, 'was Zeser Ibn Hasim.'

'I see,' Bianca said. 'And where did you hear this . . . legend?'

'Oh, it is one of those common tales that abound wherever doctors, or scholars, or alchemists are found together,' replied Leonardo. 'I heard it in a tavern by the Ponte Carraia, along with similar stories of philosopher's stones that turn everything into gold, and nonsense of that kind. And yet . . . let us suppose, or guess, or imagine if you like, certain things. Zeser Ibn Hasim, who

88

was thought to be dead long since, is alive, for I have seen him. His astronomical tables, which I studied in Rome's archives, are indeed better than all others. It follows that the notion of his once having built a clock of amazing accuracy is not so far fetched as it would seem. As for the fabulous emerald, this I have seen for myself. Very well. Then let us conclude that he did build it, at the behest of the Caliph Abd-al-Rahman. How did he escape from Accra? By sea. Who befriended him, and helped him escape? Here, the story always ends.'

'And you think it was Felippo Mendoza.'

'That,' agreed Leonardo, 'is exactly what I think. And I think that in gratitude for his life, Zeser Ibn Hasim gave Felippo the clock, or perhaps merely lent it to him, it matters not. And I also think that Felippo visited the old man regularly, here in a cave on Malta, in order to have Ibn Hasim reset the clock for him so that it always told the correct time—*the correct time in Malta*, that is.'

Bianca considered this for a while. 'I think you are teasing me.' she said finally. 'Why should he want to know the correct time in Malta, if he spent most of his life at sea?'

'Because,' said Leonardo, 'if he was in the middle of the ocean, without landmarks, it would tell him his meridian, or *longitude*. Consider again. According to Lemmo, Felippo used his quadrant to shoot the sun each day at noon, as many sailors do. They do so in order to calculate their latitude. But Felippo did something more. He would go into his cabin, shut the door, and remain there for some time. Why? To read his clock; it told him the time in Malta. And from the difference between the hour at sea—which was noon, by his quadrant—and the hour in Malta, he could compute how far east or west of Malta he might be. Thus Felippo Mendoza, alone of all navigators, could find both his latitude *and his longitude* and so, day by day, could correct his course precisely.'

'Felippo alone?'

'Yes. For he alone possessed the knowledge to do so, and a clock accurate enough for the task. Others might stumble from headland to headland along a coast, or sail down a latitude. Felippo sailed from port to port, and thereby made his fortune.'

'But all this is guesswork,' said Bianca. She sighed, and closed her eyes. 'I am not saying that it's unreasonable, Leonardo, but all you have to go on is a story, and your own imagination. Isn't that true? Admit it.'

Leonardo leaned back, resting his head in her lap once more. 'It is easily tested,' he said. 'Either there is a clock in the cabin of the *Pyramus*, or there is not. I shall go down and find out.'

'Under water?'

'Certainly. Divers for sponges do so. So can I.'

'And if you are right?' Bianca asked him. 'What will you do with this clock?'

'Return it to Zeser Ibn Hasim, who is its rightful owner.'

'And that will be the end of the matter?'

'Apart from having satisfied my own curiosity, yes.'

Bianca's eyes remained closed, though she smiled. 'It does not occur to you that you might use it to make your fortune, then, as it made Felippo Mendoza's?' she enquired innocently.

'No,' Leonardo answered her. 'For one thing, Felippo, once fortunate, is now dead.' He reached upward and laid his hand against her cheek. 'And besides,' he added, 'my fortune is already made.'

'The woman Decima now lives with them?' asked Uberto Neri curtly. 'Is that the sum of what you have to tell me?'

'As I told you,' Lemmo said sulkily, 'she came back from Zejtun with Captain Leone four days ago. She has been at the villa ever since.'

'Then they are five. What do they plan, boy?'

'How can I know?' Lemmo demanded. 'I work all day in Birgu for the boatwright Ottavio, do I not? It was Master Leonardo himself who found the position for me so that—as he says—I might learn a trade. I hate it. What do I need with a trade, Uberto? Can you not——?'

'You will do as I say, Lemmo, and disobey me at your peril.' Neri's tone was still deadly. 'It serves my purpose well enough to have you in Birgu, where you may observe the comings and goings at the wharves and thus warn me if da Vinci tries to find a ship and leave this cursed island. Equally, you serve my needs at the villa, perfoming such small tasks as they may set for you. Keep your ears alert, boy. These are orders.'

'But it is near four miles to Birgu,' Lemmo whimpered, 'and eight miles from Birgu to you here in Rabat. I spend weary hours walking, day after day. My feet are blistered, and my hands rough from Ottavio's damnable carpentry lessons. And do you care? No!'

Neri rose from his chair, sliding his dagger from its sheath, and set the blade against Lemmo's throat. 'You are but a slice away from death, boy,' he said. 'There will be no more of this trivial bleating. I have need of you only for so long as you may be my eyes and ears—at Birgu and at the villa. Do we understand each other, you and I?'

His head frozen in fear, Lemmo rolled his glance downwards towards the dagger. He nodded once. Neri withdrew the blade and sheathed it. 'Good,' he said. 'And now to Leonardo da Vinci. Tell me, where does he sleep at night?'

Lemmo gulped with relief and set himself diligently to answer the questions which Uberto Neri fired at him. At the latter's insistence, he attempted to draw a plan of the villa, though his shaking hand made it a crude affair. Eventually Neri became affable once more, and offered him a goblet of wine.

'Excellent,' he said. 'They seem to be spending their time as though on holiday, Lemmo. Would you not agree? And yet, one wonders . . . but no matter for that. Let us make sure they are not interrupted, for the present at least.'

The last grains in the upper chamber of the sand-glass ran out. Bianca turned it over, setting her gaze towards the surface of the waters just off shore. Two minutes had passed; Leonardo would surface some time before the trickling sand announced the end of the third, she knew. Yet, even after a week of his experiments, she felt a prick of relief at the sight of his form rising from the green depths of the cove, and held the glass in front of her in anticipation of his signal.

He burst from the waves, spluttering, with upraised arm, and began to kick his way shorewards with powerful, surging strokes. Rainbows of spray danced in his wake until, ten paces from the dark line of seaweed that marked the water's edge, he stopped swimming and stood upright with streaming hair.

Each day for the past week they had found their way to this inlet, to the narrow, shingled beach that was clasped by headlands to north and south and shielded on the landward side by a great wall of tumbled rocks, behind which rose a sandy bluff. It was a pretty beach, and private, well hidden from nearby Marsasirocco.

Leonardo came through the surf towards her, stumbled where the rim of the beach dipped, and laughed as he recovered his balance.

'How long?' he called to her. 'How long this time?'

'A shade more than two and a half minutes,' she told him. From the ground beside her she picked up a pebble and dropped it into a pouch. 'That will be your thirty-seventh dive.'

'Thirty-seven. Yes. And better than two and a half minutes, you say? It is progress, Bianca, of a kind—but not enough.'

'And the ship?' Bianca asked him.

'She lies at four fathoms,' Leonardo said. 'Which would not be so bad, if the door to the cabin were not jammed tight. I doubt if I am down there more than two minutes at a time, and I cannot budge it. Well, we shall have to think of some other way around the difficulty, that is all. At all events, it is cool work on a day like this, so I cannot complain.'

'It is very pleasant for you, I am sure,' said Bianca, 'since you wear only a loincloth and are free to slip into the water whenever the fancy takes you—while I must need sit here in my gown, under a sun that will surely bake my brain if it does not broil my back first, counting your pebbles and staring at your sand-glass. Cool work, indeed!'

'Every problem has its solution,' said Leonardo, smiling at her fondly, 'and we need not rack our brains overlong to find this one.'

'Leonardo . . .'

'Yes?'

'If you think I am going to undress here, you are sadly mistaken,' Bianca said indignantly. 'Supposing someone were to see me?'

Leonardo looked skywards, shading his eyes.

'Well,' he said, 'there is a sparrow-hawk up there who will undoubtedly do so, though I doubt if you will outrage his feelings by disrobing.'

'No,' said Bianca. 'No, Leonardo.'

'You are hardly so modest at night, my heart.'

'At night it is different.'

'It is colder. I will allow that,' said Leonardo.

'You know perfectly well what I mean.' She glanced across at him with lowered eyelids. 'Will it give you pleasure, Leonardo, if I do so?'

'Of course it will.'

'In that case, how can I refuse?' Bianca said. 'Since it is my purpose in life to please you.'

She stood up swiftly and pulled at the ties that held her pale green gown at either shoulder.

'Well?' she said.

Casa d'Oro: Ca' d'Oro. It had music in its very name, this House of Gold in the capital city of the Most Serene Republic of Venice. Its arches soared like Moorish melodies, the filigrees adorning them were cadences of hammered leaf; its façade shimmered, reflected in the waters of the Grand Canal, drawing the eye of visitor and Venetian alike.

Tonight, gondolas drifted in smooth procession up to the festooned landing stage at its foot, bringing with them parties of dark men and brilliant women, gay with laughter and the loose chatter of earlier and more private celebrations. All who mattered in society were there this summer evening. They came to welcome—and to take the measure of—Girolamo Riario, Count of Imola. The Pope's nephew, some murmured, smiling behind their gloves at the closer, parental relationship they hinted at. What better place than the House of Gold for an occasion that

93

must not be openly official and yet, equally, must show the approval of the Committee of Five?

Nicodemo da Parenzo, that practised diplomat, made his introductions informally upon a private balcony overlooking the canal.

'You have not met, I think,' he said. 'General Riario, this is Signor Orso Contarini, First Secretary to the Committee of Five.'

'I am honoured, sir.' The little secretary bowed.

'And I, sir. Also, I confess, no little puzzled.' Riario's tone was guarded and faintly hostile. 'I had not thought the Committee took note of my small business here.'

'Bluntly spoken, as befits a soldier,' replied Contarini easily. 'But changing circumstances alter plans, and there is certain delicate information that we must share with you concerning the man Leonardo da Vinci. I myself am lately returned from Malta, and feel I must acquaint you with certain new schemes for his disposal.'

'Oh? He is not dead, then?'

'He is a difficult man to kill, so it seems.'

'No man is hard to kill if his back is close to a knife. I was offered the service of your Messer Uberto Neri as a master of such business,' said Riario. 'I take it, therefore, that he has failed?'

'Your own efforts failed, sir, as well, if memory serves.'

Da Parenzo's voice broke in firmly. 'Please, messires. Our purposes run together. Let us not confuse them with needless argument. Rome wants him dead; so, equally, does Venice. We are sending six men to take him. He has ... information which affects our vital interests, and we intend to squeeze him for it here in Venice. When we have extracted it from him, he will be killed.'

'Indeed?' Riario said. 'And may Rome be permitted to know the reason for Venice's sudden interest in the contents of this artist's head?'

'I fear not,' said Contarini. 'I am empowered to say only that it touches no part of Rome's concerns in any way. I gather that you, sir, have sent Messer Uberto a fee?'

'I have.'

'Venice will return one half of it, since our intentions are now shared. And, as further evidence of our sincere desire for cooperation, I am also authorised to tell you that Venice will enter Rome's proposed alliance against Florence, as discussed earlier this year. Come, sir; are you satisfied?'

Riario nodded. 'A fair business arrangement,' he said. 'Rome accepts. Good hunting to you, sirs. And when you squeeze him, do so very slowly.'

... thus, Magnifico, I am now safe on the island of Malta, with Leonardo da Vinci. We live in a pretty villa with Captain Leone, and Cipriano di Lucca, and my new-found friend who is called Decima, a girl from Greece. Leonardo is working upon new experiments in science, and I am learning to cook and am very happy. And I pray most earnestly for your forgiveness: I wanted only to be with Leonardo, and lied to you in order to achieve this, telling you that I was with child, which is not true. He tells me that I did wrong, and I acknowledge it. And I pray also for your forgiveness, Magnifico, on behalf of Cipriano di Lucca, whose only crime is that he refused to leave my side when I would not enter the convent in Pisa you had appointed for me; in this he was doing no more than you had ordered. He is looking after my wellbeing no less than are Leonardo and Captain Leone. I can come to no harm, and think often of you, praying sincerely that God may ever keep you and Florence in His care.

From the Lady Bianca Maria
Visconti to her guardian
Lorenzo de' Medici, August
3rd, 1478.

The six men before him made an impressive group, Neri decided. Contarini, and Venice, had chosen well. All of them were young, catlike in demeanour, and attentive. Their weapons, designed for use rather than display, were unadorned; they exuded an air of powerful and professional competence, which was as well for himself, since he felt his own reputation was at stake.

His plans for the assault on the villa outside Zejtun, by the garden wall of which they now stood, had been worked out in detail and with exquisite care. Lemmo, at least, had done his work well. Every room in the house had been charted for the attackers. Neri had chosen the small hours of the morning for his attempt, when sleep would be deepest. His men wore black from head to toe, and carried only stilettoes in the interests of stealth and silence. In the frail light cast by a new moon, he felt confident of success.

'You know your assignments?' he asked.

'We do,' said the leader of his subordinates softly. 'Two of us to the gunner, one to the man Cipriano di Lucca, to cut their throats while they lie asleep. They are expected to be in the first room at the top of the stairway.'

'The Captain may be with his whore from Rabat,' said Neri.

'Then his friend will be alone, and will present no problem. We kill him, and three of us will then deal with both the Captain and the woman.'

'Good.'

'The rest of us will overpower Leonardo da Vinci and bind him. If the lady Bianca Visconti is with him, she dies.'

'Excellent. Should the women be found together in the middle room, you had best kill them in any case if they seem likely to raise the alarm.'

'Of course.'

Neri looked at the night sky. 'I will wait here, then,' he said, 'for it is always possible that Cipriano di Lucca may be in Birgu or Rabat. I am told that he fancies himself as a ladies' man, and it will be as well not to risk being taken by surprise upon his return.' He laughed, and added, 'Nothing has been said of your reward for this night's work, sirs. Know, therefore, that no matter what your hire may have been in Venice, I intend to give each one of you five hundred ducats if you succeed in bringing da Vinci to me unharmed. Go, then, my friends.'

Darker than shadows, the six killers scaled the garden wall, and were gone. Uberto Neri stayed where he was; he drew his sword and picked with it at the stony soil by his feet, as a man might do while thinking of other matters. He was unworried. A carefully planned attack was under way, in the hands of a group of men superbly fitted to carry it out. Had he been told that this attack was, in large measure, anticipated by its chief victim he might well have smiled in scorn.

No responsibility for what followed could be laid at Lemmo's feet. He was staying the night in the boatyard at Birgu, with Leonardo's permission and upon the instructions of Uberto Neri himself. But his reports had been detailed and accurate. That they were incomplete, since a few of Leonardo's private preparations for the defence of the villa had not been revealed to him, was neither coincidence nor any fault of his.

The killers from Venice drifted through the gardens like wraiths. Not even the sleeping birds stirred as they passed along the side wall of the villa towards the kitchen window at the rear. A razor-sharp knife cut through its hinges in seconds, and silent hands worked the shutter free of the inside latch, lowering it to the ground. As they made ready to enter the house, none of the attackers noticed that, almost before they had started upon their enterprise, they were doomed.

There was, after all, very little to notice. A tiny wedge of cork, trapped cunningly between shutter and wall, was released as the boards were removed. Once free, it flew ceilingward and out of sight, pulled by a length of fine black fishing line, which whipped along joists and rafters, through cracks in floorboards and around cunningly placed pegs, ending in Leonardo's room overhead. Here, a small brass weight—one of a row attached to the ends of similar lines—fell to a narrow ledge and, in doing so, tilted a goblet of water across the bed.

Leonardo sat up and glanced at the row of weights. It was the third of them which had fallen, thus telling him that the kitchen window had been forced.

Without a sound, he left his room. Before the last of the intruders below had even entered the building, therefore, preparations for its defence were complete.

Cipriano tapped softly for entrance to the middle of the three upstairs rooms, waking Bianca and Decima. At his instruction, they barred their door with a padded wooden beam fashioned for the purpose. After trying its security from outside in the passage, Cipriano joined Rigo Leone in the room at the immediate head of the stairs, where they waited in silence.

In the kitchen, the six assassins gathered and made their way on padded soles towards the bottom of the stairway. Unaware that their intended victims were anything but deep in slumber, they climbed to the upper floor like wraiths. Nothing disturbed their progress.

Once on the landing that ran the length of the house upstairs, they separated. Two men pushed tentatively at the door to the women's room, finding it firmly held against them and, within, as silent as stone. By pantomime, one of them was signalled to stand guard by it, while two of his fellows nudged the neighbouring door. This they found unlatched. They entered the room where, so they confidently expected, Rigo and Cipriano should be lying asleep.

Events were quick and merciless. One man darted to Cipriano's bed and stabbed the shape that lay there. In the brief instant before he died, he realised that his blade had plunged into a straw filled dummy; Cipriano chopped him down from behind with a length of leaden water pipe wrapped in cloth. Rigo's would-be assassin, moving more cautiously, turned his head at the unexpected sound of the impact, and fell dead a second later as Rigo's weapon—an identical and effective mace—crushed the side of his skull.

Outside in the passage, the three remaining killers moved past the half-open door, interpreting the muffled thuds from inside Rigo's room as signifying their companions' success. They headed for Leonardo's room at the farther end of the passage. The guard waiting outside the barred middle room turned to watch their retreating backs, and thus failed to see Rigo and Cipriano approach him from behind. They reached him just as his fellows disappeared from view into the end bedroom. Cipriano broke his arm with a swift downward blow, and Rigo laid him unconscious before his mouth had opened to shout. Pausing no longer than it took to kick his prostrate body out of their way, the two gunners raced onward.

As for Leonardo himself, he was at this moment smiling grimly as he stood in the inky blackness of a corner of his own room, while his three assailants circled his bed warily and poked at what they believed to be his motionless form.

'Damn it, the man sleeps no matter where I prod him,' breathed one of them.

'Here is no man, but a dummy,' hissed another. 'We have been tricked! Where is he?'

'Why, here, sirs,' said Leonardo gently.

In unison, the three turned to face him, staring into a darkness their eyes could not penetrate.

'Come forward, then,' suggested their leader. 'We are here in force, but do not mean to harm you unless you resist us. Accompany us peacefully, and all will be well.'

'My regrets, sirs. I do not choose to go.'

'You have little enough choice, Master Leonardo. Your companions are dead, the women under guard, and we are six armed men. Let us strike a light, then, and behave as reasonable men.'

'My friends dead, you say?' replied Leonardo. 'I think not. But let us find out, by all means.' Then, raising his voice, he spoke out. 'Rigo? Cipriano?'

From beyond the door his two colleagues hurtled into the room with upraised arms. The fight that followed was swift and savage, and proved beyond doubt that ten-inch daggers, no matter how expertly wielded, are no match for three-foot lengths of leaden piping. Rigo kicked his man in the stomach to double him over, and broke his neck immediately with a short and deadly downward blow. Leonardo's nearest assailant died at the same instant, his head crushed in. Cipriano's victim lived a little longer, gasping in the blackness as he slashed wildly to this side and that; grunts sounded, and a quick yelp from Cipriano was followed almost at once by the soft thump of a falling body.

Leonardo crossed to the bed and opened the side of a dark-lantern, casting a yellow light across the room. Cipriano was upright against the wall, with the third attacker at his feet. Blood was seeping down his sleeve, and he gripped his arm with a self-satisfied grin on his face.

'Crude weapons, these pipes,' he said. 'But I begin to find them effective, though impossible to use with any finesse.'

A noise in the passage outside interrupted him. He moved to the doorway, still holding his sleeve fastidiously, and peered out into the gloom. He could see little, except that the guard they had left for dead outside the middle room was no longer lying on the floor; he could be heard, however, in hasty and clumsy retreat down the stairs, cursing his broken arm.

'Damn me for a fool!' Cipriano said. 'I did no more than tap him on the wrist. His head was your concern, Rigo. Well, let him escape. It is all one to me.'

'Aye, let him escape,' agreed Leonardo, 'if he can.'

After searching the upper floor of the house carefully, they knocked on the door of the women's bedroom and answered the anxious voices from within it reassuringly.

Outside the villa, Uberto Neri watched the stumbling progress of his henchman across the garden towards the gateway.

'In God's name, what happened?' he demanded, as soon as the man reached him.

'They were awaiting us,' said the assassin shortly. 'All are dead save myself, or so I think. I did not stop to see.'

'Then rest, fool,' said Neri. After several minutes had passed, he spoke again. 'You are right, it seems. So much for Venice's choice of men.' He tapped his teeth with the pommel of his sword reflectively, before making his mind up. 'We had best find you a surgeon.'

'And a ship,' said the assassin. 'I must inform the Committee of what has happened here.'

'I will inform the Committee,' suggested Neri conversationally.

'You may do as you wish, sir, but I have my orders to carry out.'

'That is admirable,' said Neri, setting the point of his rapier against the man's chest, 'but I cannot allow you to do so. Farewell.'

Moments later, he was on his way back to Rabat.

Eight

AT SUNRISE, AN hour later, Leonardo found the sixth assassin curled in death outside the garden wall, his outflung arm grotesque in the early light and with ten inches of Neri's steel sunk into his heart. He had died with an expression of surprise on his face, and Leonardo thereafter spent the day sunk in thought.

In the early evening Lemmo arrived from Birgu to start his round of domestic tasks, and the five friends gathered around the kitchen table. News of the attack upon them, when they relayed it to the boy, produced a satisfying show of surprise.

'Thank God you are all safe, my masters!' he said piously. 'I am sorry I was not here to help you.'

'Thank God you were not,' retorted Rigo bluntly. 'They were killers, and I do not think you are built for fighting.'

'Perhaps not,' said Lemmo.

'At all events,' Cipriano said, 'our problems are now at an end, I suppose. Venice is not foolhardy.'

Bianca, who was looking at Leonardo, addressed him. 'What do you say?' she asked. 'You have spoken little all day. Why so?'

'Because I am thinking ahead,' Leonardo replied. 'And I am troubled.'

'We have beaten them off,' said Rigo. 'We will do it again, if need be.'

'And if they send twelve men next time? Or twenty-four? Venice has a long arm, Rigo.'

'And a weak one,' said Cipriano. 'I suggest we send them

Uberto Neri, in a coffin, and then return to Florence. What keeps us here, in God's name?'

Leonardo looked at each of them in turn. 'I have work to do in Malta, my friends,' he said, 'and I must stay. For as long as you stay with me, you are in danger. Therefore, the time has come when I must tell you all why Venice seeks to take me. I am close to Felippo's secret, and Venice knows it. They will not be discouraged until they have it, and we cannot sit here for ever waiting for their next attack. If you are with me, I know what I must do; *I will let them know exactly what I am doing, and where, and when.* For this I need your help, if you will give it.'

'Count on us, master,' said Lemmo swiftly.

Rigo motioned him to silence. 'Our answer you already know,' he said. 'But what is this secret?'

'As the lady Bianca knows, it is in the cabin of the *Pyramus*,' replied Leonardo. 'It was with him when he died, and stays with him still. I need only contrive a means of diving down and staying under water long enough to get it.'

'Staying under water?' said Rigo. 'For how long?'

'I cannot be sure. Six or seven minutes, perhaps.'

'Which is impossible,' Rigo said, 'as any fool knows.'

Lemmo could not restrain himself. 'What is it you hope to find, master?' he demanded.

Leonardo gazed at him for a while before replying. 'A clock,' he said. 'A small clock, Lemmo, that gave to its owner such mastery of the seas as man has never known before. What do you think of that?'

'All this is new to me,' Decima interrupted, 'and I am confused by it. How can a man stay under water for six or seven minutes? And how will Venice know what you are doing?'

'Why, Decima, because we will do our work in plain sight,' replied Leonardo. 'We must dive, and we can hardly do it in secret. Well, then. Let those who are curious see what we are doing—including Venice. If we are asked, we shall reply that we are seeking treasure. Those who serve Venice are not stupid, and will be delighted to wait until we have done their work for them.'

'And therefore will cease their interference,' said Decima. 'Yes, I see. I believe you are right, Leonardo.'

'Then let us eat, and go to bed,' Leonardo said. 'Tomorrow we have much to do.'

He sleeps, Bianca thought.

Side by side, they lay together in the warm midnight interlude which had come to mark the sweetly replenishing moments that followed their love-making. She rested, held between languor and wakefulness, considering for the hundredth time several long discussions she had indulged in with Decima.

Does he, perhaps, feign sleep as I do, she wondered? Is this when love begins to slip away from our grasp, freed from the body's strident demands? Does his mind stray away from me and wander towards that realm of science and reason he so often dwells in, and do I, then, lose him? Decima's point of view was simple enough. A man was either a stag in rut or he was not, and if his mind and body were elsewhere, that was not a whore's concern.

She studied him in the light of the room's solitary candle. His eyes were closed, and his face calm. Tentatively, she rolled away from his reclining form, and knelt beside him. She bent her head to kiss the hollow of his neck, and then deliberately set herself to arouse him. As Decima had promised her, she found her own initiatives vastly pleasurable.

But what did he feel, she asked of herself?

Her answer came as, drawn from his half-sleep, Leonardo's arms reached out for her. Wordlessly, he pulled her towards him and the now familiar rhythms of passion touched them both and flared into delight.

'You please me beyond measure, Bianca,' he whispered, and opened his eyes. 'And perhaps you surprise me a little, as well. But what am I, if not a student of cause and effect? Have I not observed that you spend a great deal of time in conversation with Decima? In lessons, perhaps?' He smiled at her.

'And why not?' she answered. 'Of course I have talked with her. She is an expert in matters where I am but a novice—and have you not always told me to learn whenever I can?' She lay beside him again, putting her arms closely about him, her lips by his ear. 'I do not want you to tire of me, Leonardo,' she murmured. 'Do you understand?'

'I can see that Decima, who is a good-hearted girl of a practical disposition, has been telling you a lot of nonsense,' replied Leonardo. 'What does she say?'

'That all men tire of their mistresses sooner or later. That horses and cows may couple as nature bids them, but women have to learn certain skills in order to keep their lovers interested. Why are you laughing at me? It's serious.'

Leonardo kissed her. 'Very serious indeed,' he said. 'However, Decima may be an expert in the mating of horses and cows, but she knows nothing of love.' He touched her cheek. 'How could I tire of you, my heart? We are like unknown lands, you and I, our bodies and our minds alike. We explore each other. I learn from you continually. I love you, Bianca. Hold on to that, and forget all the rest.'

'And you complete me, Leonardo. I cannot find words to tell you what I mean.'

'Nor have you need of words. They are used as brushes are used, to make pictures; but pictures are not reality, no matter how skilled the artist. Who should know that better than myself? It is true. You may paint a picture with greater skill or with less, but you cannot alter or compel reality.'

'And neither can you compel love? Is that what you are saying?'

'Yes. And you have no reason to try, Bianca. You bring me pleasure, and I thank you for it. But if Decima confuses pleasure with love, she is not the expert you imagine her to be. Do you love me?'

'Yes.'

'Then you need no teaching. Do you?'

'No,' Bianca said, and sighed contentedly. 'No, of course not.'

'It is as you ordered, sir,' said Lemmo. 'Achmet has been posted where they may see him, this past week and more. I am hidden where they cannot. That is, when I am not working for them at the villa.' He stood again before Uberto Neri, his narrow shoulders hunched high with strain.

Oblivious, Neri nodded coolly and sipped at his wine. 'And what have you seen, boy?'

'They row a little boat out to the wreck; Rigo handles the oars. Cipriano holds a sand-glass, I think, and some little bladders filled with air. Messer da Vinci takes one with him when he dives down to the ship. When he comes up they talk and he tries another bladder; a larger one or a smaller one. It is hard for me to see it all and remain hidden.'

'You confirm Achmet's report; good, good. I relieve you of this duty, Lemmo. Achmet will continue to observe and report their work in the cove. You will continue to work in their villa. All will be reported to Venice, boy. Continue your good work and I may mention you favourably. Only be very sure that they do not suspect you. You *are* certain . . . ?'

'They suspect nothing, sir! I swear it on my life!'

Neri studied the boy briefly. 'Why, so you do, Lemmo, so you do.'

'You are here early this evening, Lemmo. No work in Birgu today?'

'They gave me leave, Master Leonardo, since work is light. I came straight here, to clean the floors.'

'Then let us both work at our tasks, Lemmo,' said Leonardo kindly.

The boy's eyes studied Leonardo's work table, which bore a welter of pots and brushes, clamps and tubes. 'What are those little pipes you are painting, sir?' he asked. 'I have never seen their like before.'

'Sheeps' guts,' the artist told him. 'But I am not painting them, not exactly. This jar holds resin and turpentine; when heated, it melts. You see?'

Lemmo sniffed. 'It has a fearsome and evil smell,' he observed.

'Very true. Happily, the smell disappears when the mixture

dries—thus.' Leonardo held up a length of gut, stiffened by the varnish into a rigid, hollow tube. 'Under water it will not leak. I am fashioning a pipe long enough to rise above the surface of the sea and reach the air I need to breathe when I am beneath it.'

'Why, sir, it is a wonderful contrivance,' said Lemmo. 'And as I see that you must work in the kitchen, I will go upstairs to begin my duties. With your permission.'

'You have it,' said Leonardo. He watched the boy's departure with an oddly enigmatic look on his face. When he was satisfied that Lemmo had climbed the stairs, he closed and locked the kitchen door. Then he went to a cabinet beside the oven and drew out a brass-bound wooden box. In it were tools and gears, rasps and snips of metal, identifiable upon close inspection as the workings of a clock.

A clock, let it be said, of a most curious, not to say, original design.

'I come to you in peace,' said Cardinal della Palla gently. 'Let there be a truce between us for this hour at least.'

Lorenzo de' Medici shrugged and nodded sourly. 'Rome ever mouths words of peace, Eminence. But the Holy Father's armies form against us still.'

It was early autumn. Cardinal Domenico della Palla sat in the private library of the ruler of Florence, hands resting easily in the grey satin folds of his gown. Outside, trees were turning, the air was chill with the hint of winter. A small fire burned, warming the room pleasantly.

'The Holy Father does not know I am here,' said della Palla placidly. 'I try not to ask him a question unless I am certain of his reply. In this case, had I asked, I would have been forbidden.'

'Oh?' A faint smile touched Lorenzo's face. 'Has this, then, the barest breath of treason, Eminence?'

'By no means, my lord. I am a loyal servant of the Church in this, as in all things. But war brews. It will come to the boil if men of influence do nothing.'

'Then let the Holy Father call off his dog,' said Lorenzo irritably. 'Riario, I mean. God knows that Florence seeks no war.'

Della Palla lifted one hand. 'But you take a very hard line, my lord,' he murmured. 'Our Father in Christ would welcome even the smallest sign of your softening. It is your harsh intransigence that enrages him.'

'Yes,' replied Lorenzo. 'Had I but allowed his assassins to murder me as they murdered my brother, he would doubtless have blessed my soul even as it flew to heaven!'

'It was no plan of the Pope's, my lord,' said della Palla firmly.

'I am pleased to hear it, your Eminence. You will forgive us, however, if we keep our guns clean and our matches burning?' Lorenzo rose and leaned forward, his hands on the desk that separated them. 'We have beaten Rome's armies at Castelmonte, Chancellor. We will beat them again, if the occasion arises. Make no mistake about it.'

'Yet if Rome and Naples come from the south, my son, and Venice from the north, your city will be squeezed first and crushed later. Is this what you want for Florence?'

'Florence will fight,' Lorenzo gritted, 'not because she wants to, but because she must. Is that what *you* want?'

'No,' said Cardinal della Palla sombrely. 'If so, why should I have come here? Men will die. Women will be widowed, and children become orphans. Crops will rot in the fields and wither on the vines. We know what war brings in its train. Surely, my lord, we can find some other way? I know you to be a man who respects the force of argument. Your own military engineer has said as much to me.'

'Leonardo da Vinci?' Lorenzo grimaced. 'He may go to the devil!'

'He has not travelled that far yet. He has gone only to Malta. He has a remarkably dull ear for hearing orders that do not fit his own plans, has he not?'

'Has Rome tried to order him?' asked Lorenzo. For the first time, his features relaxed, though he did not smile.

'Perhaps not exactly to order him,' said the Cardinal. 'We tried to turn him from your service to our own, but he remained loyal to you, as you know.'

'His service to Florence has ended,' said Lorenzo.

The Cardinal sat in silence for a moment. When he spoke, it was with the intensity of conviction. 'Leonardo serves you still, Magnifico,' he said. 'It may not appear so, but I know it to be true. He guards your ward, the lady Bianca Visconti; he has seen fit to write to me and say so. I can see that they have incurred your displeasure, the more so since they are not wed, which some might think scandalous. Yet your Leonardo da Vinci is no ordinary man, and I believe your ward to be as safe with him as with yourself.'

'You speak of him as a friend,' said Lorenzo with puzzlement in his voice.

'I think so. God knows I hope so. Why, I am not sure. His mind moves in strange ways, and he says much that is wise. There are moments, my lord, when I fancy that you and I will be remembered not for ourselves, but because we knew him. A humbling thought, is it not?' The Chancellor stirred uneasily. 'What I have now to tell you may indeed smack of treason after all,' he went on. 'Rome treats with Venice even now, and there is a plot afoot to have Leonardo da Vinci murdered.'

Lorenzo sank back into his seat. 'He is in danger, then? I had no word of this.'

'But I perceive that you care.'

'Perhaps I do. I doubt that you will get me to admit it publicly.'

'Attend to me, then, my lord,' said della Palla. 'This pact with Venice may be forestalled. It needs careful planning, good fortune, and prayer. But I think it may be managed. If I do my work in Rome, will you ... soften your intransigence? Will you make some overture to the Holy Father? I came here with this hope in my heart: that we might join hands together, you and I, and do what lies in our power to protect Leonardo da Vinci and Bianca Visconti. What do you say?'

His eyes bright with concentration, Rigo watched the bobbing tip of the varnished tube, feathering the oars of the little boat to follow it as it moved. Secured to a pair of floating bladders, the tube cut through the waves, trailing Leonardo as he swam just under the surface, his body clearly visible in the pale green water.

Leonardo rose now, very near to the boat, hooking one arm over its side. He spat the hand-carved mouthpiece into the boat and removed the padded clip of spring metal that pinched his nostrils tightly shut.

'You were not down there very long,' said Rigo.

'I know,' said Leonardo, gasping great gulps of air. 'There are new problems, I find.'

'Nor did you go down very deep. I never lost sight of you, in fact.'

'As I say; new problems,' said Leonardo, swarming over the side of the boat. 'Let me pull in our tube and bladders and we will row back to shore and join the girls.'

'Your new tube will not serve, then?'

'In three *braccia* of water, yes. Yet when I dive deeper than my own height, no matter how hard I breathe in and out, I cannot seem to pull the fresh air down. A surprising result. There appears to be some sort of weight or pressure that holds the fresh air out. Most interesting, is it not?'

'I am a gunner and, because of your tests, a pilot of small boats,' said Rigo, grimacing. 'What interests me more is yonder Achmet upon the clifftop. He sits there in plain sight, like some great vulture. I like it not, Leonardo.'

'He follows Neri's orders to watch us. Since we have planned it so, let us be thankful that he is there where we can see him.'

Skilfully, Rigo manoeuvred the boat to catch the crest of the last small wave that rode them through the little boil of water that rolled up to the beach. Lemmo splashed into the light surf, holding the prow as Rigo and Leonardo disembarked. Together, they pulled the boat beyond the water's reach.

'Fourteen dives, Leonardo!' Bianca announced. 'I counted them.'

'. . . and I timed them,' said Decima. 'None more than two and one half minutes, I fear.'

'Look here,' said Leonardo, and he knelt in the sand, smoothing a rectangular portion with the palm of his hand. With his finger he then drew a line across the centre and looked up at Bianca, Decima and Lemmo. 'Let us make this line the surface of the water. When I am down here—say, three feet down—my little tube brings me fresh air in abundance. Yet, when I move but another three feet farther down—to here—the fresh air no longer reaches me. Why, I cannot say. But since the *Pyramus* lies in twenty feet of water and more, it will take me several months of experiment to find a solution . . .' He broke off.

'So much time, sir?' said Lemmo with innocent concern.

'Oh, two or three months, at least,' said Leonardo smoothly. 'Perhaps even four. Who knows?'

From UBERTO NERI to the First Secretary to the Committee of Five, His Excellency ORSO CONTARINI: I report with sincere regret the death of the six men sent here by Venice. They perished, my Lord, in an untimely and unauthorised assault on the man da Vinci. This man and his companions are engaged in diving tests, and I have them under observation. My agent has learned that they seek a certain Clock which belonged to *Il Fortunato*: the same agent remains in their trust, as steward, reporting to me daily. Our web thus holds them like flies: they may buzz in our strands, but when they recover this Clock we shall take both them and it. I remain Your Servant in all things.

Nine

OUTSIDE THE CAVE of Zeser Ibn Hasim the dog days of August had given way to the beginnings of autumn, and a thin afternoon haze filled the valley. Here, in the womb of the rock itself, there were no seasons. The old man sat motionless, as he had done before, a grey boulder washed by the stream of time and yet unchanged by it. For how many years had he done so, Leonardo wondered? Malta was timeless. Men had built temples upon it before the records of history had opened; had scratched a brief living from its meagre and sunlit soil, passed on, and been forgotten. Only the rock remained and, like the vanished temple-builders, Zeser Ibn Hasim seemed to have come to terms with it and now partook of its strength and longevity.

'A clock?' he said. 'How do you know this?'

'From assembling its pieces,' said Leonardo, 'as a clockmaker might do.'

'You speak in parables. What pieces?'

'Invisible ones. A quotation in latin, an ivory and emerald key, a story overheard long ago in Florence. A mariner who knew his position every day at noon, measuring his longitude by the passing of time, and who carried something inland, in a sea-bag, every time he visited you here in Malta.'

Zeser Ibn Hasim wheezed in ancient and appreciative laughter.

'Food,' he suggested. 'Or money, perhaps. Gifts for a mad old magician. Why should it have been a clock he carried?'

'It was,' said Leonardo. 'You are no more a magician than I am. As for madness, you wear it or slip it off like a pair of gloves. Come now, Ibn Hasim. You are a scientist. So am I, as I hope to persuade you. Does wealth interest you? It does not interest me overmuch. Neither does power, nor position, nor fame. Sir, we live each in a world within his own head, and with what we find there, which is knowledge.'

'Knowledge did not buy your clothes,' observed Ibn Hasim, 'nor yet that pin at your throat, which I perceive to be an amethyst. How much are you worth, as the world reckons such things, da Vinci?'

'At this moment? Some ten thousand florins, I dare say,' Leonardo replied. 'Though I have not counted it of late. I did not say that I avoided wealth. I claimed that it did not interest me overmuch, which is a different matter. If I am tossed a gold coin, I will—like all men—catch it. Perhaps I might cross the street to do so. But I would not stand upon my head for it.'

'And you will stand on your head for the sake of knowledge?' asked the old man, wheezing again.

'Certainly. Do you wish me to?'

'Now, by Allah,' said Ibn Hasim, 'I believe that I have met an honest man! It is a pity, then, that I must disappoint you. I have no clock, real or imaginary.'

'I know that. But you had one, and will have it again. I know where it is.'

'And where is that?'

'At the bottom of the sea. I will get it for you.'

Still Ibn Hasim did not move. His eyes searched Leonardo's face as though the shadows cast there by the candlelight might tell him something, or perhaps as a man studies his opponent in a game of skill, or chance.

'From the *Pyramus*,' he said finally.

'Yes.'

'And you propose to give it to me?'

'To return it to you.'

'I am not sure that it belongs to me. Are you?'

'I think it does. The man for whom you built it is dead. So is the man you later gave it to. Therefore it is yours.'

'Have a care with your generosity,' said Ibn Hasim. 'This

clock is worth a hundred times your store of florins, being cased in gold and encrusted with jewels. Does not your interest in wealth quicken a little?'

'By now,' said Leonardo, 'it is probably cased in barnacles and encrusted with seaweed, as well. I care nothing for its shell. Its workings, however . . .'

'Ah,' the astronomer said. 'Its workings. Its spring, and movement. Its accuracy. Trifles of that kind. Yes. You wish to retrieve it, examine it, and then return it to me?'

'Yes.'

'Then do so, with my blessing. In return——'

'I have not asked for any return,' said Leonardo.

'Do not interrupt me. I am too old to accept gifts without giving in exchange,' Ibn Hasim said. 'Let me see. What can I offer you?' He closed his eyes. 'I will give you,' he said, 'all I possess. That should be a fair bargain, don't you think? Of course, you will realise that I possess only knowledge, but that will not trouble you, da Vinci. Will it?'

'Sir, if I had hoped for a bargain,' Leonardo replied, 'that would have been its essence. I thank you.'

He rose, and turned to leave the cavern.

'Wait,' said Ibn Hasim. 'Who killed Felippo Mendoza?'

'Venice killed him. I am not sure who, precisely, held the knife. Is it important?'

'Not to me,' the old man answered. 'But perhaps to you. Are they watching you?'

'They are.'

'Well?'

'Sir,' said Leonardo, 'Venice is a powerful city, and her servants are many. If they see me with a clock, and wish to take it from me by force, I cannot prevent them from doing so. I can only trust in Providence, and my wits.'

'Which are considerable, I have no doubt.' Zeser Ibn Hasim raised his hand. 'Go with God—your own, or mine, or another's, it matters not—until we meet again.'

From the valley outside the hidden entrance to the cave, Leonardo walked eastwards for an hour until he was overlooking Marsasirocco. He was, unusually for him, carrying a small sack over one shoulder; a sack whose contents he might have shown to Zeser Ibn Hasim for the latter's amusement if he had not been anxious to get on with the next portion of his day's task.

He looked beyond Marsasirocco, carefully scanning the cliffs and headlands around the cove where the *Pyramus* lay. Throughout the previous weeks the dutiful Achmet had watched constantly their comings and goings in the cove, which annoyed Rigo but troubled Leonardo not at all.

Today, however, was a different matter, and that was why he had left his appointed task until this late hour.

When he was satisfied that the Turk—if he had been at the cove at all that day—had returned to his master with nothing of interest to report, Leonardo made his descent from the high ground and worked his way slowly around to the *Pyramus*, arriving on the beach as the light was fading. He stripped, and plunged into the sea with the sack he had brought with him, swimming briskly out to the small cork float that marked the position of the sunken vessel. Here, without further ado, he tilted up his heels and dived, his descent assisted by the weight of the sack and its contents, until he felt the anchor-chain of the *Pyramus* against his forearms. He grasped it, pulled himself a fathom deeper towards the anchor itself, and carefully tied the sack to the bottom link of the chain by means of the length of twine which sealed its neck. After checking that it was secure, he jack-knifed for the surface again, reaching it—he noted with approval—with plenty of breath to spare.

He turned onto his back and kicked placidly towards the shore. The air was chilly. He dressed as quickly as possible, and set off at a run in the direction of Zejtun and the villa, where he was greeted with cries of outrage and the cold remains of his supper.

'I trust you have had a pleasant day,' said Rigo with heavy sarcasm, strolling in from the balcony with Cipriano. 'What the devil have you been doing, may we ask?'

Leonardo laid aside his knife.

'Reaching decisions, among other things,' he replied. 'Where is Lemmo, by the way?'

'How in God's name should I know? In Birgu, I dare say,' said Rigo. 'Though I hear from Ottavio that he will never make a shipwright, being somewhat delicate. I cannot see why you set him to a trade. He was far better employed as our steward, to my mind, though I confess he is beginning to irritate me with his attentions.'

'A milksop,' said Cipriano, airily.

Rigo looked his lieutenant up and down, in an offensive manner.

'I have, at times, heard the same remark made about you,' he said.

'Possibly,' Cipriano agreed, not a whit put out by this challenge. 'But I will wager that you have not heard it said twice, lard-belly, within reach of my ears.'

'If you two are about to brawl with each other,' put in Decima, who was sitting with Bianca by the fireside, 'oblige us by doing so in the garden, and not here.'

Leonardo wiped his platter with a piece of bread, swung his leg over the bench, and stood up.

'You would oblige me by not doing so at all,' he said. 'Though I realise it's several weeks since you've been able to exercise your muscles in a fight. The time has clearly come when I must point out that Lemmo is a spy. Uberto Neri's spy, to be exact.'

'*What!*' Rigo said.

'I will believe it readily,' said Decima at once. 'Did I not tell you he was a thief, and worse, Rigo? Not that you listened to me, of course.'

'But he was Felippo Mendoza's adopted son,' Rigo said.

'That may be,' said Leonardo.

'He was broken-hearted when we first came upon him.'

'He certainly appeared to be, I agree. He has also wept copiously, and at will, ever since,' Leonardo said. 'None the less, I think that Felippo died at his hands.'

'A murderer?' said Cipriano. 'He has too weak a stomach for it.

You stretch your imagination too far, Leonardo. Why, I'll wager that the sight of a drop of blood makes him fall over in a faint.'

'Again I agree,' Leonardo said, 'except that his own life was at stake. I believe he was left behind by the men who tortured Felippo Mendoza in order that, as their accomplice, he might search the cabin before the *Pyramus* sank. When he heard us come aboard, he was forced to silence Felippo at once so that his betrayal should not become known. After finding out who we were, since our Lemmo is nothing if not an opportunist, he seized his chance to join us.'

'You're sure of all this, are you?' said Rigo.

'Quite sure. Cast your mind back, Rigo. How long were we at the House of Ten Pearls before Uberto Neri and his men found us there and attacked us? How did they know we were there at all? And when they attacked us again, here in this villa, did you not find their assault singularly well-planned? One might have supposed they were familiar with the place—as no doubt they were. Again, why has Lemmo always been so insistent upon accompanying us wherever we went? Nearly every day, during these past weeks, he has toiled from here to Birgu and back again, supposedly in order to be at our service of an evening. A long walk for such a delicate lad, when he might have found lodgings near the boatyard instead. Mind you, his walking has been even more extensive, since I imagine that he has also tramped to Rabat every now and then to report our doings to his masters.'

'If you knew all this,' said Rigo with indignation, 'why did you not send him packing?'

'Yes,' interrupted Bianca. 'Leonardo, he has seen almost everything we have done! He knows . . . well, about the *Pyramus*, for instance.'

'My dearest heart,' said Leonardo, 'he knows exactly what I want him to know, which is why I have not got rid of him. As for our diving at the *Pyramus*, there was never any hope of keeping that a secret, as we have already seen.'

'I will break his neck when he returns,' said Rigo. 'Before God, I will!'

'I beg that you will do nothing of the kind. I have not nursed our young friend Lemmo along all this while in order that you might kill him in a fit of temper. Matters are coming to a head, and there is one more vital thing which it is essential for him to hear—and to report.'

'And what may that be?'

'The fact that we are going to retrieve a clock worth several hundred thousand florins from the cabin of the *Pyramus*, on the afternoon of the day after tomorrow.'

After a lengthy silence while all present considered this, Cipriano spoke up.

'I have a question,' he said.

'Let us hear it, by all means, Cipriano.'

'I have always thought of myself as being tolerably quick-witted,' said Cipriano, 'but I do not quite see all ends of this. Do I take it that Venice has some passing interest in this clock of yours?'

'She does.'

'In fact, Venice will be quite prepared to slit all out throats for it. Would that be fair?'

'Undoubtedly,' agreed Leonardo.

'What, then, happens when we have retrieved it?'

'We disappear. We shall, like foxes, go to ground.' Here Leonardo took Bianca's hand in his. 'And I have to tell you, my heart, that you and Decima cannot be with us when we do so. You will find a separate, and secure, hiding-place of your own. I have already arranged it for you.' Seeing Bianca about to protest, he hastened on. 'It is not that we wish to be parted from you,' he said, 'but simply that you are too easy and tempting a target for Venice. Let them find us, and we can fight them off. Let them take you, and they would have a hold upon us that we could not possibly resist. Do you see?'

'Yes,' said Bianca levelly. 'I do see, indeed. Very well.'

Cipriano coughed, pointedly.

'Forgive me,' he said. 'All this is admirably conceived, but it does not quite satisfy my curiosity. The day after tomorrow, you say, we are going to retrieve this clock?'

'Yes.'

'From the *Pyramus*?'

'If I have not badly miscalculated.'

'And you propose to tell Lemmo this, in order that he may alert our dear friend Uberto Neri?'

'He shall overhear it in conversation between all of us, tonight. Rigo, I think you had better go down to Zejtun and stay there until well after midnight,' Leonardo added, 'since we cannot afford to have our discourse spoiled by the sound of your teeth grinding in rage. Besides, your face is too honest. The rest of us can deceive master Lemmo well enough, I think.'

'Ah,' said Cipriano, his face clearing. 'Now I see. We deceive him. We are not, in point of fact, going to retrieve——'

'Oh yes,' replied Leonardo. 'We are going to retrieve it.'

'And the day after tomorrow?'

'Precisely so.'

'Why, then, by the blood of Christ,' shouted the infuriated Cipriano, 'I know what I would do if I were Uberto Neri! I would give you no chance to go to ground! I would collect together a dozen men, or twenty, at the very instant you appeared above the waves with a stupid grin on your face and holding your damned clock in your hand——'

'You will give yourself a seizure,' said Leonardo. 'Calm down, and listen.'

'Excellent,' Uberto Neri purred. 'Most admirable. Lemmo, my dear lad, if I have seemed harsh towards you of late, it is because I have been anxiously awaiting this piece of news you bring us. They are going to dive, you say?'

'Yes, Uberto. They are going to use an apparatus of tubes. I have seen parts of it, but I do not quite understand it.'

'No matter,' said Neri. 'But it will be tomorrow afternoon? You are sure of this?'

'Quite sure,' Lemmo said. 'They were talking about it until late last night.'

Uberto Neri glanced across the salon. By the balcony window, now repaired, sat Orso Contarini once again. He had reached Malta from Venice but three days since, and had made plain his displeasure with Neri. With him, now, was an elderly man in a fur-trimmed robe, grey of beard and bald headed. Contarini had introduced this worthy as Dr. Magnus Bembo of Utrecht, but had not thus far explained his presence at the Venetian outpost in Rabat. Both men wore expressions of satisfaction, though Contarini's manner, when he spoke, was still far from cordial.

'Take them,' he said.

'At the beach, Excellency?'

'Naturally at the beach,' said the envoy with irritation. 'Why take the smallest risk of their escaping? And I care not whether you kill them or not, so long as you bring the clock to me, here.'

'I can see no difficulty,' said Neri.

'There should be none,' Contarini replied. 'None the less, Uberto . . .'

'Yes, sire?'

'Look yonder, if you will.'

Neri turned his head. Beside the main door to the salon, a halberd was standing upright, set in a socket of masonry.

'Do you see it?' The voice of the Secretary of the Committee of Five was conversational, yet the hair prickled at the nape of Uberto Neri's neck. 'Shortly after dusk tomorrow,' said Contarini, 'I shall be sitting in this chair, as I do now. And I shall be looking at one of two things as I sit; either at a clock which used to belong to a sea captain called Felippo Mendoza, or else . . . Uberto . . . at your head, impaled upon that pike you see before you. Venice is becoming impatient with you. I suggest you keep it in mind.'

Ten

THE FOLLOWING DAY was brilliantly sunny, with a fresh breeze from the west.

By the third hour after midday Leonardo, Rigo and Cipriano had launched their work-boat from the beach in the cove beyond Marsasirocco, and were a hundred and fifty paces offshore. As before, the two gunners were to act as Leonardo's support at the surface, while he himself undertook the dive. He sat in the stern of the boat, carefully uncoiling and laying out his equipment.

This he had now modified. After long thought, he had decided that one breathing tube was insufficient. Below a certain depth, so he had discovered, it seemed that he could not draw sufficient air into his lungs through it to sustain him. He had at first imagined that this was due to the collapse of the tube under the pressure of the surrounding water. The tests of the last few weeks had shown him that this was not the case. The tube of gut, when stiffened by the varnish he had applied to it, stayed open even at a depth of several fathoms, and the flow of air through it unimpeded. He therefore concluded that the difficulty lay in the fact that, beyond a certain length of tubing, he was no longer inhaling fresh air from the surface, but simply rebreathing the stale air expelled from his own lungs. This air, evidently, lacked some vital principle necessary to the body, and hence must continually be replenished. Thus, he reasoned, *two* tubes were needed; through one of them he must breathe in, and through the other he would blow out the dead air from his chest. Trials had shown him that this system worked, and he had made himself a face mask of beaten copper, which held the lower ends of the two pipes.

He was fitting this mask over his nose and mouth when Rigo tapped him on the shoulder.

'They are here,' he announced. 'Though I cannot see them.'

Leonardo looked up. Beyond the shoreline and the stony beach no sign of movement could be observed, but above them an agitated collection of gulls and cormorants wheeled, crying noisily. Leonardo lowered the copper faceplate and grinned.

'So they are,' he agreed. 'Well, let us not disappoint them.'

Beyond Rigo, who was at the oars, Cipriano finished tying the bow line to the cork float that would keep them roughly in position above the sunken ship; he settled his back against the gunwale in apparent boredom. Leonardo took off his shirt. He handed the open ends of the twin tubes, with their small supporting bladders, to Rigo, and slipped over the side into the water, holding the mask in one hand. Submerged to his shoulders, he hooked his left arm through a loop of mooring line attached to the rowlock, trod water, and refitted the mask to his face, tying it behind his head with a pair of narrow thongs. He signalled to Rigo, who passed down to him a belt pouch containing several fist-sized stones and a knife.

Leonardo fastened these at his waist. He would now have sunk but for the support of the rope which held him up, and the knowledge gave him a slight and temporary feeling of insecurity. He inhaled deeply through one of the tube ends that protruded inside the mask, raised his left arm to release himself from the rope, breathed out through the other tube, and began his descent to the sea floor and the waiting *Pyramus*.

Above him, Rigo paid out the tubes with care, making certain that they developed no kinks that might cut off the flow of air through them. Since they possessed their own buoyancy, this was no hard task. They eventually floated away from the boat's side, their ends well above the gentle surge of the tide. As sponge divers might reckon it, the dive was hardly a deep one; but its duration would make it unique, and Rigo watched the drifting bladders closely.

The bright afternoon sunlight penetrated deep into the sea. Leonardo, checking the fit of his mask as his feet touched the side of *Pyramus*, found that he could see fairly well. During his descent he had kept his hands at his waist, ready to jettison the weighted belt at once should anything go amiss with his breathing gear. All seemed in order, however, and he relaxed. His chest was labouring slightly with the unaccustomed effort of drawing air downwards from the surface. Through his mind there flashed the notion of supplying it under forced pressure, perhaps with a pair of bellows. He dismissed the idea for the time being, and began his slow and careful approach to the cabin.

In the event, things went more smoothly than he had dared to hope.

The cabin door, canted almost to the horizontal by the heel of the wrecked ship as it lay on the sand, he already knew to be jammed. He drew his knife, and cut away the thin trailers of weed that obscured its hinges. These were of bronze, and riveted to the planking of both door and jamb. He wasted no more time upon them, but pulled himself upward to the handle instead. He probed gently for the tongue of the latch, and disengaged it. Levering at the door's edge, he felt it give slightly, and then stick. But his blade was beneath it, and he found enough clearance to gain a purchase on it with his fingertips, and then his palms. He braced his feet against the cabin front, and heaved mightily. The door gave way, releasing whorls of mud and grit where it had been forced into compression against the lintel, and swung downwards. A shoal of small fishes, their sides glinting turquoise and silver, darted out of the gloomy sea cave beyond it.

Leonardo paused. The muscles around his rib cage were aching, and he found it hard to concentrate on sucking at one of the tubes inside his mask, blocking its end with his tongue, and then breathing out through the other. Water had leaked around the edge of the copper sheet where it pressed into his cheeks; he blew, hard into the interior of the mask itself and drove it out again. But despite these difficulties, he knew that he had been under the sea for longer than any man had remained there before—it seemed to him like an age—and yet he was no worse than uncomfortable.

Grasping the edge of the door frame, he pulled himself inside the cabin. Somewhere near him in one corner or another, would be the loathsome and bloated thing that had once been his friend, Felippo Mendoza. He wondered how long it would take for a corpse to be stripped down to tidy bone and ligament by predatory fish, by crab and squid. He put the thought from him, hoping that he would not touch whatever might be left of *Il Fortunato*.

The cabin table, its legs anchored to the floor planks and thus on its side, was ahead of him. He swam into the darkness and found it. It was the table's under side that interested him, since he had reached—partly through deduction, partly through guess-work—certain conclusions about the cabin's contents and their arrangement. He remembered only the table itself, a bunk and a crude locker as furnishings.

Working by touch, he found his conclusions correct. The table top was a handspan thick. He felt beneath it—or rather, as the ship now lay, at one side of it—and his fingers encountered what he was looking for; a rectangular depression, a sliding flap, and behind the flap the hard and irregular outline of something the size and shape of a small lantern. With the tip of his knife he picked at the wooden clamps that secured this object; they loosened, and he pulled a clock out of *Il Fortunato's* hiding place.

His instincts immediately told him to swim away from the cabin, into the sunlight, and to head for the surface; but his mind insisted that he made certain of his trophy before doing so. Cautiously, he propelled himself backwards from the table and allowed himself to float in the doorway. The sea was fast becoming turbid with particles of dislodged silt but he could see, now, what he had felt in his grasp. Dim and fugitive fires leaped and died as he turned it over; gleams of crimson and green and blue, overlaid but not completely obscured by salt film and slime.

He realised, suddenly, that he had been holding his breath, and exhaled forcefully through his discharge tube.

There remained, now, one essential thing for him to do.

With the clock of Zeser Ibn Hasim in his left hand and the knife in his right, he swam along the hulk of the *Pyramus* and located her anchor chain. To this was still attached the canvas sack he had brought down here two days before. He picked open its mouth and removed from it a second clock—the one he had constructed himself at the villa over several weeks of patient effort. It was a workmanlike affair in steel, bronze, and tin, a thing with a certain functional beauty of its own. He let it fall gently to the sand by the buried fluke of the anchor, and pushed the jewelled timepiece of Ibn Hasim into the sack in its place. Sealing the canvas once more, he left it tied, as before, to the lowest link of the chain.

Now, at last, he was ready.

He retrieved his own clock from the sea bed, cut the thongs that held his diving mask in place, and released the stone-weighted belt from around his waist. Then he took a last deep breath from the inlet tube between his teeth, tore the mask away from his face, and thrust for the surface of the sea above him.

In the boat, Rigo caught sight of the rising stream of bubbles which preceded Leonardo, and kicked Cipriano on the shin. The latter, apparently asleep, sat up at once and looked about. Five yards from him, Leonardo broke surface with his arms thrashing, and held the clock above his head in jubilation. He spat, blew his nose between his fingers, and dog-paddled towards them.

'I have it!' he shouted.

'So I see,' Rigo said. He leaned over the gunwale and took the instrument.

'Well,' said Leonardo, 'on with the masquerade, my friends— but have a care.'

'Your audience is gathering,' put in Cipriano, who was looking over Rigo's shoulder towards the shore a hundred and fifty paces away. Leonardo had pulled himself into the boat and was rubbing his hair briskly with a cloth. He stopped doing so in well-simulated astonishment.

From the low ridge at the back of the beach some twenty men had appeared, and were forming the beginnings of a semicircle. In this formation they advanced, until they were at the water's edge. In their midst stood Uberto Neri, with the Turk Achmet at his right hand. Several of the men carried arbalests.

'Efficient,' commented Leonardo. 'Our Uberto is improving somewhat with experience.'

'I like not their crossbows,' Cipriano said.

'Nor I. But remember that they will want the clock first and foremost, and ourselves only as a side dish. Are you ready?'

Rigo and Cipriano nodded.

From the shoreline, Neri called across the water to them.

'Surrender!' he said. 'Or we shoot you down like dogs!'

Cipriano leaned over the bow of the dinghy and cut the mooring line. Leonardo picked up the clock from the bilges, and held it up.

'Is that what you want?' he asked.

'Yes,' called Neri. 'Give it to us peacefully, and we will spare your lives!'

Leonardo thereupon made a pretence of conferring with his companions. Then: 'Very well,' he said. He nudged Rigo, who bent to the oars and began to propel the boat slowly shorewards. When they were some twenty yards from the men grouped on the beach, Leonardo signalled him to stop rowing and hold the boat steady. He came to the bow and addressed Neri.

'How did you know?' he asked in mock chagrin.

'Never mind that,' Neri replied.

'Was it Lemmo?' suggested Leonardo.

'Very perceptive of you, if a little late in the day,' said Neri. 'It matters only that we are here, and hold you at our mercy. Give me the clock, and we will leave.'

'Send your Turk hither, then,' said Leonardo. He raised the clock suggestively. 'We come no closer. And I can smash this toy before you move.'

Neri bit his lip at this threat, and turned it over in his mind for a while. Then he signed to Achmet, who strode forward into the water and stopped a few feet from the boat, the sea surging about his chest.

'Give it,' he commanded.

'Do not let it fall,' said Leonardo, tossing the clock towards him. Achmet staggered, off balance, and caught it. As he floundered, Leonardo, Rigo and Cipriano launched themselves over the sides of the boat and made for its stern, thus assuring themselves of a shield against any missiles. Neri shouted, but was prevented from taking action by the Turk, who had turned clumsily towards the shore and was struggling up the sloping sand.

Leonardo and his two companions, supported by the boat's counter, kicked hard with their legs and drew it gradually, but with gathering speed, out to sea. Crossbow bolts hissed into the waves at either side of them and thudded into the planking, but within seconds they had made sufficient headway to ensure that the only way to reach them would be for their opponents to swim after them. But as Leonardo had reckoned, they did not do so. They had, after all, achieved their object, which was the taking of the clock.

None the less, he refused to allow Rigo or Cipriano to climb into the dinghy until they had cleared the mouth of the cove, a swim which took them a good half an hour. By the time they finally came to land, which they did—prudently—at the quay of Marsasirocco itself, their enemies were nowhere in sight.

From Marsasirocco, they marched west and south. It was a long march and a weary one. The afternoon gave way to an angry sunset and then to a night of parched and angry wind that dried the saltwater from their clothes and left them itching.

Near midnight they reached their goal, a ruined temple some distance inland from the island's precipitous southern coast. During the last two hours of their journey they had each carried a heavy supply pack, which they had concealed a mile or so from

Zejtun on the previous day. Once arrived, therefore, they let these fall from their salt-raw shoulders gratefully, and Leonardo set about building a fire of brushwood trimmings while his companions explored the hiding-place he had chosen.

From a military standpoint at least—as both Cipriano and Rigo agreed—their position could hardly be better. They were a league or more from the nearest house. The gaunt remains of the walls that surrounded them made the place a natural fortress, a stone maze of roofless chambers and passageways in which three men might hold off any assault but the most massive. If their enemies should discover them, which seemed very unlikely, an entire company of troops would be needed to seal off their escape by night. Meanwhile the tumbled prehistoric slabs and archways still offered them shelter—of a sort—from wind and rain.

Satisfied with his inspection, Rigo returned to the merrily crackling fire.

'It will serve for a day or two, at any rate,' he pronounced.

Leonardo, who had removed his shirt and was halfway out of his breeches, grinned.

'For longer than that,' he said.

'Not if we go back to Marsasirocco—now—and collect that old fool's clock,' said Rigo. 'In three days' time, God willing, we can all be quit of this damned island.'

'Rigo, you are a glutton for punishment. You would go for it tonight, after the march we have just made? I think not.'

'We can have it safe in our hands by dawn,' Rigo pointed out.

'And be fatigued beyond measure,' said Leonardo. 'Tomorrow or the next day will do as well. Have patience, Rigo.'

'No,' replied the gunner. 'Uberto Neri and his friends are happy for the moment. So why wait?'

Cipriano approached the fire. 'Exactly,' he agreed. 'Never put off what can be done at once. That is the tactician's argument. Mind you ... speaking for myself, I would have been satisfied with the emerald in that key of your——'

'Not mine,' said Leonardo. 'It belongs to Zeser Ibn Hasim. Had you forgotten?'

'Well and good,' said Cipriano in exasperation. 'In God's name, then give him his emerald and his clock, and let us be gone!'

'In a month from now,' said Leonardo remorselessly. 'Did you imagine I had chosen this place for a night's sleep? I need four weeks.'

Rigo, who had stripped, crushed his clothing into a ball and threw it violently to the ground.

'*Why?*' he demanded furiously.

'Because I am not done with Zeser Ibn Hasim. Because I did not come to Malta to find a jewel, or a clock, but to study the art and science of which they are a part. That old fool, as you are pleased to call him, has spent fifty years in perfecting a system of navigation. How many years did it take him to teach Felippo Mendoza how to use it? Five? Ten? If this clock of his is worth a hundred times ten thousand florins, then the manner in which it is used is yet worth a thousand times more.'

'Oh, yes,' said Cipriano sceptically. 'Because knowledge is priceless, I dare say, as you are always telling us.'

'Idiots!' cried Leonardo, in a passion. 'Knowledge may be priceless to me, but can I not drive it through your thick skulls that *this* piece of knowledge is beyond imaginable price to others? Is Venice hounding us for the sake of a little learning, think you? Does she seek to murder us because we are professors of astronomy? Is Uberto Neri a scholar? Is Orso Contarini? What in the name of Providence do you think is happening here—a twittering quarrel between schools of philosophy? Go to sleep. I despair of you!'

Taken aback at this outburst, his two friends remained silent. Leonardo continued, more gently.

'Listen,' he said. 'They have a clock, and a good one. I built it. It is not the clock they seek, but they cannot know this until it has been examined by experts. Since there are no experts here, they must send it to Venice for study, and await a reply from Venice. That reply will undoubtedly make them as mad as a nest of hornets, but their fury is five weeks away at least. I will take four of those weeks, and I promise you that we shall be gone by the time they realise that we have fooled them. That is all there is to it.'

In this confident belief, Leonardo was wrong. At the very moment he was speaking, Dr. Magnus Bembo of Utrecht was presenting his report to Orso Contarini in Rabat.

'Sirs,' he said simply, 'Venice has been duped.'

Uberto Neri started to his feet in rage and disbelief. Across the table from him, however, Contarini seemed less perturbed.

'You cannot be mistaken in this?' he said.

'Impossible,' Dr. Bembo replied. 'Did you not bring me here with you because I am an authority on time and clocks? It was very sensible of you.' Dr. Bembo's speech, like his temperament, was heavily influenced by his origins; he was a phlegmatic Low Countryman. He was holding Leonardo's clock a few inches from the end of his nose, rotating it between square and competent fingers. 'A nice piece of work,' he went on. 'Very nice. But nothing is unusual about it, and it will not keep good time for long, I think. It is driven by a spring, you see, and not by weights. And so, as this spring unwinds, it exerts less and less force upon the wheels and the mechanism ... you understand ... and the clock runs slower and slower. This is well known. Now I would say ... I would think this has been made recently, fine workmanship surely, but of no value except as a toy. I have seen many such, and none works properly.

'And so,' Dr. Magnus Bembo concluded, 'If this is the reason you have brought me all the way from Venice, then it is a pity. What I would like ... I would like to have seen this other clock, this wonderful one that you have told me——'

Neri, in ten swift paces, had crossed the salon and was gripping Achmet by the throat.

'You fool!' he screeched.

Orso Contarini sighed. 'Uberto,' he said, 'you tire me. Always, when a mistake is made, it is someone else's. Never yours. They have cheated you again—and, through you, myself. But I do not make the error of continually underestimating them. That is why I brought Dr. Bembo here. Come, Achmet.'

The Turk shook himself free of Neri's grasp and obeyed.

'Achmet,' said Contarini, 'did they have another clock with them?'

'No, my lord.'

'Not concealed upon their persons? Or in the boat?'

'No, my lord,' repeated Achmet stolidly. 'They were in breech-clouts, and I could see from where I stood in the surf that the boat was as bare as they were.'

'Thank you, Achmet.' Contarini turned to Neri again. 'Then it is still in the cove, Uberto. Under water. And Leonardo da Vinci believes that he has delayed us by this move, which I grant was a clever one.' He sighed again, softly. 'Take my men and yours again, Uberto, and find the clock. I am a reasonable man, even when provoked. You may have until dawn.'

By the fire, Leonardo lay asleep. Cipriano was on watch, and had completed his tenth careful circuit of the temple walls when he was intercepted by Rigo. The latter held a warning finger to his lips.

'I am leaving,' he whispered. 'Do not wake him until morning, since he is tired and I am in no mood for argument.'

'And what are you about?' asked Cipriano.

'I am going to fetch that pox-ridden clock,' said Rigo. 'Our young genius there may think his tactics sound, but you and I know better, eh, Cipriano? The longer we wait, the greater the risk.'

'Agreed,' Cipriano rejoined, 'but you are no diver.'

'I have no need to dive,' said his captain, 'since it is tied to the anchor chain and thus may be pulled from the sea. I shall be back before noon, God willing. In the meantime you may amuse yourself by trying to knock some sense into him. Farewell.'

With this, Rigo slung an empty pack loosely over his shoulder, slipped into the shadows beyond the wall, and was gone.

He made good time to Marsasirocco, setting his course by eye in the cloudy and uncertain dawn. Once arrived at the village and its quay, he debated briefly with himself whether or not to take the boat around the headland to the cove. He then concluded that he would do better to drag loose the anchor from the beach itself, where his stance would at least be firm. He took a line from the dinghy, coiled it around his waist, and set off overland. It must be said that his knowledge of sea matters was scanty, since to break out an anchor—more especially after months of silt had washed over it—might well have been a task beyond even Rigo's massive strength.

But now time ran out for Rigo. He was still staring out to sea, searching for the small buoy that marked the position of the *Pyramus*, when he was seized from behind by Achmet. Roaring defiance, he half turned, and Uberto Neri set the tip of a dagger underneath his chin.

'Well,' said Neri. 'Back so soon? It is not as much as I had hoped for, but perhaps it is enough.'

Rigo counted the men who surrounded him, and decided not to waste his breath.

'Speak,' said Neri. He drove the dagger's point upward by a fraction of an inch, and blood began to trickle down the blade of it. Rigo said nothing. Neri twisted his fingers sideways. Steel grated against the bone of the gunner's jaw, slid minutely, and opened a vein. The trickle of blood became a pulsating gush, and Neri took the stiletto away. He stood back, and looked into Rigo's eyes. 'Florentine,' he said, 'you are a dead man. *When* we bury you, and how long you will scream before we do so, are matters which are up to you.'

They took him to Rabat by cart, with his elbows pinioned behind his back and a sword at his breastbone. Seeing him Contarini was at first disposed to hang him out of hand. But Neri had other plans.

'If we have him, he will tell us where the clock is hidden. And also, sir, we may have Leonardo da Vinci into the bargain, and thus redeem all we have lost so far.'

'Perhaps,' said Contarini. 'What do you say, Captain Leone?'

131

'That you are a greater fool than I am,' answered Rigo, 'although not by much.'

Contarini smiled unpleasantly.

'We shall see,' he said.

Leonardo kicked at the stones of the beach impatiently.

'Blood,' he pointed out to Cipriano. 'Then he was down here, and they took him. It is my fault.'

'How so?' asked Cipriano. 'You were asleep, and he came of his own free will. And what of me, if it comes to that? I could have stopped him.'

'True. But the fault does not lie in that, only in my own miscalculation. If they have taken him, then they must know that we have tricked them. How they discovered it I cannot guess, but they do know. Four weeks?' He laughed bitterly. 'I had only a day, and was too stupid to realise it. Either Rigo is dead, or a prisoner.'

'If he was killed, then his body is missing,' observed Cipriano.

Leonardo squatted and turned over a pebble splashed with crimson. He scraped at the dried blood with his fingernail. 'I know,' he said, 'and it gives me hope. But we can find out for certain.'

'By what means?'

'We can see whether the clock is still there or not,' said Leonardo, pointing out to sea. 'If it is gone, then Rigo took it before they found him; and if so, then Venice has it now. In which case they may indeed have killed him, having no further use for him.'

'And what if you find it still there?' Cipriano said.

Leonardo was already taking off his cloak. 'Then they captured him before he tried for it,' he said, 'and he will not have told them where it is. In that case, they will have kept him alive . . . at least for the time being.'

Twenty minutes later, Leonardo swam to shore, towing the sack and its precious contents behind him.

'He is a prisoner, then,' said Cipriano, helping him ashore.

'Without a doubt.' said Leonardo.

'Good. Then it is easy. We go to Rabat and reclaim him. It will be a pleasure.'

Leonardo shook the water from his hair and began to rub it with his cloak. 'Not so fast,' he said. 'He will not be at the villa in Rabat. If I were in Neri's place, or in Orso Contarini's, I would not hold a prisoner anywhere so obvious.'

'What, then?' demanded Cipriano. 'What do we do?'

'We wait. It is the hardest task of all. We wait a message, since there will be one. A demand, an ultimatum. It is not hard to read Venice's mind. We must return to Zejtun; or at least I must return there. Perhaps you should join Decima and the lady Bianca.'

'No,' said Cipriano. 'Where you go, I go.'

'Then we'll both go to the villa, since it is there they will deliver their message . . . when it comes.'

The fishing port of Birgu, like the ancient capital city of Rabat, was dominated by Venice rather than by its Spanish owners.

A poor and sprawling community built around one of Malta's several northern inlets, Birgu consisted in the main of clay and wattle houses, though two sides of the market square were in rough-hewn stone. It possessed a customs house and a causeway for launching boats; for the rest, a tangle of dusty tracks lined with shops and workplaces overlooked the harbour itself, about which had sprung up a haphazard collection of shipyards and fishing shacks. In another part of the world perhaps, these latter might have been made of boards. In Birgu, the struggling chief port on an island almost devoid of trees, timber was an imported luxury, and every scrap of it went for the repair of boats.

The sole wooden establishment of any size was the Venetian warehouse on the outskirts of the village. Situated a good quarter of a mile from the noisy central waterfront, this was a fair-sized citadel in its own right, as Venice had intended it to be. Venice had thought nothing of shipping huge beams of oak, the planks, the roof slats, all the way from the Italian mainland. Nor had

Venice seen fit to erect her stronghold on dry land, but had instead hewn to her own traditions and built it offshore, supported on massive pilings. At its seaward end, its own quay gave shelter to a small fleet of lighters. At the opposite, shoreward end, a drawbridge could be raised, thus preventing access from the short pier from the land.

This fortress-like design was a sensible precaution, since the silks and spices it contained, the ingots of tin and gold awaiting trans-shipment from one Venetian carrack to another, would have bought the town of Birgu twice over. At the same time, it reminded Malta of the power and the wealth of Venice.

In a half-empty storeroom at the seaward end of this building, Uberto Neri talked softly to Rigo. Their conversation had been going on for several hours, and the marks of it showed redly across the gunner's face and back in a pattern of raised welts and trickles of blood. The conversation had also been onesided, though this was not through want of effort on Neri's part.

Neri had now lost patience.

Rigo was seated in a heavy chair, his feet shackled to ring bolts in the floor, his arms fastened by leather straps to the table before him. Occasionally, for only a second at a time, his head would loll against his shoulder. When it did so Achmet, who stood beside him, slashed at him with a short whip in what was by now a gesture of futile desperation.

'How deep is it?' asked Neri. 'Tell us only that, and for the present you may rest.'

Rigo made no reply.

'Very well,' Neri said. He reached across the table and took the whip from Achmet's hand. Instead of using it, he set it aside, and his voice grew persuasive and conversational. 'You are a strong man, Captain Leone, but stupid. If Leonardo da Vinci were present, he would tell you that your position is hopeless. But since you are clearly resolved not to betray his trust, let us have him here and speak with him ourselves. Is that not sensible?'

To this, Rigo said nothing whatever.

'We will, therefore, write him a note of invitation,' pursued

Neri, 'or rather, you will. Come, man. We shall have him in the end, and your gunner-companion with him. Why not now, while there is yet time to bargain? Write to him. You are not betraying him by doing so. He is a free agent. What do you say?'

Rigo turned his head and spat.

Neri stared at him coldly and without blinking for a full minute. Then: 'Bring me a knife, Achmet,' he ordered. 'Let it be a sharp one, and heavy. And, Achmet . . . set a kettle of pitch to boil on yonder brazier while you are about it. We may yet find a use for your hot coals.'

The Turk left Rigo's side. Neri sat on the table, swinging his foot. He tested, with some care, the wrist-straps that held Rigo's hands extended in front of him.

'They tell me,' he went on, 'that Florence has not seen a gunner as skilful as yourself for many a year. Is that true? Not, of course, that such things are of any great concern to me. Are you right-handed, Captain Leone? I ask because your compatriot Leonardo da Vinci—as many of us have observed—appears to favour neither hand, which might put me in something of a quandary if I had him in your place. Which I do not, or at least not yet . . . ah, thank you, Achmet.'

The Turk was holding out to him a short, triangular-bladed butcher's cleaver. Neri tested its edge with the ball of his thumb. 'And now,' he said, 'let us have matters clear. Thanks to Master da Vinci and his trickery, we are still seeking a clock. I say again that it is aboard Captain Felippo Mendoza's sunken ship. You, perchance, may tell me if I am right in this and—if so—its exact whereabouts. But perhaps I do you an injustice. It may be that you do not know, since it was after all Master da Vinci who dived for it, with his clever apparatus of tubes. Very good. In that case, it is to Master da Vinci I must address my questions, and you may serve me equally well by getting him here. In order to do this, you will write him a message. I care not what you say in it, so long as you convince him. Well?'

Rigo raised his head and looked the Venetian directly in the eyes.

'Convince him yourself, pig's dung,' he said.

Neri uttered a sudden, shrill giggle.

'And why not?' he said. He raised the cleaver swiftly and swung it downwards, burying its edge in the table top with a dull thump.

At the instant of the knife's descent, Rigo felt only a minor and bruising twinge of pain. His mind took in Achmet's deep bray of laughter, but that was all. Then he looked down at his right hand. His little finger, and the stumps of his three remaining ones, had curled back in an unconscious reflex. Half an inch from their ends, the iron blade stood upright in the wood and, immediately beyond it, the top joints of his severed index, middle, and ring fingers lay severed.

Neri wrenched the cleaver out of the table.

'Untidy,' he said. 'But we shall do better next time. You can still write, gunner. What do you say?'

Rigo set his teeth, wrenching his wrist to and fro against the leather band that held it. His struggle was instinctive and useless.

'No?' asked Neri. He swung the blade up again and, as he did so, Achmet moved behind the imprisoned man and ground his thumbs into the sensitive pressure-points at either side of his neck. The gunner's arms extended convulsively, his fingers splaying in reaction, and Neri brought the cleaver down for a second time. A moment of numbing darkness swept over Rigo, and he shook his head, half blind.

'Unfasten the strap,' Neri ordered, 'and bring the pitch-kettle.' The Turk obeyed, and Neri lifted the mutilated remains of Rigo's right hand from among the pieces of bone and gristle that surrounded it on the table-top. Blood was spurting from the whitened knuckle-ends, and the Venetian allowed them to fall once more and wiped his own fingers fastidiously on a kerchief. 'We have crippled you, Captain,' he said. 'We can cripple you further, but I should not care for you to bleed to death while we are doing so.'

Achmet brought the bronze pot to the table and set it down. The burned, resinous smell of pitch filled the air between them.

'My surgery is still poor,' Neri continued, 'but I think we should cauterise your wounds before proceeding further. You are of no further use as gunner to Florence, but perhaps you may find a living as a beggar when we are done with you. And now, have you anything to say?'

Rigo raised his right arm in reply to this, and briefly surveyed the shattered ruin at its end. Then, of his own volition, he quickly plunged it into the molten black fluid, searing the stumps of thumb and fingers in a single instant of fiery agony.

'Go back to Venice,' he gritted, 'and to your mother, who sells herself in its sewers. I have nothing to say.'

Eleven

BY THE EVENING of the second day following the capture of Rigo, Leonardo had grown gaunt and hollow-cheeked with a desperate anxiety which he did his best to conceal from Cipriano di Lucca. The latter, stamping furiously about the villa, could barely be restrained from rushing to Rabat with drawn sword and attempting to take the Venetian headquarters there in single-handed assault.

Leonardo sat on the villa's balcony with the clock of Zeser Ibn Hasim before him. Meticulously, he had taken this to pieces, and now was cleaning every spring and pinion of it with loving care before replacing them in the jewelled case. He did this to occupy his mind as much as for any other reason, while ever and again Cipriano would pause in his restless wandering to rail at him for his inactivity.

'And what the devil would you have me do?' Leonardo demanded of him finally, tension thinning his voice. 'How many supporters of Venice are there in the streets of Rabat, and Birgu, and Marsasirocco? What would it avail us to seek him? It is enough that they have Rigo; if they have me—and this,' he laid his hand on the gleaming clock, 'they have won everything. It may come to that, I know, but not yet.'

'And if there is no message?' shouted Cipriano. 'What of your tactics then?'

'Then I am wrong, and have lost a friend,' Leonardo replied. 'And do you suppose I have not considered it? I have not so many friends that I can afford the loss of any of them—including

138

yourself, Cipriano. *But I command here.* Is that understood? So it was agreed, and so it is. Mine is the responsibility.'

Cipriano stopped pacing and flung himself down on the wooden bench beside the table. He became calmer.

'It is your damned fiddling with that thing that annoys me,' he said. 'Well. Rigo is too tough a chicken to die yet awhile, I dare say. I am sorry, Leonardo. I know that you are as distressed as I am, and it is doubtless the intention of those sons of whores that we should go to pieces with the strain of waiting. But tomorrow . . .'

'Yes,' said Leonardo. 'Tomorrow it may be time to give up hope.' He changed his line of thought. 'At least Bianca and Decima are safe enough,' he said. 'At least we have that much on our side.'

'In a whorehouse?' said Cipriano. 'I don't doubt it was a brilliant idea on your part, but your notions of safety are peculiar.'

'Safer there than here.'

'I dare say. As for that,' said Cipriano, 'the lady Bianca has never tired of telling me that all Italy is a whorehouse, though there can be few women who are given the chance of examining such opinion at first hand. If you are satisfied, so am I—though what Lorenzo de' Medici might feel about her lodging is a different matter.' He sat up suddenly. 'Hello,' he said.

'What?'

'Our young friend Lemmo is coming up the hill,' said Cipriano. 'I wonder that he has the courage to do so.'

Leonardo at once rose.

'Thank God. Rigo lives!' he said. 'This is what we have been waiting for. Who more likely to bring us a demand from Venice than Lemmo?'

'And who more likely to take a foot of my sword blade in his ribs,' said Cipriano sourly. 'Pox-ridden little bastard.'

'Peace,' responded Leonardo.

A few minutes later, Lemmo appeared beneath the balcony and called up to them. He was swaggering.

'Who is within?' he asked.

'The two of us,' Leonardo told him. 'Who else? Come up here, Lemmo.'

'No harm must come to me,' said Lemmo cockily.

'Nor will it, boy. Come.'

'Very well, then.'

Lemmo climbed the steps to the front door to join them on the balcony. He carried a small casket of sandalwood, which he placed on the table.

'A gift from my masters,' he announced. 'And a message with it.'

'Well?' asked Leonardo.

'Open the gift first,' Lemmo said. 'Those are my instructions.'

Leonardo broke the seal and lifted the lid of the box. It was lined with satin and contained a carefully-folded package of crimson silk. He removed this and laid it beside the casket before unwrapping its several layers. As he unfolded the last of these he took a pace backwards, staring whitely.

Before him, obscenely, lay the pieces of Rigo's right hand on a sheet of oiled silk. The grisly morsels of flesh were pale and wax-like, contrasting foully with the black pitch that coated the ends of some of them.

Fighting for self-control, Leonardo laid the silk back over those ghastly remains. Behind him, someone was vomiting noisily. He turned to see Lemmo, plainly unprepared for the sight of the contents of the casket he had brought. As Leonardo stared balefully at him, he sank to his knees and hugged his stomach. Beyond him Cipriano, as though in a stupor, was crossing himself repeatedly.

Leonardo stirred the kneeling boy with the toe of his boot.

'Get up,' he said. Lemmo obeyed him.

'I . . .' he said. 'I . . . I swear . . .'

'I care not what you swear,' said Leonardo. 'He is alive?'

Lemmo seized at the question. 'Yes!' he said. 'Yes, he is alive, sirs, I swear it!'

'And what is your message?'

'Sirs, sirs,' cried Lemmo, 'I did not know they had done—this. Holy Mother of God, I did not!'

'The *message*,' said Leonardo.

'Yes, yes, the message. You are to wait here until noon

tomorrow,' Lemmo said. 'Achmet the Turk will come with four men . . . and if you wish to see your friend alive, you are to accompany them unarmed. That is the message I was to give you. God in heaven——'

'Stop the mewling, Lemmo,' said Leonardo. 'We have enough here without any protestations of yours. You have delivered your message. Go back and tell your masters that we will comply with their orders—and go swiftly. Your life hangs by a hair.'

Lemmo turned at once and ran from the balcony. When he appeared on the garden path below, stumbling in his haste to be away from the horrid gift he had been carrying, Leonardo beckoned urgently to Cipriano, who was standing quite still as though in shock. His lips were moving slightly and his eyes were fixed upon nothing, the whites showing around their pupils. Leonardo walked around the table and kicked him, hard and unceremoniously, in the shins, and the gunner started from his trance.

'What?' he asked. 'What is it?'

'Buckle on your sword,' commanded Leonardo, 'and stop standing there like a stricken sheep. We have work to do.'

'What?' repeated Cipriano. He still seemed dazed.

'Your sword,' Leonardo said, picking it up from the tiles and thrusting it into its scabbard. 'You have spent two days begging for action. Now you shall have it.'

Cipriano made an effort of will, thumped himself on the breast-bone, and recovered. 'I am ready,' he said. 'Before God, I am ready. What do we *do*, Leonardo?'

'Follow Lemmo, at a careful distance. We have an opportunity in a hundred, if we seize it. They are expecting us to sit here like obedient dogs and await their summons tomorrow. Therefore . . .'

The furtive beginnings of understanding stole across Cipriano's face. 'Lead on, then,' he said. 'Since you are in command. For myself, I am in the mood to kill some Venetian dogs!'

Their task was made easier by the fact that Lemmo, hurrying on his way, was too shaken to look about him. He passed through

Zejtun like a thief fearful of being apprehended and took the road that led towards Birgu. Leonardo and Cipriano, who had remained outside the village on the slope of the hill in order to observe the direction in which he left it, thereupon set off across the open country. They got a sight of their quarry every now and again at a bend in the road or a ridge crest, and closed gradually in on him as he neared the northern coast in the failing light.

From behind Birgu itself, they watched Lemmo's progress towards the harbour and then around it. He broke into a run as he drew near the pier that formed a link between the huge Venetian warehouse and the shore. He crossed the drawbridge and disappeared within the building. The drawbridge was then hauled up—by what means they could not, at this distance, make out—and the warehouse door closed behind him.

'Good,' Cipriano said. He had, by now, quite regained his usual airiness of manner, and his tone suggested that so far as he was concerned everything was straightforward. Leonardo glanced at him curiously.

'What do you suggest?' he asked mildly.

'It is simple,' Cipriano replied. 'You will agree that Rigo must be in there?'

'I will agree, at least, that it is more than likely.'

'Very well. Now in Ottavio's boatyard down there,' Cipriano pointed to the cobbled slipway a little to their right, 'is a cannon.'

'A *cannon*?'

'Yes. He pulled it from a Genoese galley not long ago, for repair. I have seen it.'

'I had forgotten your familiarity with all that goes on in Malta,' said Leonardo. 'Well?'

'When it is dark,' said Cipriano confidently, 'we will steal it, together with its powder and shot. If we haul it over there . . .' he gestured again, this time at the side of the headland overlooking the warehouse, 'we can blow them to pieces. Ten shots, or a dozen will do it. The . . .'

'Hold hard,' put in Leonardo. 'Have you thought? Twenty shots or fifty, will make no impression on that building, except to

142

smash a few unimportant holes in its walls—that is, unless this gun of yours is so large that the two of us cannot move it an inch. Dear God, it is no wonder that I find Rigo and yourself as like as two peas; give you a cannon, and nothing can withstand you! We shall do nothing of the kind.'

Cipriano made a sour face. 'What then?' he demanded.

'First of all,' said Leonardo, 'we will do nothing for an hour or two except consider, and observe. Have you not noticed that warehouse is the size of a small fort?' He sat down on the thin grass and stared through the gathering gloom.

'Forts are taken by cannon,' persisted Cipriano.

Leonardo made a heated and highly indelicate suggestion concerning cannon, and invited him to hold his tongue. 'Count the men,' he said.

Cipriano, subdued, sat down beside him. After a while: 'Eight,' he said. 'Two at the drawbridge, and six more on the staging by the side of the doorway.'

'And more inside, let us assume,' Leonardo said. 'Four are in the personal uniform of Orso Contarini, so there is no doubt that they have Rigo there, to my mind.' Whereupon, he lay back and closed his eyes.

A long while later, Cipriano nudged him.

'Are you asleep?' the gunner enquired.

'Thinking,' Leonardo said.

'To some purpose, I hope. It has been dark for hours.'

'Quite right,' responded Leonardo. 'It is time we moved.' He got up and brushed himself. 'You said there was powder in Ottavio's yard?'

'Three barrels. I am glad you have come round to my way of thinking at last.'

'I haven't. Not exactly.' Leonardo had already begun to pick his way down the ridge towards the sleeping town and its harbour. Cipriano followed, and five minutes later they climed over the low wall of Ottavio's boatyard together. Once inside, Cipriano looked around, and led Leonardo to a corner where a rusting and pot-bellied bombard stood beside a pile of old timber. Leonardo surveyed this weapon.

'That?' he asked. 'Is that your cannon?'

'Somehow it does not look quite so effective as I had thought,' admitted Cipriano, unabashed.

'I thank God I did not include it in my plans,' said Leonardo quietly. 'Where is the powder?'

'Here.'

Leonardo pried off the lid of a small keg with the point of his dagger and sniffed professionally at its contents. 'It is fair enough,' he said.

'I did not realise you were such an expert in gunpowder,' observed Cipriano sarcastically. 'Give it to me. I am the gunner, not you.' He seized the keg from his companion, who laughed.

'Make me a fuse, then,' Leonardo said.

'With what?'

'With rope, and powder, of course. It is very simple. You cut a length of rope, untwist the strands, rub powder in between them, and then twist them up again. After that——'

'I know how to make a fuse, thank you,' said Cipriano. 'Where is your rope?'

'We are in a boatyard,' said Leonardo patiently. 'One, moreover, with which you claim to be familiar. I will not ask why this particular boatyard should have captured your attention, but there it is.'

'I was tupping a wench,' said Cipriano, 'and therefore the materials for fuses were not on my mind at the time. Her husband——'

'Find a rope, and make a fuse,' said Leonardo. 'We have not got all night for your tales of sexual conquest.' He left Cipriano and went across the yard to the slipway. Several dinghies lay about, though all were in various degrees of disrepair. He gazed across the inlet towards the Venetian warehouse on its pilings; it lay several hundred yards distant, across moonlit water. He returned to Cipriano.

'We have to swim,' he said.

Cipriano, who had unearthed from somewhere a piece of tarred rope, was worrying apart its fibres with his teeth. He stopped, and spat fragments of hemp. 'I cannot swim,' he said in an offhand manner. 'Nor do I propose to learn now.'

It was curious, Leonardo thought, how the best-laid and most dashing of schemes was liable to founder on some trivial difficulty like this. He could, he supposed, swim out to the warehouse, bring back one of the Venetian lighters that were moored in its lee, and then row Cipriano out again, but the chances of doing so without being seen in the moonlight seemed slender.

'We will float you,' he said calmly. 'Now bring the fuse, two kegs of powder, and your flint and steel over to the slipway yonder. I'll see what can be done.'

He went back and chose a boat whose bottom, at least, was fairly sound. After launching it, he slid into the sea, rested his weight on its gunwale and turned it over. It floated sluggishly with several inches of its keel and bilges protruding above the water. When he dived, he discovered a sufficient air space beneath its hull for his purposes. The fuse, he thought, was bound to get damp; this would not matter as long as it did not become sodden. The two unbreached powder kegs were bound to be airtight, as were all such kegs, since otherwise their contents would spoil in misty air or rain.

Cipriano, arriving at the slipway a few minutes later, was unenthusiastic when Leonardo explained what he had in mind.

'We shall drown,' he said.

'Nothing of the kind,' replied Leonardo. 'We have enough air to breathe under there, and it is not very far.' He took the fuse from Cipriano, lifted a gunwale of the overturned dinghy, and manoeuvered the length of blackened rope into the bilge without immersing it. Holding it clear of the water with one hand, he allowed the boat to wallow back to its original attitude, accepted one of the kegs from Cipriano, and prepared to dive. 'Come,' he said. Cipriano hesitated, then joined Leonardo in the darkness beneath the keel. 'Lean your arms on the thwart, and keep still,' the artist said, and pushed off with his feet.

They were compelled to find their target blindly, and twice during their progress Leonardo was forced to emerge from beneath the upturned hull to correct their course. At last, however, they bumped gently against the nearest of the huge piles that supported the warehouse. Leonardo at once grabbed his companion by the collar, ducked him forcibly, and hauled him under the gunwale, clamping a hand over his mouth when the gunner surfaced outside the boat and gasped for air. Once Cipriano was clinging safely to a cross-timber, Leonardo was able to right the boat and at the same time extract the fuse and the powder kegs, none of which had suffered greatly from their journey; the tarred surface of the fuse rope had kept its interior dry.

Leaving Cipriano to support these items clear of the water as best he might, Leonardo swam from piling to piling until he reached the row of lighters moored behind the transverse quay at the seaward end of the warehouse. One of these, he was happy to find, contained barrels of lamp oil and pitch. He untied it from its mooring and eased it cautiously beneath the staging. Footsteps sounded above him, and he held his breath; but the paces were measured and deliberate, and receded without a break in their rhythm. He hitched the lighter to a piling out of sight and swam back to collect Cipriano.

Together they made their way through the network of struts and braces that supported the warehouse, sometimes half sub-merged and sometimes climbing entirely clear of the water, until they could pull themselves aboard the lighter. Here, Leonardo noiselessly pried open the tops of both powder-kegs, and inserted half of the divided fuse in each. All was ready.

'Flint and steel,' he said softly.

'Cipriano produced these, and a tinder box, from his waist pouch. All were wet, but on opening the box Leonardo found enough dry pieces of tinder to burn. 'Get up to the roof,' he said, 'and I will join you there in a while.'

He watched Cipriano swarm up the piling to which they were moored, pull himself nimbly over the protruding edge of the warehouse staging, and disappear overhead. He dried the flint and steel, and after some persistence struck a spark; within a minute or two he was able to hold a glowing chip of tinder against the end of each fuse in turn and blow them into spitting life.

Powder fuses were notorious both in the unreliability and their speed of burning. As soon as he was sure that both were lit, he ran to the prow of the lighter and climbed to the deck of the warehouse, where he stood upright to look for Cipriano. The latter beckoned to him from the eaves above, and pointed, indicating a shuttered window whose sill could be used as a step. Leonardo mounted this, grasped Cipriano's downstretched arm, and a moment later was lying beside him on the sloping tiles.

'How many men?' he asked softly.

'Two, I think,' said Cipriano. 'They are by the drawbridge.' He nodded towards the shoreward gable, some thirty paces distant.

They were halfway along the roof, moving in crouched silence, when from below the muffled roar of a bursting powder keg reached their ears. Immediately, hoarse cries of alarm sounded within the warehouse, followed by a second explosion which announced that both kegs had now been fired. Smoke began to spread across the water, obscuring the dim shapes of the moored lighters behind the quay.

'Wait,' Leonardo said, resting his hand on Cipriano's shoulder. 'Fire is our ally; give it time to grow into a more powerful one.'

Carefully, they inched their way towards the gable that overlooked the drawbridge. By the time they reached it, Venetian men-at-arms were swarming out of the twin entrance doors below them, running to right and left along the sides of the building in search of the fire. A dull crackling of wood hinted that the staging itself had caught fire, and a rim of burning oil was starting to drift outwards from around the pilings.

'Now,' Leonardo said.

A lull in the activity beneath them gave them their opportunity. They still did not know how many men opposed them, but they could see only one guard who had remained at his post by the raised drawbridge. As Leonardo spoke, some primal instinct for danger made the guard look up at the roof, and he shouted an incoherent warning as Leonardo and Cipriano descended on him like dark and sky-borne devils, choking off his scream and hurling him into the waters below.

Cipriano would have made at once for the warehouse doors, but Leonardo seized his arm.

'The drawbridge!' he cried, and ran for one of the winches that supported it. He slashed at the rope with his sword edge, while Cipriano did the same at the opposite winch. The drawbridge leaned, gathered momentum, and fell with a resounding crash, bridging the gap between warehouse and shore; but the few seconds of delay this had cost them meant that they now faced three Venetians who had been slower than their fellows in leaving the building and now stood in the doorway, uncertain of what was happening.

Their hesitation was fatal. Cipriano hurled himself at them, spitting the nearest like a chicken with the force of his charge. Leonardo ran another of them through the arm and knocked the third sprawling. Before the Venetian could rise, they were past him and running down the central corridor of the warehouse.

At either side, doors gave on to storerooms and offices. All were empty; in one of them Leonardo caught a glimpse of truckle beds and hanging uniforms. Twenty paces ahead they reached a timber archway, beyond which lay the main bay of the warehouse. This extended for its full width from side to side, and was stacked everywhere with bales and chests. It was also, as they saw at once, directly above the oil-filled lighter that was the source of their fire. Almost in the centre of the room a blackened hole, edged with tongues of flame and smoke gaped like the mouth of hell. Even as they watched, a pyramid of casks tottered at its fiery margin, collapsed, and fell through it into the sea below, together with a ten-foot length of floor beam.

'God's blood!' Cipriano exclaimed in awe. 'Have you not over-done things a trifle here? We came to rescue Rigo, not to fry him along with ourselves!'

They skirted the roaring chasm, feeling the floorboards hot

beneath the soles of their boots, and reached the far side of the room in safety. Here they were faced with an archway similar to the one by which they had entered, and a pair of ornate brass-bound doors. Evidently, Leonardo thought, the plan of the warehouse must be symmetrical, with a central store for heavy cargo and smaller rooms at either end. He kicked at the doors, slamming them open against the walls of the passage beyond.

As he had foreseen, this corridor indeed ran for a further twenty or thirty paces. It was sealed at its farther end by a massive ironwork grille, which served to make the seaward end of the warehouse secure. Its existence, however, meant that unless they made haste they were trapped. Their exit at this end of the building was barred, and behind them was a growing inferno. If there should be windows in the rooms at either side of them, these must infallibly lead them straight into the arms of their foes.

All these thoughts passed through Leonardo's mind in an instant, and were gone. None of them seemed important when compared with the sight that greeted him as the doors flew apart at the very end of the corridor and hard by the iron grid that blocked it as a means of escape there stood a figure holding a ring of keys.

It was Uberto Neri.

He was in the act of unlocking the farthest side door on their right, and turned at once to look in their direction. He fumbled, and dropped the keys. As he did so, a jarring explosion sounded from behind Leonardo, and the whole building seemed to lurch sideways and tilt on its foundations. A powder-magazine, Leonardo thought: there must be one somewhere in a stronghold such as this. But his feet, as though of their own will, were already carrying him at a run towards the Venetian at the far end of the passage, where Neri was standing with drawn sword, the keys now lying unheeded at his feet. Hard on Leonardo's heels, Cipriano was shouting, his voice half drowned by a rising and angry crackle.

Had they reached him together, their charge uninterrupted, they would have killed Neri at once. But they were barely halfway to him when the fire, driven by its own remorseless laws and heedless of the affairs of mere mortals, took a sudden hand in matters. Burning oil from the lighter underneath the building had spread far and wide, so that the whole warehouse sat above a sea of flame like a pot on a roaring stove. The blast from the magazine had torn off a huge section of the roof and thus provided a chimney draft for the flames, which at once tripled in their destructive force. It seemed to Leonardo that the floor under them became a griddle, while the thin wall at their left burst asunder like charred paper and filled the corridor with a turmoil of hot smoke that tore at their lungs like acid. The building lurched again. Leonardo was thrown to the ground, and as he struggled to regain his stance Neri thrust desperately past him and was gone. He heard Cipriano shout again, but could not see him through the rolling blackness.

Then, finding the bunch of keys still lying where they had fallen, he forgot his companion and set himself to the task at hand. The second key he tried upon the locked door at his right fitted, and turned; he drove his shoulder against the door, and burst through it into the room beyond.

Rigo was in a corner by the window. He was standing upright among the remains of a straw mattress, his right arm inside the breast of his tunic; a chain on his left wrist held him fastened to a ring-bolt set into the wall. He was deathly pale, and swayed, but at the sight of Leonardo he produced his usual indomitable grin.

'Well,' he said. 'What have we here? A gunner? Two of them, by Christ!'

Leonardo turned his head briefly and saw Cipriano, grinning likewise as he slapped at the sleeve of his doublet, which was smouldering. Relieved, he crossed the room and picked up a low wooden bench, which he at once smashed like a battering ram into the wall beside the chain bolt. The planking split, and Leonardo wrenched at the chain with all his might. Bolt, ring and all flew out of the wall, and he draped the chain around his neck and gave Rigo his arm for support.

'What of Uberto Neri?' he asked Cipriano.

'Dead, without a doubt,' replied the gunner. 'He ran past me before I could stop him, and then found he could choose between the fire back there and myself. He chose the fire.' He was still in the doorway, and beyond him in the passage an ominous, flickering orange glow gave emphasis to his words. 'Rigo . . .' he said, and then stopped, as though alarmed at the thought of seeming, for however short an instant, serious. Instead he addressed Leonardo. 'I dare say you have considered how we are to get out of here, have you?' he asked.

'Through the window,' said Leonardo.

'Good,' Rigo said. He looked around him. 'What in the devil's name have you done here?'

'He lit a fire,' replied Cipriano, 'but I think it has run a little out of hand.' With this, he lifted the bench and beat out the window frame with it. Thrusting his head out, he peered to right and left. Against a hideous yellow glare, he could see a few remaining Venetians running hither and yon as though panic-stricken; one had jumped into the sea behind the moored lighters and was thrashing in desperation, surrounded by the burning oil on its surface. The warehouse was leaning dangerously. Flames towered through its roof, whirling upwards a fountain of sparks, drifting cinders, and pieces of fiery debris, while over and around everything a pall of greasy smoke billowed.

He withdrew his head.

'Why, it is a rout,' he declared. 'They would hardly notice us if we had three heads apiece. Shall we go?'

He set the bench under the window, and climbed through. Together, he and Leonardo extracted Rigo from the room as carefully as they could, and propped him against the wall outside, where he closed his eyes and seemed about to collapse. Leonardo shook him.

'Can you walk?' he asked.

Rigo nodded, but his eyes stayed shut. Cipriano took his left arm and put it around his own shoulder, while Leonardo did likewise with his right, from the bandaged end of which blood was beginning to seep. Thus, as well as they could, they made their way along the canted side of the building, across gaps in the deck that breathed flame and past fallen and blackened lintels. Near the middle of the warehouse, where their fire had first taken hold and therefore blazed most strongly, they could hear its howling behind the wooden wall.

Beyond this point, the heat lessened somewhat, so that sweat ran down their faces. They paused at the corner by the draw-bridge; a soldier in the livery of Orso Contarini looked directly at them without recognition and then turned away to make for the bridge; another ran half-heartedly towards them only to stop at the sight of Cipriano's drawn blade. He might, perhaps, have attacked them, but above him the gable end sagged suddenly, cracked, and fell inwards with a rumble. Broken glass showered down on the man and a firebrand struck his helmet. His caution turned to fear and he, too, fled.

'Did I not tell you?' Cipriano said. 'A rout. They are demoralised.'

Beyond the drawbridge a confused murmur of voices from the shore told them that the inhabitants of Birgu had come to watch the holocaust. Cipriano laughed, and Rigo at last opened his eyes and drew upon some reserve of strength. He took his arms from around his companions' necks, stood upright, and began to march towards the bridge.

'Where to, friends?' he asked them. 'I have been three days without wine, which is three days too long. Where to?'

Twelve

'GIVE ME MORE brandy,' Rigo said. 'And a pox on you.'

'By all means,' said Cipriano, reaching for the flask which lay on Decima's bed. Decima slapped his wrist sharply.

'He has had too much already,' she said.

'Oh? Personally,' rejoined Cipriano, who was himself somewhat tipsy, 'that is to say, speaking for myself, you understand . . . I cannot wait for him to drink himself to sleep. He has not been brilliant company of late.' He hiccupped, and prodded Rigo in the chest. 'You are alive,' he said profoundly. 'Remember that.'

'Aye,' answered Rigo. 'Alive. But now comes the reckoning. Where was I? I asked you for more wine, pretty-boy, did I not?'

'You are asking to have your skull broken.'

'What!' exclaimed Rigo. 'You would strike a one-armed man?'

'Rigo,' Decima said gently. 'Rigo . . .'

'Leave him,' said Cipriano. He prodded the Captain-Gunner again. 'You have the best of the bargain. What about Uberto Neri?'

They were sitting, as they had been doing for five days now, in Decima's room at the House of Ten Pearls. Rigo had spent the first twenty-four hours unconscious, and all except Cipriano had feared he would die; but he was now recovering slowly in body, though not in mind. Occasionally he would smile, and seem his old self again, but for the most of the time since he had regained his senses he had been—as now—morose, and drunk.

'I thought he was dead,' Rigo said.

'Then you have not been listening,' replied Cipriano. 'He is not dead, though I believed he was. I had it from the foreman at Ottavio's boatyard. He has gone to Venice with Orso Contarini, and they say half the flesh is burned from his face. Of course,' added Cipriano cheerfully, 'he may die yet.'

'And I care not whether he lives or dies,' said Rigo. 'Damn his face. What has *he* lost? He is nothing but a pox-ridden assassin, and a poor one at that, whereas I am a Captain of guns. Or I was.'

Downstairs, in a room behind Madame Olympia's own quarters, Leonardo was squatting on the floor crosslegged, surrounded by drawings. Once he had assured himself that Rigo would survive, he had kept out of his way, having much to think about. The departure of First Secretary Contarini in disorder, together with the stricken Uberto Neri and two thirds of the Venetian force on the island, pleased him a good deal. It was true that Achmet the Turk was still present, but on balance Leonardo felt he had been offered a period of reasonable safety, something which for many reasons he badly needed.

Bianca was lying on her stomach beside him, looking through a sheaf of papers. Some of these bore portraits and caricatures, while the remainder were diagrams of mechanisms of one kind and another, interspersed with anatomical studies of hands in various attitudes.

'Who is this?' Bianca asked, holding up a cartoon.

'Him? That is Pignatelli, the baker,' Leonardo replied. 'He was here the night before last, as I recall.'

'So he was,' said Bianca, laughing. 'I should have recognised him at once. He wanted to take me to bed, and broke six wine flasks when he could not have me. Is that why you've made him look so furious?'

'Well,' said Leonardo, bending down to kiss her upturned mouth, 'it was a golden moment, and I felt it should be preserved for posterity. Incidentally, I have been meaning to ask you . . .'

'What?'

'Madame Olympia must be giving her clients some reason for your . . . er, unavailability. I wondered——'

Bianca laughed again, blushing. 'We're supposed to be sisters,' she said. 'Decima and myself, that is. We're Circassians, and we've only just been brought here. And, well . . . you see, we're also supposed to have some kind of disease—I'm not quite sure what, but anyway . . . why are you looking like that, Leonardo?'

'I am trying to imagine how I shall explain all this to Lorenzo de' Medici.'

'You won't have to.'

'I think I will,' said Leonardo, 'and fairly soon, too. But never mind. Bianca, I am going to need your help this afternoon.'

'Of course.'

'Rubbish!' said Cipriano. 'Arrant nonsense, and I begin to weary of listening to it. What do you suppose will happen? Is there a single gunner in Florence who will think the less of you because you have lost a hand? Of course not! You are their Captain, and mine. Why in the devil's name should you imagine all this is changed?'

But Rigo, who was now sitting bolt upright in his chair with the brandy flask clutched in his left hand—was not so easily comforted. He had reached that state of pitiless clarity achieved only by the very wise, and the exceedingly drunk.

'Listen,' he said, and belched solemnly. 'Listen. That is how it will begin, because you are all good fellows. But how long will it last? Six months? A year, perhaps? A man cannot trade for ever on what he has been. It is what he is that counts. Eh?' He squinted at Cipriano. 'A pox on you, pretty-boy. Eh? What do you say to that?'

'You are drunk,' said his lieutenant.

'Yes, you are,' Decima said.

'Strike me, pretty-boy. Why not? Strike.'

'No,' said Cipriano.

'There you have my argument. Listen, Cipriano . . . Cipriano, you're a damned fine gunner. But listen to me. You will not strike me, because I have only one hand. You see? So it will be in Florence. I am Captain-Gunner for two reasons; all men are what

155

they are for two reasons. One: because Lorenzo made me so. Two: because, when it comes to the touch, I can beat any man to a pulp. That is, I could, before...' He lifted his healing stump. 'Let me tell you something,' he went on doggedly. 'How long since you joined the gunners?'

'Six years,' said Cipriano. 'Why?'

'And you are the son of a haberdasher.'

'We have been through all that,' Cipriano said, with patience.

'Haberdasher,' said Rigo. 'Because when you joined us, we all called you "Pretty-boy". You remember? And what did you do?'

Cipriano fingered his nose. It was broken, and lent an air of ruggedness to his otherwise handsome and rather delicate face. 'I fought you,' he said. 'And beat you ... except for Scudo, who is no man, but rather a mountain upon legs. None the less he stopped calling me by that name.'

'You did not beat me,' said Rigo, slyly.

'That was because you chose not to bait me,' said Cipriano with a grin. 'Which was prudent of you.'

Rigo drank from the flask. 'Well,' he said. 'What was I saying? Yes. You are my lieutenant-gunner for two reasons. You lay a cannon better than any man I know. But also you have thrashed everybody soundly, and they respect you for it. You see my point? I was Captain-Gunner to Florence by right. I will not stay so through pity, or tolerance, or memory of what I once was.'

At this Leonardo, who had been standing at the door for some while, came into the room.

'Take those bandages off,' he said lightly, 'before you die of remorse.'

'Ah,' said Rigo, looking up. 'Ah! My—sh—shurgeon. How are you, friend surgeon? Eh?' He began to unwind the strips of cotton cloth from his right arm.

'A good deal the better for not being forced to listen to your drunken maunderings,' replied Leonardo briskly. He sat down and examined Rigo's proffered stump. It was pitch-smeared, scarred and hideously distorted, having been severed directly through the wrist joint. He sniffed at it for putrefaction, but there was none.

'Ha,' said Rigo. 'If you are tired of my complaints, friend surgeon—cure me!'

'That is what I propose,' Leonardo replied coolly.

'What?'

'I said, I propose to cure you. I offer you a bargain, Rigo. Are you too drunk to listen to it?'

'What bargain?'

'A new hand.'

'Oh, no doubt, no doubt,' said Rigo with deep cynicism. 'A hook, with which I may lift buckets, if I choose. I have seen them.'

'A hook be damned,' said Leonardo. 'I am talking of a hand, not a hook. A hand with which you may pick up a grape without bruising its skin. How does that strike you?'

For reply, Rigo raised his left arm and hurled the brandy flask across the room to shatter in a corner. 'Do not mock me,' he said.

Leonardo looked at him long and hard. 'Rigo,' he said, 'have you ever known me to promise what I could not deliver?'

'It is not possible,' Rigo muttered, lowering his eyes.

'It is. All things are possible, at a price.'

'Including miracles? What price?'

'A small one, for a man like yourself,' said Leonardo. 'Pain.' He took a charcoal stick and with it drew a circle around Rigo's forearm, about a hand span below the elbow. 'I shall have to shorten it . . . to hereabouts.'

Suddenly Rigo sobered up.

'You mean, cut off more of it?' he demanded.

'Yes.'

'Why? I have lost enough of it already.'

'Not so,' Leonardo said. 'Look at it. You have lost the hand, and it's a butcher's job. I can do nothing with it now; it is too flat, and the bones will begin to stick out from it in a while. I need to fashion you a tidy, well healed stump before I can build what I intend to mount on it.'

Rigo looked down at the blackened circle, and attempted

bravado. 'Well,' he said, 'you are the engineer. The pain will not trouble me overmuch, if you do the job swiftly. What is one hack more or less?'

'You do not yet understand,' said Leonardo. 'If you are thinking of a single clean blow with an axe, you are mistaken. That is how such things are done on the battlefield, but it will not serve me. I propose joinery, not rough carpentry. An hour of careful—and painful—work, and another hour of stitching to follow. Perhaps longer. That is what I meant by a price. Can you withstand it?'

'Dear Jesus,' Rigo said softly. 'How do I know? You are talking of a longer time than those Venetian dogs took over their ... carpentry.'

'I know,' said Leonardo.

Decima got up from the bed and came forward. 'Leonardo,' she said, 'are you sure? You can truly do this thing?'

'I can, with God's help.'

'And when you have done, you can give him a hand—of sorts?'

'When I have done,' Leonardo answered, 'he will be able, with his right hand, to pluck one of your eyelashes without your noticing. I do not promise that it will *look* like a hand, since it will be a piece of machinery, nothing more. But it will be a delicate piece, and a strong one.'

'Then do it,' said Decima.

Rigo turned. 'Woman,' he said, 'I did not ask you to take my decisions for me.'

'Then tell him he may not,' said Decima, calmly. Rigo looked at his right arm, and scraped thoughtfully at the charcoal circle Leonardo had drawn around it. He nodded.

'When?' he asked.

'Here, and now,' said Leonardo. 'That is, unless you would like to think it over for the next day or so.'

'No, by Hades,' the gunner said. 'Let us get it over with.'

'Good. Then drink some more brandy,' said Leonardo. 'Decima, can you find us another bottle? A large one,' he added reflectively. 'I have all that I need downstairs. Bianca will help me—and you too, Cipriano, if you will.'

Cipriano swallowed. 'I am,' he said, 'somewhat drunk myself.'
'You will sober up quickly enough,' Leonardo said.

'Rigo ...?'
'Yes?'
'We are ready to begin. Are you comfortable?'
'Yes.'
'Then go to sleep. Dream of cannon, if you wish.'
'The pox take you, sawbones. Get on.'
'Decima?'
'Yes, Leonardo.'
'Take his left wrist in your fingers ... so. Can you feel his heartbeat?'
'I can.'
'Tell me if it alters. And watch his breathing. If he asks for drink, give it to him unless I tell you not to. Cipriano?'
'What?'
'See that he does not move. I have his shoulder firm with this strap, but he is a powerful man; and the pain will reach him even as he is. You understand?'
'Yes.'
'Very good. Bianca, will you set fire to the brandy in that dish, please? And, when the flame dies, give me the shorter of the two knives that lie in it. If I ask you for thread, give it to me quickly, since I shall need it to tie a blood vessel. For anything else, there will be no great haste. Keep the chasing irons hot in the flame there, always; they are for searing the smaller veins. More than a cupful of blood lost, and he may be done for.'
'I can hear you, sawbones,' Rigo croaked. 'Keep your good cheer to yourself.'
'Go to sleep. Bianca? Thank you. Now ...'
'Holy Jesus,' whispered Rigo. 'Sweet Christ! *No!* No. Have I told you how it was with us at Ravenna? Well ... thus it was ...'

'Lean on him, Cipriano. Lean on his back. *He must not move his shoulders!* Bianca?'

159

'Yes?'

'Give me that fine saw. You see what I must do? I have cut these two flaps of skin and muscle, so . . . and now I must shorten the bone ends beneath them, so that I can build a soft cushion of flesh to fold over them. Is he bleeding there, at your side?'

'Very little, Leonardo. A trickle.'

'Sear it for me, will you? You see where it is coming from?'

'Yes, I can see it. Just here . . .'

'Good. Sear it. That's right.'

'They had a ravelin,' Rigo murmured, 'and a forward redoubt. Were there two redoubts, Cipriano? By God, there were two; my mind is slipping. Or was it only one. Never mind. Well, said I, if we can have them in no other way, then it must be a mine. Cipriano?'

'Lie still.'

'What is he doing? By Christ, it *burns*!'

'Lie still, idiot! There were two redoubts, and your mine was a failure,' said Cipriano, 'as I knew it would be. Tesoro lost his whiskers in a backfire. He had only just grown them, with considerable labour. He blamed it on you, and he was quite right, of course. My advice at the time . . . Decima? Decima?'

'He has fainted.'

'Thank God for that, then,' said Cipriano.

'How is he, Decima?'

'Still alive.'

'We are almost done now. Bianca, can you hold his arm in just this position, and keep it steady, do you think?'

'Yes, I can.'

'Give me the canvas needle first, then, and a long thread to it . . . thank you. By the way, Cipriano, after all that, what *did* happen at Ravenna?'

'We won,' said Cipriano. 'That is what happened.'

'Well,' Leonardo said, 'we have won here, also.'

'Rigo. Rigo . . . Rigo?'

'Leave him,' said Decima. 'Let him sleep it off.'

'He can sleep when I am certain that he will not stay asleep for ever,' said Leonardo. 'He has enough brandy in him to kill three ordinary men. *Rigo!*'

Rigo stirred, snored, and turned on to his back. The strap that had been holding him face downward on Madame Olympia's table had been loosened. He half opened one eye, and passed a leathery tongue over his dry lips.

'My head splits,' he said.

'Good.'

'And my mouth feels like a shrivelled fig.'

'Excellent.'

'What the devil am I doing? I need a drink.'

'No, you don't,' Leonardo told him.

'Well,' said Rigo, 'when are you going to get on with it, saw-bones? Eh? A pox on you, is what I say.'

'It is done,' replied Leonardo, 'and I am pleased to tell you that you seem much recovered already. Thank you, Bianca, my heart. My thanks, Cipriano. Decima, look after him well.'

'I shall,' said Decima. 'Have no fear of that.'

The weeks that followed were untroubled ones. Christmas came, was celebrated at the House of Ten Pearls with cheerful abandon, and was gone; winter laid its hand on Malta, and turned the sea from blue to sleety grey.

Leonardo debated with himself—and with Cipriano—whether or not to return to the villa above Zejtun in the absence of their foes. But he decided against it, and as a result Madame Olympia made a small but satisfactory profit from their lodging. She was happy to do so, since her custom fell off at this season in any case. Furthermore, she had developed a passion for Rigo; she was flattered continuously and outrageously by the flamboyant Cipriano, and she sat up until all hours discussing philosophy— one-sidedly—with Leonardo, trying (so she announced) to put some flesh on him by force-feeding him with chicken.

For his part, Leonardo listened to her views with half an ear, and indulged in metal working the while. Ten days after rebuilding the stump of Rigo's arm to his liking, he fitted it with a conical socket of leather and wood which was attached by means of buckles to the upper arm and shoulder. Rigo found it uncomfortable, but Leonardo forced him to wear it day and night, his orders being enforced by Decima. A week later he was ready to fit the first of a series of attachments to its lower end. This was a gunmetal hook split lengthways, so designed that its two halves could be pulled apart, pincer like, by a thin cord that ran in grooves. The upper end of this cord was fastened to the shoulder harness in such a way that when Rigo raised his arm and extended the elbow joint slightly, the hook would open; it was closed again by an opposite movement.

Rigo at first thought this clumsy, and protested vigorously at the new skills involved in using it; but after being shouted down by Cipriano on the one hand and Decima on the other, he agreed to practise. Within days he found that he could pick up a thin spike, and a little later was challenged by Bianca to thread a sewing needle, using both the split hook and his sound left hand. It took him only a minute or two to succeed in this, whereupon Cipriano hammered him on the back and plied him with drink.

On the morning following this triumph, Leonardo left Rabat with a small, heavy muslin bag, announcing that he would be back by nightfall. He walked to Zejtun, and then, following a path to which he had become accustomed, to the valley wherein lay the entrance to the cave of Zeser Ibn Hasim.

He found the obstructing boulder in its mouth already standing aside, and the interior of the cavern lit by a multitude of candles and a roaring brushwood fire. The old astronomer, smiling faintly, offered a chalice of wine, which Leonardo accepted.

'Since this is your last visit,' Ibn Hasim said, 'the Prophet will grant us indulgence. I wish you health and long life, of which in any case you are assured.'

'I did not say that this would be my last visit,' Leonardo replied, and the old man smiled more widely.

'You did not say you were coming at all,' he pointed out, 'and yet the door was open. How is your friend, the gunner?'

'Much improved. And your entrance door is always open to me, Ibn Hasim. I assumed that you always saw me from afar. Isn't that so?'

'I hardly stir from my home in here,' answered Ibn Hasim, 'and I have better things to do than stand watch for your approach. But I am kept informed of this and that.'

Leonardo drank from the chalice, a little puzzled.

'By whom?' he asked.

'By nobody that you would recognise,' said Ibn Hasim, and at once changed the subject. 'I see you have brought my clock.'

'Yes,' Leonardo said. He removed it from the muslin bag and set it on the narrow table between them. 'I have cleaned and repaired it, and it runs well. A beautiful piece of craftsmanship. The bearings and pivots are unworn; I had never before seen them fashioned from jewels. It loses time remarkably steadily, as of course I knew it would. The one I built to deceive Venice...'

'Yes?' said the astronomer.

'It was a mere plaything compared to this. But I believe that while making it I have discovered a principle whereby such clocks need not lose time at all. Are you interested?'

'Indeed,' said Ibn Hasim courteously. 'The difficulty has always been that the tension of the mainspring decreases as it unwinds; do you mean that you have found a way to overcome this?'

'I have,' replied Leonardo. 'Here. I have drawn it in my notebook... you see?' He laid his portfolio on the table and drew a candle across for better light. 'Here is the spring,' he said. 'It is contained within a helix... and this is in turn connected to this second cone by means of a small chain, thus... and thus. As the spring unwinds, the chain acts on a larger and larger diameter of this second cone—so—and thus its reduced force is compensated by the longer leverage it exerts on the mechanism. I have not built it yet. I will confess that my eyes and mind are better tools than my hands. But once I have made the computations, it will work. Do you agree?'

Ibn Hasim glanced casually at the drawing he had made.

'Yes,' he said. 'It is well conceived. If I were a younger man, I would build it myself.' He gazed at Leonardo for what seemed like a time without end. 'Will you build it, do you think?' he asked.

Leonardo smiled in his turn. 'Those who visit you,' he said, 'whom I would not recognise . . . can they not tell you whether I will, or will not, do so? For myself, I cannot tell. A man must learn to understand himself, and I am a better thinker than a maker of things. Well?'

'You do not scoff at my . . . visitors?'

'My lord,' said Leonardo, 'we come from different worlds, you and I. If I do not mistake your words, you claim a familiarity with time as a whole as it runs past us, and not with that portion of it which eddies about us now, or an hour ago. Science, whom I serve, tells me that this is impossible; but you have been studying time longer than I have. Moreover, I do not reject out of hand what I do not at once comprehend.'

'Yes,' said Zeser Ibn Hasim, as though communing with himself. 'Yes. Do you know, I have waited a long time to meet you? How old are you?'

'Twenty-six.'

'So young? Well, it is no great matter. You will not build your clock, but that is no great matter either. You will build little, save what you need for your immediate purposes—as with your cannon, and the clock with which you have deceived Venice, and . . . things of that nature. In this much you are right. It is for you to think, to imagine, and to reach out; but when it comes to more than this, you will always find yourself distracted by further reaching, further thought, and further imagination. You already know this. Are you reconciled to it?'

'No,' said Leonardo. 'Are you reconciled to your life, my lord?'

'I was not,' said Ibn Hasim, 'but I believe I am now.' He pushed the clock towards Leonardo. 'Take it,' he said. 'As a gift from an old man to a young one.'

'Thank you.'

'It is nothing.'

164

'And the calculations that go with it?' Leonardo said gently.
'The system of navigation?'

'Why,' said the astronomer, 'do you wish to sail around the world?'

'No. But others may.'

Ibn Hasim rose, in his customary gesture of polite dismissal.
'The calculations will be here when you need them,' he said. 'I
would discuss them with you now, but you have other things to
do; more things than you realise. Come back in a year, or two, or
ten. They will be here. I bid you farewell, Leonardo da Vinci,
since we shall not meet again—except, *Insh'Allah*, it be in a
world which is neither yours nor mine.'

'I am going to Florence,' said Leonardo.

'When, my heart?'

'Next week. Will it make you unhappy?'

'A little. Can I not come with you? No, you do not need to
answer. You'll be back soon?'

'Before spring. You will be safe here.' Beyond the wall of their
room, someone was strumming inexpertly on a lute. Laughter
sounded in the courtyard. Love in a whorehouse, Bianca thought;
a strange place to find it, but then all places are alike to lovers. 'If
I had wings . . .' Leonardo said beside her.

'Why are you going?'

'To ask Lorenzo de' Medici if I may marry you.'

Thirteen

LEONARDO ARRIVED IN Rome in late February, under a lowering sky that threatened snow. He made his way directly to the Lateran Palace, where the Apostolic Chancellor, Cardinal Domenico della Palla, was far from welcoming.

'Rome is still dangerous,' he said, 'and you are not automatically protected from harm within these walls, my son, as you seem to imagine.'

'The outward severity of your Eminence,' said Leonardo innocently, 'fills me with both shame and disquiet. Underneath it, however . . .'

'Leonardo.'

'Yes, your Eminence?'

'Oh, nothing. Nothing. You have come here, I assume, to return the book you stole from me last June?'

'It is here, and unharmed.'

Cardinal della Palla rang a handbell. 'You have ridden far, from your appearance,' he said. 'I can offer you a little cake, and some Bergamese wine provided by our Captain-General, Count Girolamo Riario. He is in Venice, by the by—or perhaps you knew that?'

'I have been in the south, your Eminence. But I thank you for the intelligence.'

When they had eaten and drunk together, the Apostolic Chancellor brushed crumbs from his robe and relaxed his countenance somewhat. 'And the lady Bianca Visconti?' he inquired.

'She is well. I am on my way to Florence to ask for her hand in marriage.'

'You will not get it,' said della Palla, promptly and with certainty. 'But I can only approve of your intentions. Now, as to Venice . . .'

'My Lord,' said Leonardo 'why this pressing concern with the affairs of Venice? I am a poor scholar and an artist, and although it is true that Venice has recently offered me patronage——'

'Do you know what you are?' said the Cardinal suddenly. 'A gadfly. Sometimes, in the long watches of the night, I believe that God Almighty in His wisdom has visited you upon me as a trial of my patience. You are impudent beyond measure. You are an unrepentant sinner. You are a free thinker and a rebel who teeters on the edge of heresy. You are irritatingly flippant. Authority is a laughing stock to you. You are clever, outrageous; you have a certain charm which I am at a loss to understand, and at least in a strictly military sense you are Rome's enemy.'

'But not yours,' said Leonardo.

'That may be,' replied the Chancellor, a little too hastily. 'It does not answer the question of why I am prepared to put up with you.'

'I had always supposed, my Lord, that it was from natural affection.'

For some reason Cardinal della Palla appeared to find difficulty in speaking. Finally: 'Is that what you feel towards me?' he asked. 'Affection?'

'My Lord,' Leonardo said simply, 'though we have known each other for barely a year, yet I think of you as a father.'

The Cardinal made a show of brushing his robe again. 'And your part in this life of sorrow, I take it, is that of the Prodigal Son,' he said. 'Be that as it may . . . I was speaking of Venice. You have come from the South, you said. You must, then, have seen the armies of King Ferrante of Naples?'

'I passed through their lines, my Lord.'

'Rome is allied with Naples,' said the Chancellor, 'and Girolamo Riario is seeking further alliance with Venice. If he succeeds it will go hard with Florence, don't you think?'

Leonardo considered for a while. 'Florence is a nettle,' he said.

'It matters not how many hands reach out to grasp her; all will be stung in doing so.'

Della Palla rose and crossed to the window. 'I do not approve of war,' he said.

'I know that, my Lord.'

'It can be prevented.'

'How?'

'By Lorenzo de' Medici. Leonardo, if opportunity presents itself, I would like you to do something for me. Advise Lorenzo to come in person to Rome, and make formal obeisance to our Holy Father, begging forgiveness both for himself and for Florence. If he will do this, I believe that all may yet be saved.'

In a dark and sour smelling room in Venice, Girolamo Riario looked down at the figure that lay on a bed, swathed in bandages from crown to waist.

'Fortunately, Uberto,' he said, 'we may yet have him. Does that gratify you?'

Blindly, the man on the bed turned his head. His voice was cracked and barely audible.

'How?' he asked.

'Rome has fingers everywhere,' Riario said. 'Even in Malta. Fingers, perhaps, more subtle than those of Venice. But Venice has bungled, and paid for it. My informants tell me that the contents of your warehouse in Birgu were valued at something over seven hundred thousand florins. You bungled too, Master Uberto; and you, too, have paid a heavy price. Never the less, take heart. You shall have your revenge—here in Venice.'

The burned man on the bed made no reply to this.

'Therefore have patience,' said Girolamo Riario, 'the more so since I hear your surgeons arriving. No doubt their attentions will be painful, but I am sure you will survive. I bid you good day.'

'Out of the question,' said Lorenzo de' Medici. 'The lady Bianca is barely sixteen years of age. And in any case ... well, let us leave your situation aside. The answer is no.'

'Sir,' said Leonardo, 'when would she have married the Prince of Savoy? This year, or next? She was betrothed to him, whatever her age may be.'

Lorenzo de' Medici pricked the surface of his library table idly with the point of a fine stiletto. 'Since you killed the Prince of Savoy,' he said, '*that* question does not arise—fortunately for all of us, I dare say, since he was a most unpleasant man. But there is not the smallest chance of my giving you the consent you ask for. I am quite sure that you know this already, and you are not one to waste time in fruitless argument. If I did not know you better, I would even suspect you of trying to make a gallant gesture in order to prevent my having you thrown into a dungeon, where you belong, as surely as the lady Bianca belongs in a convent. However that may be, the matter is closed. Do you understand?'

'For always?'

'I did not say that. Continue to serve Florence, and who knows what rewards the future may bring you? I would not forbid you to speak to me again a year or two from now—that is, assuming for the moment that this is not merely a passing and deplorable liaison between a man of persuasion and a beautiful child.'

'It is not,' said Leonardo, 'and, as to that, she is less of a child than you think.'

'Do not anger me,' said the ruler of Florence. He drove the stiletto more deeply into the table, and left it standing upright. From outside the window of the great library in the Palazzo Medici the street sounds of Florence reached their ears faintly in the silence that followed. Eventually, Lorenzo pushed his chair back and motioned with his hand. 'Sit down,' he said. 'You have spoken your piece, and there are other things I wish to discuss with you. My Captain-Gunner, for one. He lost his hand?'

'He is well,' Leonardo said, taking a seat, 'and his spirits are as good as his health. Yes, Venice removed his right hand, and I have replaced it with another. He will serve you as he has always done.'

'Venice,' said Lorenzo, as though to himself. 'Venice, Naples, Rome.'

'True,' said Leonardo. 'Ferrante of Naples is assembling an

169

army thirty thousand strong in the Volturno valley, near Capua. And Girolamo Riario is in Venice.'

'I know. Do you think I have neither ears nor eyes? There is a Medici Bank in Venice too. What you have not explained to me is why Venice and yourselves came to be at odds in Malta.'

'That is a long story,' Leonardo said, 'and perhaps a difficult one to understand.'

'Tell it,' commanded Lorenzo de' Medici.

The afternoon had passed, and a cold dusk was beginning to thicken over the palazzo gardens. Florence lay between winter and spring, and the paths and flower beds were as yet bare, though the walls about them held out the wind.

'A clock, then,' Lorenzo said. 'Very well. And Venice is prepared to kill you for it?'

'Just so,' answered the artist. 'You must not think of it as merely a clock, sire. The handiwork of Zeser Ibn Hasim you may hold, and see, it is true; but the work of his mind is another matter.'

'A better way to navigate a ship, then? Would that be fair?'

'I think I have failed to impress you,' said Leonardo. He paused in their walk, and sat on a bench. After a moment's hesitation, Lorenzo joined him. 'Magnifico,' Leonardo went on, 'will you allow me to paint a picture for you? A picture of the imagination. In this picture, all men are born without sight. They come into the world blind, they live blind and die blind. They learn to travel from room to room by touch; they avoid by practice the awkwardly placed chair; in an unfamiliar hall they feel about them with slender staves. They have known nothing else. Can you understand this picture, Magnifico?'

'Go on.'

'Into this world, then, there comes a man—a very wise man— who has invented *eyes*. He offers sight to the men of our imaginary world, though they can comprehend the gift of sight only when they have accepted it from him. What would you then say? That they had been given a better way to move from room to room, and nothing more? Would you not rather say that their lives had been utterly changed, from that day forward, in a manner far beyond understanding . . . *their* understanding? And if he were to ask them a price for the boon of sight, what should that price be? Could any man pay it? No. So it is with what I obtained from Zeser Ibn Hasim, no more and no less.'

Lorenzo de' Medici set his chin against his fist. 'Thank you,' he said. 'And now, let me think awhile.'

They sat in silence while the night gathered about them, until a servant came to the arcade at the far side of the garden and began to light the torches there.

'Malta is dangerous,' said Lorenzo. 'But so is Italy, to the south of us. Is that why you have not brought this clock with you, Leonardo?'

'It is, sir.'

'And the lady Bianca? I presume that my Captain-Gunner and his lieutenant are her security?'

'I believe so. Venice has retired to lick her wounds for the present,' Leonardo said, 'though the Turk of whom I spoke is still in Rabat.'

'And where is she?'

'The lady Bianca?' Lorenzo looked at him in exasperation, and Leonardo summoned as much nonchalance as he could find. 'Sir,' he said, 'she is in hiding. In a brothel, as a matter of fact.'

'I ask your pardon,' said Lorenzo ominously, 'but I am not sure that I heard you. *Where* is she?'

'At a whorehouse in Rabat. It is really quite comfortable,' Leonardo went on, 'and a first-class centre for intelligence, which thus ensures her safety there. She——'

He stopped. In the dim light of the torches it seemed to him that Lorenzo de' Medici might be having an apoplectic seizure, until he eventually perceived that the ruler of Florence was laughing.

'Well,' said the latter, 'whorehouse or nunnery, it is all one, I suppose. Who in Florence knows of this?'

'Nobody except the two of us,' said Leonardo.

'Then take care that none hears of it,' Lorenzo said, 'or I give you my word that I shall hang you by the heels until the brains burst from your head. Tomorrow you will return to Malta. You will take with you a company of infantry, and bring both the lady Bianca and this clock of yours back here forthwith. Those are my instructions.'

'Not infantry,' said Leonardo.

'What, then?'

'Give me twelve gunners and two of the cannon I built for you last year.'

'For escort duty? I think not.'

'Sir,' said Leonardo, 'if we do not return in safety, whom will you hold responsible?'

'You.'

'That is what I thought. Therefore give me the escort of my choice. What do I need with a company of pikemen? I am a gunner—of sorts.'

'Are you, by God?' Lorenzo exclaimed. 'Yes, now that I come to think of it, I dare say you are. Very well. Pick your own men, and do as you see fit.'

In the city of Rabat, Lent marched its solemn road towards Easter, and a certain friar came to the House of Ten Pearls— though not, it is at once necessary to add, in search of its pleasures.

Madame Olympia, as devout as might be expected when actually faced with a servant of Mother Church, agreed readily that if any of her sinful charges were numbered among the faithful they should surely be allowed to accept his advice and ministrations.

Cipriano di Lucca, ever a man with a tender conscience, parted with five florins in exchange for an indulgence. Rigo called him a fool, and worse.

Bianca Visconti, under the friar's soft persuasion, went with him to confess her sins at the Church of Santa Caterina, disguised in a borrowed cloak and wearing a mantilla to conceal her face.

Her penance was severe, and one which she might have had the wit to foresee, but did not. Achmet the Turk and three men took her from a side chapel while she was at prayer, and by nightfall she was lying in the hold of a chartered Genoese trading schooner, sailing northwards for the toe of Italy.

Fourteen

THE MEDICI GUNNERS, under the command of Leonardo da Vinci, arrived at Marsasirocco on the Thursday after Easter.

It had been twelve days by ship from Piombino, their port of embarkation in Tuscany, as they had been forced to heave to and ride out a storm between the fire-capped island of Stromboli and the Calabrian coast. Ercole Molfetta, the captain of their vessel, had worried endlessly about the two guns they carried. Each of these—barrel and carriage together—was but the weight of two men; but during the tempest they had broken free of their lashings and slammed to and fro in the hold. All twelve gunners, toiling like demons in the rolling darkness, had finally wrestled them into immobility and secured them once more.

Now, as they manhandled the cannon from ship to quay, Leonardo plied obsessively between one and the other. He had to be sure that the ranging mechanism of each, the precision-cut screws and seating blocks, the quadrants that marked the elevation of the barrels, had not been damaged by the hazards of their journey. They had dropped anchor in the bay by mid-afternoon, but the sun was sinking before he had convinced himself that all was well with his brain-children—those deadly, precise and manoeuvrable little artillery pieces; six alone had been needed to take the fortress of Castelmonte last year.

Leonardo had chosen Marsasirocco as their port of entry not out of any desire for secrecy—twelve gunners and two cannon, he knew, could have faced down any Venetian force that remained in Malta—but because the overland march to the villa would be shorter from Marsasirocco than from Birgu. But it was at Birgu that Rigo had spent day after day awaiting Leonardo's return with heavy and anxious heart, and so the gunners had almost reached Zejtun itself by the time they saw his approaching figure in the dusk, dishevelled and out of breath.

Shouldering aside the clamorous greetings of his men, Rigo made his way at once to Leonardo's side.

'Bad news,' he said without preamble. 'The worst possible. The lady Bianca has been taken.'

It was as though some invisible titan had seized Leonardo's heart and body in a careless grip. About them, the gunners fell silent.

'How?' he asked, bitterly.

The gunner told him. Together they walked away from the rest, and Leonardo sat down on a sloping boulder to hear the end of Rigo's brief tale. 'A friar?' he cried. 'By Almighty God, I am the greatest fool that ever lived! Rome and Venice. Cardinal della Palla told me that Riario was in Venice—and I, blinded by my own cleverness, thought only of Florence and political strategy. Why? Why did I not turn about at once and come back here? And you have no word of what they have done with her?'

'None,' Rigo said. 'But we have the Turk, and our little weasel friend Lemmo. We took them on the road between Rabat and Birgu on the very night she disappeared. It was a chance meeting, and even now I am not sure we were right to waste time in capturing them. Had we pressed on instead to Birgu, as we intended, we might have saved the lady Bianca; but they seemed to be fleeing, and we thought . . .'

'You did well,' said Leonardo. 'In your place, I would have done the same. Where are they?'

'In the cellar above.' Rigo pointed towards the distant villa. 'They have said nothing . . . yet. Lemmo is afraid of Achmet, and perhaps I do not have about me enough of the look of a man who would cut them to pieces, as Achmet did to me; I do not know. I would kill him with pleasure, but I dared not. I have been waiting for you.'

'Yes,' said Leonardo. 'So you have. As always, my friend, I

thank you. And now bring your men, and see that they are made comfortable. They have come a long way, and hard.' He stood up, feeling rage wash over him in a sudden spasm, and ran uphill towards the villa.

Ten minutes later he flung wide the cellar door and set the point of his sword against Achmet's throat.

'Where is she?' he demanded.

The Turk's eyes flickered sideways for an instant towards Lemmo, who was cowering in a corner. 'Put your sword up, Florentine,' he said with contempt. 'We are your only hope.'

Leonardo made no movement. 'Achmet,' he said softly and terribly, 'hear me well. I will take Venice apart with my bare hands, brick by brick, if it brings me one step closer to her. Where is she?'

'Safe,' the Turk said. 'Which is all you need to know. For the rest, you need only listen to my orders, and obey. We have her, and you must know our price: yourself. Think of Captain Leone—and then consider whether, despite your sword and your empty threats, I do not have you in the hollow of my hand.'

'Leonardo,' said a deep voice behind him.

He turned. In the wide arched doorway which he almost filled—stood Scudo, the largest, strongest, and most good-natured of the Medici Gunners. He came forward and laid a hairy paw on Leonardo's arm. 'Come,' he said. 'We must talk with you. All this,' he gazed around, taking in the still crouching Lemmo and the Turk, 'can wait a little. Eh? If you please.' He added no explanation to this, but tightened his grasp meaningfully. His fingers were like the jaws of an enormous vice. 'Come,' he said, again.

Leonardo lowered his sword. There was little else he could do. Scudo urged him out of the cellar, closed the door, and barred it. At the end of the passageway, Rigo was sitting on a stair.

'You see,' Scudo went on, 'me and the Captain, we have been talking. Fellows like this Turk, I have seen many of them. Wrestlers. You cannot hurt them, so he will never tell you what you want to know.'

175

'And you cannot kill him either,' put in Rigo. 'For excellent reasons.'

'No,' agreed Leonardo. Now that he was out of the cellar, he found he was shaking. He had allowed anger and despair to overwhelm his judgment, and he knew it.

'So we thought,' Scudo said genially, 'that I should reason with him. It is up to you, of course.' He leaned against the wall of the passage and scratched his belly. He was two hundred and fifty pounds of muscle, bone and sinew, and he smiled gently and with the happiness of anticipation. 'What do you say?' he asked.

For the first time since hearing Rigo's news, Leonardo felt himself relax. He even managed an answering smile, and rubbed his upper arm where the giant had gripped it. 'Well,' he said, 'it is some time since I last straightened a horseshoe for sport, and I may be somewhat out of condition; yet your reasoning might convince me, Scudo. On the other hand. I would guess that Achmet outweighs even you by some fifty pounds.'

Scudo spat on the floor, and widened his grin. 'Fifty pounds of Turkish fat,' he said. 'Wait here.'

He levered himself off the wall, and walked down the passage.

At the sound of the drawn bolt, Achmet rose from his seat. Scudo entered the cellar, stopped and beckoned.

'Come here, mannikin,' he invited. 'Come, eater of filth.'

The Turk's eyes narrowed. There was no mistaking the big gunner's intentions. Achmet did not exactly consider him foolish, but his mind began to fill with glee. He had faced many men of like size—even bigger—across wrestling mats laid out on the tiles of courts and palaces here and there in the world. All had looked at him with the same confidence. All had been defeated. Some had never wrestled again; and a few had died. Here was one more in a long line of victims, that was all. Nor did Achmet foresee any need for subtlety. He kicked off his shoes, the better to gain a purchase on the earthen floor and advanced to meet Scudo.

The gunner stood still, rubbing his palms against the front of his thighs as a man will do before lifting a weight or taking in hand an axe.

He had watched Turkish wrestlers perform, had himself stood against one or two for a purse of a few florins. He knew quite well what a man of Achmet's enormous size and weight would do sooner or later: he would simply wrap his arms around the chest of his opponent, and start to squeeze the life out of him. Scudo sighed, and raised his arms shoulder high.

'Well, scum,' he said. 'Let us try you.'

This deliberate invitation—apparently virtual suicide—might have given the Turk pause, but did not. A small fire of blood lust had kindled itself in the back of his mind, as it always did at times such as this, and it drove him, machine-like, to accept what was offered him. He shuffled forward slowly, reached out, and drew the gunner to his breast. He clasped his intertwined fingers behind Scudo's back, and began inexorably to tighten his hold.

He did not, at first, exert all his strength. That is not the way of the bear hug, whose user waits until his victim is forced to exhale before applying the full force of the grip, thus preventing him from drawing in his breath again. After that the sequence is inevitable. There is a struggle—rib cage against constricting arms—which is at first strong, then desperate, and finally weak and futile. The victim's lungs scream for air, and find none. He becomes feeble. The vessels in his neck and face stand out. His eyes close. His spine breaks. Finish.

After a minute, Scudo spoke.

'Are you done, wind-bag?' he asked with apparent curiosity. 'Is that the sum of it? Why, there are girls in my village who would laugh at so puny an embrace, if they could stand the smell of you, which they could not.'

That his opponent could speak at all was an offence against nature, and Achmet became enraged. He shifted his forearms, and strained, but to no avail; he might as well have been wrapped around one of Scudo's siege guns for all the effect he was having. His eyes bulged, and his tendons cracked; his whole frame shook with effort. Sweat began to pour down his forehead.

Scudo smiled. He drew his raised hands apart, held them

poised, and then clapped them against the sides of Achmet's head, breaking one of his eardrums. At the same time and with the practice of timing learned over years of back alley brawling, he lifted his left foot and scraped the instep of his leather boot down the front of the Turk's shin from knee to ankle. As though for good measure, he broke his nose with a head butt. Achmet's arms flew open, and he reeled back in agony.

'And *now*,' said Scudo.

He went to work upon the task of destroying his foe with an awful and seemingly careless deliberation, showing neither malice nor spleen as he did so. His approach was like that of an expert logger felling a very large tree, and reducing it to useful lumber. Neither the pace nor the depth of his breathing altered by so much as a fraction as he chopped, kicked and shouldered his way into the Turk's very vitals. Once, in squealing animal fury, Achmet seized the gunner's forearm and sank his teeth deeply into the muscles. Scudo paid no great attention to this, only taking the opportunity it presented of holding his opponent by the scruff of the neck and running his head into the stone wall of the cellar four or five times. When Achmet let go, Scudo continued his work with the same clinical precision as before.

In ten minutes Achmet had been reduced to a pitiful, blubbering ruin. He knelt in a corner opposite Lemmo—who had remained silent and wide-eyed throughout the Turk's terrible beating—and hunched his arms protectively over his face. Scudo stood over him, reached down, and patted his cheek as though he were a fractious child.

'Now—talk,' said the gunner.

A few minutes later, he went out of the cellar, leaving the door ajar, and rejoined Rigo and Leonardo at the foot of the stairs.

'The lady Bianca is in Venice,' Scudo announced. 'But he does not know where.'

'That is not much,' said Rigo, disappointed.

'Well,' Scudo said, 'I can go back and reason with him further, I suppose, but I doubt that he has anything more to tell me.'

'It is something. Even though we already suspected it, it is something,' Leonardo said. 'They might, after all, have taken her to Rome instead.'

'What of Lemmo?' said Rigo. 'Perhaps——'

'Nay,' Scudo interjected hastily, 'I do not reason with field mice.'

'I was not thinking of that. I was thinking that he might be frightened enough . . .'

He was interrupted by a single, terrible, bubbling scream from the cellar. All three men turned as one and started down the passage, but they had taken only a few steps when Lemmo staggered out in front of them, clutched at the door frame, and then collapsed. As they reached him Leonardo saw that a thin pink foam was dripping from the corner of his open mouth. Lemmo hugged his body, panting, and seemed to choke.

Scudo stepped over him and strode into the cellar. In the middle of the room Achmet now stood upright, his lips drawn back from his teeth like a mad dog, with a ferocious, lunatic glare in his eyes. He clenched and unclenched his hands, threw back his head, and howled in what was either a foreign tongue or no tongue at all. Scudo reached him in three paces, and drove the hard edge of his hand against the Turk's exposed throat. The wild ululation was cut off instantly; Achmet clutched at his gullet, toppled, and lay still. His breath rasped twice, and stopped.

In the passage outside, Leonardo knelt by Lemmo and felt for his ribs. His entire chest seemed to have been mangled like the flimsy wires of a birdcage beneath the wheels of a cart.

'I . . . tried to help him,' the boy whispered. His entire frame was racked with a fit of coughing, and a trickle of bright red blood mingled with the pink froth at his cheek. 'Crushed me,' he said, with a forlorn surprise in his voice. 'I was only . . .'

'Rest,' Leonardo told him.

'Shall I die?'

To this Leonardo made no reply. Lemmo struggled to sit up, and failed. His eyes were already glazing over. Leonardo wiped the corner of his mouth, and waited. When he spoke again, it was almost as though—for the first time in his life—he did so as one man speaks to another, clearly and without pretence. 'You were kind to me,' he said, and then: 'She is in the Casa Albano. I do not know where that is,' and his eyes closed.

By midnight, two more graves had been dug in the shallow soil beyond the garden wall. Leonardo da Vinci was sitting at the focus of a semicircle of gunners on the terrace. Lanterns burned smokily here and there, picking out the flash of teeth and illuminating a face or two in the surrounding darkness. Leonardo looked at these faces, recognising each in turn with a sense of comradeship, and more.

For the most part, they were harsh faces, etched with powder, coarse-skinned, reflecting highlights that seemed to shine with the glare of fire on bronze. They were from the gutters of Florence, from those sour alleyways and poverty-stricken retreats that had given them birth. By the wall, Tomasello Cennini reamed at a nostril with his forefinger. Next to him stood Agnolo Fulvio, a seasoned gunner and Rigo's second-in-command, with his hand on the shoulder of Piccio Berignalli. In the middle of the semicircle were Marco di Carona and Giunta di Lenzo, the first light artillerymen in the world's history to have laid their guns in the dead of night by means of ballistics rather than by trial and error. Beyond them was Balestraccio, who had broken a toe before the taking of Castelmonte last year and so (after months of preparing for it, and to the laughter of his friends) had never joined the assault. At his elbow sat Guccio Berotti and the baby-faced Tesoro di Veluti, whose brother had died a prisoner on Castelmonte's wall.

All these Leonardo knew well. He had achieved with them that familiarity which is found only by those who have fought alongside one another. They had met him as an artist, cheerfully derided him for trying to teach them their own craft, and had finally accepted him as one of themselves, as a gunner and thus as something more and better than a friend. Whatever he demanded of them, with Rigo's consent, they would do.

'So we'll take Venice,' he told them. 'There are fifteen of us, and two guns. Why not?'

Tomasello Cennini removed his forefinger from inside his nose. 'Of course,' he said. 'When, and how?'

'That, I will tell you tomorrow,' said Leonardo. 'There is certain information I need first, and I can get it only from their headquarters in Rabat.'

'They may object, of course,' said Cipriano thoughtfully.

'So they may,' Leonardo said. 'God grant that they do.'

In this pious hope he was to be disappointed. Together with Cipriano, Agnolo Fulvio and five others, he marched to Rabat on the following morning. On the outskirts of the town he found the gateway to the Venetian villa swinging ajar. There was no sign of any guard beyond it. Villa and grounds gave the immediate impression of being abandoned, and so it proved. They broke open a side door with ease, and entered the house. Their footfalls rang on the marble floors, but no answering challenge met them as they went from room to room.

'They must have caught wind of our arrival,' said Tesoro di Veluti, 'and they have discovered pressing business elsewhere.'

In this judgment he was quite correct. Their leaders had left for Venice after the sack of the warehouse in Birgu. Those Venetians and local mercenaries who remained in Malta formed a token force at best, and upon receiving the news that two Florentine cannon had arrived on the island they had promptly disbanded.

It took Leonardo only a short while to uncover the entrance to the chartroom behind the master suite. In it he found exactly what he was looking for—a map of the city of Venice itself, drawn to handsome scale and complete with the names of its streets, canals, and principal buildings. Imprudently, the last person to have studied it had underlined the name of Casa Albano, thus proving the truth of Lemmo's last words on earth. The building was apparently situated on a backwater near the Rio San Polo, Leonardo noted. He rolled the chart and such other documents as he thought useful into a bundle, and returned with his comrades to their own headquarters.

There, he disappeared into his room for the space of an hour or so, and then called a brief tactical conference.

'We shall take Venice on Ascension day,' he announced to the assembled gunners. 'And now, who is the prettiest among you, do you suppose?'

'Tesoro,' said a dozen voices, almost in unison.

'I agree. Tesoro, have you any great objection to playing the part of a girl?' asked Leonardo.

'Amongst this lot?' said Tesoro. 'Every possible objection.' He added an explanation remarkable for its crudity, especially from one so young. 'However,' he said, 'I take it you have some important reason for suggesting it?'

'I have,' said Leonardo. 'You are going to be a Muse.'

Fifteen

CAPTAIN ERCOLE MOLFETTA of the Florentine caravel *Juno* spent the next few days puzzled and uneasy. He had been engaged by Lorenzo de' Medici in person and placed by the latter under Leonardo's command, but he had bargained only for a sea journey from Tuscany to Malta and back. Nothing had been said about Venice, nor—as was beginning to become clear to him—about risking the loss of his ship. Nor did he understand the purpose of the small fishing boat which Leonardo had purchased in Marsasirocco and hauled overland to Birgu, where the *Juno* now lay at anchor. Day and night the gunners, under Cipriano di Lucca had worked on this sailing craft, repainting her in brilliant reds and yellows and decorating her gunwales and transom with gold leaf. Her short mast had been cut through at the step by Leonardo, who then proceeded to remount it in swivelling tabernacles, so that it could be raised or lowered rapidly and at will.

Leonardo had told him that the boat was to be shipped as deck cargo on the *Juno*, but had not explained why. Nor had he explained the bolts of muslin and silk in scarlet, turquoise, and blue, the rolls of ribbon and lace, all of which had been stowed in the forward hold. Captain Molfetta held his tongue, however, until the day when Leonardo informed him that their course to Venice must be the shortest one possible, and by open sea all the way.

'That cannot be done, unfortunately,' said Captain Molfetta. He then gave a brief explanation, in landlubbers' terms, of why this was so. 'To Cape Passero in Sicily, and then Syracuse,' he said. 'Then the eastern coast of Calabria, the Golfo di Taranto, Cape

Santa Maria, and so to the Strait of Otranto. That is our course. After that I shall coast up the Italian peninsula and, God willing, bring you all safe to Venice.'

'No,' said Leonardo. 'That would be far too slow. From here we'll sail north east directly to the Strait of Otranto, and then change our heading ninety degrees to the north west. We'll take the centre of the Adriatic Sea all the way, and be out of sight of shore for practically the whole journey.'

'And who will navigate?' asked the captain with an edge of sarcasm.

'I shall,' replied Leonardo. 'Tell me, does Venice patrol the Strait?'

'She does, and thoroughly,' said Molfetta. 'From Otranto to the opposite coast of Dalmatia is about twenty leagues. Venice keeps four galleys stationed there, crossing and recrossing the Strait continually.' He laughed. 'Venice believes the Adriatic to be her sole property by right, though she disputes its entrance with the Turks at times.'

'Thank you,' said Leonardo. 'In that case, we must time our arrival off Otranto so that we can slip through by night.' He then went on to question Molfetta closely as to the speed of the *Juno*, her ability to sail on the wind, and sundry other matters. Molfetta's opinion of his passenger's ability in seafaring skills rose more than a little. 'You have an octant?' Leonardo asked him.

'Of course,' replied Molfetta. 'But it is of little use unless I can find my daily meridian, which is impossible.'

'I will find your meridian every noon,' said Leonardo, and left him.

On a spring evening some days later the gunners were ready to sail. Decima came down from Rabat with a gorgeous escort of her companions from the House of Ten Pearls, and kissed Rigo goodbye.

'I'll be here when you return,' she told him. 'And therefore look after yourself, and Leonardo. Have a care with the girls in Venice. They are sluts, one and all.' With this she wept a little, and then went with her friends to exclaim over the newly decorated fishing boat which now rested in blocks on the deck of the *Juno*.

'We'll weigh anchor at dawn, then,' announced Captain Molfetta to Leonardo a little later, 'and I hope you know what you are doing.'

Leonardo took his shoulder and turned him about, so that he faced the open sea.

'Be prepared to sail sooner,' he said. 'Look.'

A mile or so offshore was a carrack in full sail, making good speed towards Birgu. An hour later, it dropped anchor at the side of the inlet, opposite the *Juno*, and a dinghy was lowered over its seaward rail.

Leonardo, Cipriano, and Rigo stood on the principal quay of Birgu harbour, and watched the bumboat approach them. In it was a handsome, pleasant-looking Venetian, resplendent in uniform and somewhat pompous of manner. He disembarked, and strode towards them in a businesslike fashion.

'Which of you is Leonardo da Vinci?' he inquired.

'I am,' said Leonardo.

The Venetian held out his hand. 'Your sword, then, if you please,' he said. 'We are ready for you aboard.'

'Your pardon?' said Leonardo, courteously.

'Forgive me,' the Venetian said. 'I should have introduced myself. I am Captain Francesco Moldano.'

'And I am happy to make your acquaintance,' said Leonardo. There followed a short silence, during which the Venetian's face set into a frown of slight annoyance. It appeared that he was awaiting some response. When he got none, he began afresh.

'You are the Florentine bandit, Leonardo da Vinci?' he said.

'I am certainly Leonardo da Vinci. I am not sure about the rest.'

'Then I am here to accept your surrender, and to take you with me to Venice,' said Captain Moldano. 'My orders are from Signor Orso Contarini.' He looked from Leonardo to Rigo, and then at Cipriano. 'Your own instructions must have been clear concerning me,' he went on with a hint of desperation. 'Or else why are you here, awaiting me?'

'*My* instructions?' said Leonardo.

'They were given you by the equerry of Signor Uberto Neri, were they not? A Turk?'

Leonardo's face cleared. 'Achmet,' he said. 'Of course. I am afraid, sir, that he became indisposed before he was able to give me any instructions from Signor Contarini. It is no wonder we seem to be at cross purposes here.'

'Well, it makes little difference, I dare say,' replied the Venetian. 'Since you are here.' He seemed to think the matter was now cleared up perfectly satisfactorily. 'Sir, you are required—upon penalties which are known to you—to give yourself up to the mercy of Venice and of His Excellency Signor Orso Contarini, and to accompany me on my ship here and now, unarmed.' He held out his hand again. 'So, if you please . . .'

Leonardo smiled at him.

'Sir, I have no intention of doing anything of the kind,' he said. He pointed towards the *Juno*, which lay a little farther along the shore to his right. 'I have, as you see, business of my own with Venice.'

'In that case,' said Captain Moldano briskly, 'I must use force.' He gestured in the direction of his dinghy, where an arbalester could be seen fitting a bolt to his weapon. Cipriano at once drew his sword, and Rigo took a step towards the Venetian, who recoiled nervously.

'Little fellow,' said Rigo pleasantly, 'look closer at our ship. Fore and aft you will see two cannon. We will blow your damned carrack out of the water if we catch so much as a glimpse of your face, let alone any weapon, five minutes from now.'

Captain Moldano looked towards the *Juno* again and licked his lips.

'You would not dare,' he suggested.

'Dare?' said Cipriano. 'Look further along the shore. Those spikes of charred timber are all that remain of a warehouse that once belonged to Venice. But Venice annoyed us, and we burned it. A carrack more or less will add little to the score.'

They turned to leave, but the Venetian cried after them. His face was bewildered.

186

'Sirs!' he called. 'Did I hear you say your business was with Venice?'

Leonardo stopped. 'It is,' he said.

'You are sailing *under arms* to Venice? Why, in God's name? Your ship is tolerably fast, but I can outrun her; I can have ten ships, or twenty, and the shore batteries at the Lido, opposing you when you arrive there. Whatever you have in mind, it is pure madness, I assure you.'

Leonardo walked back to where he was standing, and patted him on the shoulder comfortingly. 'I wish you a safe and speedy voyage,' he said. 'Farewell.'

The *Juno* slipped out of Birgu shortly before midnight, broad reaching before a westerly breeze. The Venetian ship was still at anchor, showing a light or two, when they drifted past her. She showed no other sign of activity. The gunners sang several verses of an offensively dirty drinking ballard, and Scudo broke a window in her after cabin by tossing a four-pound cannonball through it from a distance of twenty-five paces. Giunta di Lenzo farted deafeningly. The *Juno* heeled as the offshore wind caught her sails, and vanished into the darkness of the Mediterranean.

In the master quarters below Leonardo was conferring with Rigo, Cipriano, and Agnolo Fulvio. The clock of Zeser Ibn Hasim stood on the cabin table before them.

'Just the same,' Leonardo said, 'we now have no time to waste. The race is on, my friends. For they have seen us and our guns. They are convinced they can outsail us to Venice. They would be right, but for the fact that they must sail coastwise, while we shall run a direct course of two straight legs. We have this,' and he touched the jewelled timepiece softly so as not to upset the delicate mechanism that purred within it, 'as did Felippo Mendoza just as he was, so shall we be first to port. I care not whether we reach Venice two days ahead of them or one, or twelve hours. It will be enough that we get there before they do. But we shall have to take our chances in the Strait of Otranto, daylight or dark; we cannot afford to lose half a day beating about and waiting for nightfall to slip through the Venetian galley patrols there.'

The *Juno* sailed north-east for four days and nights, under an almost cloudless sky. Leonardo pampered the clock, winding it at noon and at midnight with its ivory and emerald key, tabulating its accumulated error each time he did so. Each day Captain Molfetta took a sun sight, to obtain his latitude, and Leonardo worked out the longitude on a wax tablet. Molfetta accepted his daily figures with the scepticism of a man too old and well practised to change his ways, and offered private prayers to St. Paul.

On the afternoon of the fifth day land was sighted off the port bow by the look out at the masthead, who announced an hour later that it was undoubtedly Cape Santa Maria, the heel of the Italian mainland. They were twenty miles south of Otranto and about ten miles offshore. Captain Molfetta abandoned some of his scepticism, since his amateur navigator had put them within a dozen miles of their intended position.

They were also, it seemed, well placed to pass through the Strait of Otranto that night, though Leonardo himself would have been the first to admit that this was purely by good fortune.

But their fortune did not hold. An hour before sunset they saw, approaching from the east, the low shape of what was clearly one of the Venetian galleys they were seeking to avoid. It was farther south than Molfetta had expected, and appeared to be making a course from Kerkira to Otranto. It was heading directly into the wind, but since it was powered by the sweeps of sixty paid Genoese oarsmen, this made little difference to its rate of progress. It would intercept them before sundown. Examining the galley through his small pocket telescope, Leonardo saw that it was signalling, by means of sunlight reflected on a mirror, to some other vessel that lay ahead of them, probably just off the point of Otranto itself.

'Now what?' said Rigo.

'We do as we planned,' Leonardo replied. 'They have no right to stop us. Captain, will you alter course a few degrees to port?

We'll try to outrun them, if Providence wills it so. But if we cannot, then we must beach.'

Half an hour later the second galley emerged from behind the headland they were approaching, and the matter was settled. It bore down towards them rapidly. The second Venetian patrol craft was a bare mile away, astern of them and to starboard, so that they had no escape route.

'Beach,' said Leonardo. 'If they will not treat us as innocent voyagers, who are we to disappoint them?'

Captain Molfetta and his crew turned the prow of the *Juno* slowly into the wind and headed for the shore. They dropped anchor some twenty paces from a long and desolate beach that stretched north and south as far as the eye could see. Using a bow anchor and kedge, they manoeuvred the ship until it lay broadside-on to the shore, while the gunners disassembled their two cannon—a procedure which, after long practice in battle and out of it, took each gun crew some eight or ten seconds only—and lowered them into a pair of waiting boats. These they rowed to the beach, where the crews replaced the wheels on the gun carriages, spiked them to the axles, laid the barrel trunnions in the slots designed to receive them on top of the carriage wings, and loaded the reassembled weapons—all behind the cover afforded by the hull of the *Juno*.

Meanwhile the two Venetian galleys approached in stately fashion, backed their oars about three hundred paces offshore, and lowered their own anchors. Shouts echoed across the calm water. Captain Molfetta affected not to understand what these shouts might mean. Finally, three boats were lowered from each galley, and these began to fill with armed men.

Leonardo, from the waist of the *Juno*, watched these warlike preparations happily. He was not hoping for a massacre. The fact was, however, that the galleys of Venice, Genoa, and Turkey were known to be the fastest moving ships in the Mediterranean, mainly because they did not depend upon the vagaries of wind and weather. The carrack of Captain Moldano, which they had not seen since they left Birgu, did not worry him ;but the galleys did.

The *Juno* had only to lie becalmed for twenty-four hours, and all the navigational skill in the universe could not prevent these sleek greyhounds of the sea from beating him to Venice.

Therefore, it was the ships themselves which must not be allowed to escape the consequences of their own folly.

He walked across the deck of the *Juno* to its shoreward rail, and called to Rigo.

'Ready,' he said.

At once the Captain-Gunner shouted his swift orders. The two gun crews deployed to right and left under their respective commanders, Agnolo Fulvio and Cipriano.

Their targets were large and helpless. Cipriano sent his first shot home into the right of the two galleys just above the waterline. Agnolo (to the ribald jeers of Cipriano's crew) overestimated his range and succeeded only in clipping the gunwale of the other ship amidships. His second shot, fired fifty seconds later, splintered her keel.

After ten salvos, fired in as many minutes, both galleys were reduced to pitiful shattered hulks. Oars floated beside them, and among the wreckage could be seen the heads of swimmers.

'Load with grape,' said Rigo calmly.

The rowing boats full of soldiers, which had at the beginning of this barrage turned back towards their mother ships, were bobbing about between the flotsam and the beach. Eventually, it dawned upon their leaders that no other course was open to them save that of heading for shore, since at sea they had nothing left to return to. Meanwhile, cries of rage and confusion filled the air, and redoubled in volume when Agnolo Fulvio raked the surface of the water between two of the oncoming boats with a lethal torrent of grapeshot. At once all six boats stopped again, rising and falling with the gentle swell.

Awkwardly, a makeshift banner of truce was raised in the prow of one of them. To this Leonardo responded by raising his arms and signalling Rigo to cease fire. The boat which bore the truce flag floated into the lee of the *Juno*, and its officers spoke to Leonardo, who was leaning over the rail.

'Mother of God!' the Venetian said. 'What weapons are those?'

'Merely cannon,' replied Leonardo briskly. 'They are both loaded with grapeshot now. Would you care to attempt a landing against them?'

'No,' said the officer. 'We are not bent on suicide. But . . . Christ's blood, man, we meant only to board and search you!'

'A worthy aim, no doubt,' said Leonardo, 'but we are in a hurry and you have failed in your purpose. There is little more to be said, but we have no wish to kill you. We can do so, to the last man. I suggest that you beach about five hundred paces down yonder,' he waved towards the south, 'and disturb us no further, since we must be on our way.'

'But we shall be marooned,' objected the officer.

'Alas, that is true. Yet, I daresay your colleagues on patrol will find you tomorrow, or the next day,' Leonardo said. 'If they do not, there is a carrack of yours following us which must pass this spot within three days from now. Well?'

'Agreed,' said the Venetian, whose orders did not include fighting pitched battles against madmen armed with cannon of almost unbelievable power and accuracy. 'But you must realise that I shall be forced to report this . . . this . . .'

'Disaster? Outrage?' prompted Leonardo kindly.

'Whatever you choose to call it. I must report it to Venice as soon as we return there. It is an act of war.'

'Yes, I know,' said Leonardo. 'Good day to you.'

The *Juno* was under way again by nightfall.

The Casa Albano, which was now the prison of Bianca Visconti, was a decayed building whose back rose three stories above a small, shallow and muddy backwater not far from the Rio Marin. It lay at the heart of the Sestriere di San Polo, a region of Venice on the left bank of the Grand Canal which thrived in the main upon small trading and craftsmanship.

Its owner, Giancarlo Albano, was one of the city's most powerful—and most loyal—merchant princes. Perhaps it would be truer to say that he had been; for, ruthless when a young man, shrewd in middle age, he had now sunk into a rich and somewhat eccentric senility. He had never married, and he lived in seclusion, amid orchards and tinkling fountains, on the Isola Giudecca. The building that had once contained the heart of his commercial empire, the Casa Albano, was at present leased to none other than Orso Contarini, who found certain aspects of its construction ideal for his purposes.

Chief among these was the fact that Giancarlo Albano, in his sixties, had developed an unreasonable fear of robbery. He had therefore bricked up the windows of the lower floor of the building and set iron bars across those of the second and third floors. The only access to the courtyard around which the house was constructed was, therefore, a narrow gateway that gave onto a blind alley. The rooms surrounding the central court were disused, dusty, and filled with the useless remnants of half a century of trading. Orso Contarini had cleared these out, and installed in their place a platoon of his personal militia.

Bianca Visconti was confined in a suite on the uppermost floor at the back of the house. She had two windows which overlooked the noisome canal below, if she cared to survey it, together with a bed, a chair, a chamberpot and a Bible. Her water and her meals were brought to her by a crone who seemed to be a deaf-mute. For exercise, she could take twelve paces from one side of her sleeping quarters, through an open doorway, across the empty second room of the suite, and another twelve back again. During the month of her imprisonment she had become pale, a little thinner than formerly, and somewhat lethargic. She was not bored, recalling Leonardo's statement that those who cannot stand their own company are poor in spiritual resources.

She wished that Leonardo might come for her, and was afraid that he would do so. She knew why she was in Venice.

One morning in early summer, she received two visitors. The first was Girolamo Riario. He was accompanied by Uberto Neri, whom she had never seen and would not now have recognised in any case. His face was hidden behind a mask of brown velvet, and he walked with a slight limp.

'Good morrow, my lady,' said Riario. 'I trust we find you well?'

'Well enough, sir, I thank you.'

'Good. You have not been ill used?'

'Ill used?' said Bianca, coldly. 'I have been imprisoned, which is enough to bring the wrath of Florence upon you—and upon Venice, for the matter of that.'

'Perhaps,' replied Riario. 'Perhaps. And what of your lover's wrath? Is that not more terrible than the wrath of Florence?' He laughed bloodlessly. 'But no. He will be here soon, my lady, and I have the feeling that he will come among us like a lamb rather than a lion.'

'You have news of him, then?' asked Bianca, as calmly as she could.

'He is on his way here, by carrack. He has a small debt to repay. My friend and I—may I present Signo Uberto Neri, lately of Malta—thought you might be interested both in what he owes, and the manner of his payment. Uberto?'

'Yes,' said Neri; he raised his hand to the lower edge of the velvet mask that covered his face. Swiftly, he peeled it away. As he did so, Bianca turned white, despite herself.

His nose had been entirely burned off, leaving two dark holes in the centre of what had once been his face. Through these ghastly orifices his breath whistled laboriously. His left ear was also gone, as was the flesh of his cheek on that side. Red, smooth and angry, the tight scar tissue of his mouth and eye socket stretched tightly across the bones of his skull, and from it his single eye glared as though with a life of its own.

'Yes,' said Riario. 'The surgeons say it will improve, but not by much. You see before you the result of the last meeting between my friend Uberto and Leonardo da Vinci. What the outcome of their next meeting may be I leave to your imagination. Maria!'

As Bianca sank down on the bed, appalled, the aged attendant shuffled into the room.

'Fetch the lady Bianca a glass of wine,' said Girolamo Riario. 'She has been somewhat overcome by the heat. Good day, my lady.'

Sixteen

THE SUN ROSE over Venice on Ascension day, 1479, with the promise of a well-nigh perfect early summer morning. It burned the fugitive mists from the Lagoon, and gilded the towers of the Arsenal, the cupolas of the Basilica di San Marco, and the delicate Gothic pinnacles of the new Ducal Palace. It chased the shadows from streets and waterways already humming with joyful activity, and gladdened the hearts of those notables who were starting to assemble in the loggia of the Ca' d'Oro in order to watch the procession of boats along the Grand Canal that would occupy most of the hours before noon.

Chief among these dignitaries was the Doge of Venice himself, the illustrious Giovanni Mocenigo. Later in the day he would be transported to the Ducal Palace, there to board the *Bucintoro*, the State Galley of Venice, to be rowed in it towards the Lido. After the Patriarch had blessed the waves, Mocenigo would cast into them a golden ring, thereby proclaiming Venice's indissoluble marriage with the sea that supported, protected and enriched her.

By his side, now—at least for the few brief moments necessary to pay their respects to him—were both Girolamo Riario, Count of Imola (who was seeking alliance with the Republic of Venice) and Lorenzo de' Medici, *Il Magnifico*, Ruler of Florence (whose intention was to frustrate any such joining of purposes between his actual and possible enemies). Roman and Florentine bowed to each other upon relinquishing the Doge's hands. As they did so Riario looked with hatred at the man who had torn the stronghold of Castelmonte from him and made him a laughing stock,

194

while Lorenzo in his turn saw Rome's Captain-General for the violator and murderous carrion he undoubtedly was. If the Doge himself was amused by their coldly elaborate and insincere greetings, he gave no sign of it. They retired at once to opposite sides of the loggia, and gazed out over the broad waters below.

Mounting higher in the sky, the morning sun also shone down upon the throng of gaily decorated gondolas, barges, skiffs, punts and workboats which were thrusting about at the northern entrance to the Grand Canal, by the Campo Sant'Andrea. The opening procession of the *Festa della Sensa* would not begin for at least another four hours. But already this widest reach of the city's great central waterway seemed carpeted with craft of all sizes, as though a man could walk clear across it from one bank to the other and never get his feet wet; as, indeed, he well might.

Without reckoning the Steward's canopied vessel and those of the spectators, there should have been present three hundred and sixty-five boats of one kind and another, one for each day of the year, all of them gaily decked out. In fact there were three hundred and sixty-six, though the Steward, a nervous, overworked, and somewhat mannered individual—was unaware of this.

The Medici Gunners took care to keep well out of his way.

Their fishing boat, now unrecognisable as such, carried an allegorical tableau entitled (had anybody asked) 'A Pastoral Scene, With Muse'.

Its brilliance of design would surely have earned it a prize. Considering its designer and the talent at his disposal, this was no wonder. In the prow sat Tesoro di Veluti, the youngest of the gunners. He had been compelled to garb himself as Clio, the Muse of Heroic Deeds. In this role he was beyond question ravishing, as his friends repeatedly informed him—though, since he was holding aloft a polished cannon ball as a symbol of exploits great and small, they took care not to approach him too closely while they told him so. Those same friends were variously dressed as Bucolics, Satyrs, and Heroes, while Leonardo himself had chosen to represent the poet Homer.

He looked, and felt, sleepy, though this would pass. He had

spent the whole of the night in conversation with a glass blower on the island of Murano, which lay some half an hour distant from their present station. The *Juno* had docked there late on the previous afternoon. Leonardo's purpose in talking with the craftsman was to make certain that he would be familiar with every detail of the Festival proceedings, since his plan of action depended upon precise timing. Now he observed the passage of time carefully and a little anxiously, by means of the brightly jewelled clock that stood openly before him on a small table.

There was another such table on the short bow deck of the boat, immediately behind Tesoro di Veluti. Both tables were draped in crimson silk, and hidden beneath each of them was a cannon, though the sight of these warlike machines was not allowed to intrude upon the serenity of the rustic tableau above them.

The actual rescue of Bianca did not trouble Leonardo's mind unduly. His scheme for winning her freedom was bold, possibly even foolhardy. It relied in the main upon brute force, swiftness and surprise. God and Providence being with them, the venture would succeed; if God or Providence decided otherwise then there was in any case no hope for any of them.

His true difficulty lay in the fact that once they had freed her, they would find themselves in the middle of an alarmed and hostile city with every hand—and every eye—against them. As with so many surprise operations, the problems involved in reaching his target were outweighed a thousandfold by those of getting away from it afterwards. His stratagem for doing so involved a safety margin—if they were to escape alive—of not more than six minutes. It was with some care, therefore, that he studied the clock of Zeser Ibn Hasim. It had brought him to Venice from Malta ahead of his enemies; and now it had a further and still more vital part to play.

At a quarter to eleven, a bell tolled. The hubbub among the milling boats died down, and a fanfare of trumpets sounded from the Fondamente della Croce, a little way past the bend in the canal, ahead of the leading vessels. On hearing the first trumpet blast Tesoro di Veluti stood up, almost by reflex, but Leonardo waved him down again.

'We have an hour to wait,' he said. 'We do not want to be the first in this cavalcade, but rather the two hundred and fortieth. Had you forgotten? Occupy yourself by counting the boats as they enter the canal.'

'I am sorry,' Tesoro said, and took his seat again.

'It's hardly the lad's fault,' said Cipriano, who was standing beside Leonardo in the guise of a shepherd. 'Trumpets commonly call the start of battle, after all.'

'Not on this occasion,' said Leonardo. 'Patience.'

In the loggia of the Ca' d'Oro, the Steward was moving from among his guests, brimming with an enthusiasm which he strove, unsuccessfully on the whole to share with them.

'It will not be long now, my lords,' he announced. 'The first boat should pass us about five minutes from now.' He consulted a list, beautifully written on parchment. 'It will be the barge of the Goldsmith's Guild,' he added.

'Really?' said Girolamo Riario, who was the Steward's present victim. 'And how long will this procession take?'

The Steward looked at his scroll again, with reproach. 'It will be finished, my lord, at half an hour past noon,' he said.

'Good God,' said Riario impatiently.

At this moment he was approached by a page, and at once excused himself from those about him. In a side room he found one of his aides, who saluted him.

'My lord,' said the aide, 'I have to inform you that the carrack of Captain Moldano has been sighted five miles off Chioggia, and will anchor here by nightfall.'

'Good,' said Riario. 'Take a skiff at once, if you please, and cross the canal before this damned procession reaches us. Give your news to Signor Uberto Neri. He has little enough to amuse him, poor fellow, and the arrival of Master Leonardo da Vinci in chains will at least give him some cause for pleasant anticipation.'

At a quarter of an hour before noon, precisely, the Pastoral Scene With Muse jockeyed for position in order to take its place in the cavalcade down the Grand Canal. Since they had no right to be there at all, the Florentine gunners' neighbours fore and aft were inclined to dispute their intrusion, the more so since many of those present were now *in fragia*, a Venetian phrase for cheerful insobriety.

'Hey, beautiful,' said a leather worker. 'Pretty one! What do you think you're doing, eh?'

To this the Muse Clio, whom he was addressing, deigned no reply, raising instead the middle finger of her left hand in a time-honoured gesture. The leather worker laughed, and offered her a wineskin. Tesoro leaned over the prow but was prevented from accepting this offering by the sudden forward surge of the boat, which was impelled by the oars of Balestraccio and Giunta di Lenzo. The gunners were on their way.

Seven minutes later, they had rounded the first bend in the canal and were passing the Church of San Simeon Piccolo. Here they fell out of the procession and bore towards the canal bank that lay on their right. The mouth of the Rio Marin, which was their objective, was crowded with spectators in skiffs, who showed surprise at seeing one of the passing column of vessels swerving to leave the cavalcade. As their boat forced its way past, Leonardo courteously informed them that they had sprung a leak and must accordingly retire. This announcement was greeted with jeers from the men and commiseration from the women, but they were allowed passage, and were soon drifting down the Rio Marin itself, past the Church of San Simeon Profeta.

It was now six minutes before noon.

In the dim courtyard of the Casa Albano, Piero di Fossombroni—a mercenary and at present *squadretto* in the service of His Excellency Signor Orso Contarini—looked around his platoon of archers and swore. Like all of them, he would rather have been out in the streets and waterways of the city enjoying the festivities. Guard duty was a tedious business; it was a task they had been performing for more than a month, and their discipline was becoming lax.

No one could deny, however, that the courtyard of the Casa Albano was an easy place to hold—assuming that one had an enemy against which to hold it. It was surrounded on three sides by galleries, and the only access to it was through the narrow, peeling door in the middle of its fourth side. It did not, Piero di Fossombroni considered, require some fifty men to hold the damned place. Dust was blowing here and there, raised in small eddies by the trapped breeze. Above him another score of cross-bowmen strode about the galleries, while a further contingent of foot soldiers spent most of their days lolling in the overheated rooms beyond the arcades at either side.

Girolamo Riario's aide, who had earlier knocked for entrance and been admitted, appeared on the gallery towards the back of the building; he looked down into the courtyard with distaste. By his side stood Uberto Neri, at sight of whom many of the assembled soldiers crossed themselves. His velvet mask gave him, so they thought, the appearance of a walking corpse, or perhaps of Satan himself.

The aide spat over the gallery wall. Piero di Fossombroni swore again, monotonously. The dust settled in the meagre sunshine. Noon approached.

At three minutes to twelve Tesoro di Veluti had put down the polished cannon shot he was holding; he was now removing his costume as the Muse of Heroic Deeds. He tossed aside the woven chaplet of myrtle which had been scratching his temples for the past five hours, unwound from about his shoulders and waist some dozen yards of white and blue muslin, and emerged gratefully from this cocoon as a gunner.

Their boat had left the Rio Marin and was now being urged through a maze of backwaters, deserted except for an occasional seagull or a swimming water rat. The populace of the region was gathered to a man along the banks of the Grand Canal, and had left the poor wharves and chipped façades of the Sestriere di San Polo silent and untenanted. Leonardo had foreseen that this might be so. He had no real objection to fighting an artillery battle surrounded by onlookers if he were obliged to, but was none the less glad to see that he need not.

The canals along which the gunners were proceeding grew narrower and dirtier. Once Leonardo—his eyes upon the clock in front of him—feared for an instant that they had lost their way. But a few seconds later they turned a corner and found themselves in an unnamed and brackish pool, one side of which was the towering rear wall of the Casa Albano.

By good fortune, this pool was moderately wide; its banks had silted up through long disuse and the distance between them was now some seven or eight paces. To starboard the Casa Albano rose sheer from the black and oily surface of the water for three stories, capped by the slightly overhanging gables of three ancient cargo hatches. It seemed both impenetrable and blind, an effect produced by the bricked in windows eight feet above the waterline and by the accumulated grime behind the heavy bars of those on the upper two floors. Its wall had once been faced with yellow stucco, but now showed bare masonry over most of its hundred foot width. Beyond it, at the closed end of the pool, a crumbling pier marked the end of an alleyway, from the depths of which a cat screamed unseen defiance at this invasion of her territory. Otherwise, all was still.

Carefully and quietly, then, the gunners eased their craft against the yielding mud of the bank opposite the building they sought to take. Rigo and Scudo lifted the table top away from the bow cannon, uncovering the four-foot bronze barrel and the screw mechanism that controlled its elevation. At the stern, Agnolo Fulvio and Cipriano did likewise. Both guns were already trained over the starboard gunwale, since Leonardo's careful study of the maps of Venice had shown him that this was the direction in which they would have to face. He walked the length of the boat between one cannon and the other, checking the swivel mounting of the lowered mast as he did so.

Rigo lit a slow match from a canister of glowing tinder, and nodded.

'Sixteen minutes,' said Leonardo. 'No more, or we are lost, Rigo.'

'Look after your own affairs,' Rigo replied. 'And stop fussing like a mother hen over her chicks. All we need from you is your signal.'

Three floors above them, Uberto Neri was leaning with his back against the door of Bianca's prison. He toyed with his mask. Bianca, as was her habit, paced the floor without looking at him.

'Good news, madam,' said Neri. 'It grieves me that you are unable to be out and about in our city at this joyful time; but I bring you good news.'

'And what news is that?' asked Bianca, outwardly disdainful yet with a sinking heart.

'News of Leonardo da Vinci. He will be here soon, Bianca. Therefore rejoice.' His breath hissed behind the velvet. 'How much we all envy you! To have a lover who will surrender himself to disfigurement or death, for your sake alone! Madam, we are spellbound by your beauty and your innocence, and yet . . .'

'Surrender?' interrupted Bianca with disdain. 'I do not believe it.'

'Whether you believe it or not, my lady, it is true. If fortune smiles upon us, you shall see him tonight and judge the truth for yourself. Or perhaps I should say misfortune. For misfortune—like myself, little one—can smile no less than fortune, though her smile may not be as pretty.' He fingered his mask again.

Distracted by his words despite all she might summon to resist their implication, Bianca had strayed to the window. She glanced out of it; she would have looked anywhere at that particular moment, save at Uberto Neri, whether he wore his mask or not.

Through the dusty panes of glass, therefore, she looked down . . .

'Oh!' Bianca said.

Neri mistook the reason for her exclamation, and pressed home his advantage. 'I am sorry to have distressed you,' he said.

Distressed me? she thought. *Distressed* me? Nothing could now distress her. She longed to wave, she burned with the desire to raise her hand in even a momentary gesture. She knew she must not; she must, in fact, do anything in her power to keep Uberto Neri from looking out of the window where she stood. She decided to offer him the gratification he clearly sought.

'You are horrible,' she said, faintly. 'Horrible!'

'No doubt,' Neri replied. 'My face, so to speak, is my misfortune.' He moved away from the door, and came slowly towards her. Bianca watched him as (so she fondly hoped) a rabbit might watch a stoat. She raised a hand to her neck, turned from the window, and sank down on her bed. This show of weakness delighted Neri, who stood over her. 'And tonight,' he said, 'as he has done to me, so shall I do to him, little Florentine.'

'I am a Milanese,' said Bianca. Her mind was awhirl. A moment ago his words, his obscene gloating, the knowledge of the terrible things he had done and would undoubtedly do, had possessed the power to thrust her into despair. Now, all had changed; he was nothing, less than nothing. 'I'm sorry,' she said. 'What did you say?'

Uberto Neri looked down at her with sudden suspicion, and then turned towards the window. But he was too late.

From the Church of San Giacomo del'Orio nearby, a chime of bells rang out.

It was noon.

Seconds later, from across the city, came the boom of a signal cannon, followed by another from the shore batteries of the Lido, in greeting to the sun's zenith. Then, incredulously, Neri felt the foundations of the building shake, and a blast of shattering sound rose from somewhere beneath him. Bianca threw back her head and laughed aloud in joyous triumph.

'Leonardo is early, I think,' she said.

With the slow match gripped between the split halves of his hooked hand, Rigo Leone stood back from the bow cannon and shouted for his crew to reload. He breathed in that scent which was more to him than all the perfumes of the East—the pungent and sulphurous tang of burned gunpowder whose smoke billowed all about him.

The air was full of flying masonry chips. Brown dust mingled with the powder smoke and rolled across the surface of the pool. The boat rocked, its port gunwale driven hard against the yielding mud by the recoil of Rigo's weapons, then regained an even keel. At his right, beyond Leonardo, Agnolo Fulvio pushed the breech of the other cannon fractionally to one side and turned the range screw, while his loader dropped a second ball into its tilted muzzle. Leonardo, assisted by Scudo and Piccio Berignalli, was manhandling the boat's lowered mast from where it lay fore-and-aft. The three began to tilt its end over the starboard rail.

The smoke cleared, and Rigo could see his target. His ears sang from the thunderous twin explosions confined within the walls of the canal. A wall of masonry at six paces is hardly a target in any real sense, Rigo thought to himself. He surveyed the rent which his shot, travelling at some five hundred feet per second, at virtually point-blank range, had torn in the fabric of the Casa Albano. Agnolo's shot had driven home ten feet to the right of his own, and had smashed a similiar breach, but neither was big enough—and then his gun was ready again to hurl destruction. He held the slow match to the gummed and powder filled quill that Leonardo had designed to replace the usual touch-train. The cannon bellowed, leaped, rolled backward, slammed against the far gunwale, and was hauled forward by its crew.

Brute force, Rigo said to himself; it is not what these guns were built for. They were designed to throw four-pound shot for a thousand yards and strike no more than a foot from their point of aim, but no matter. He shook his head, and beat the dust from his shoulders with his left hand. Glancing at Leonardo once more he thought, the man is a gunner and yet he is not one; he is one of us and my friend, and the woman he loves is held captive, in danger. And yet he sees that rage will not serve him, he sees the end and the means all together; he moves coolly, unhurriedly, his mind is not cluttered—as mine is—with the sense of power that

203

cannon give to the gunner. For him these beautiful weapons he has designed are tools to get him what he wants, while for me they are something different. They are my fists, my hands, my fingers; I reach out with them and destroy, batter, breach, rip asunder my enemies, not human enemies but inanimate ones: walls, turrets, gates, redoubts. Be damned to grapeshot, he thought, to hell with it; any fool can cut down ten, twenty men, fifty at a time with grapeshot; it may be necessary but it is not gunnery.

This is gunnery, Rigo told himself, looking again through the smoke and seeing that this time Agnolo's second shot had pounded home exactly where his own had struck, offering a rent twelve feet across and eight high towards which Leonardo was already extending the boat's mast to act as a gang plank. He is passionless, thought Rigo fondly, as a saint is passionless or an angel perhaps; untouched, calm, serene. Yet I know this is not the whole truth about him. It is rather that his passions are greater than ours, that he conceals them even from himself in order not to be torn apart by them; he will never make his peace with the world, but he may succeed in making peace with himself. Without hesitation he has brought fifteen of us against a city in order to win back Bianca Visconti, whom he loves; and the proof of our love for him is that we followed him. And what, Rigo wondered, does that tell us about him, and about ourselves?

In the courtyard, Piero di Fossombroni and his defending force were in dire confusion.

His crossbowmen and archers lined the walls of the galleries overhead, ready to discharge their bolts and shafts. The courtyard was as secure, as easily defensible, as it had always been, but no assault upon it was being made. The rear wall of the building had been breached, but none here in the courtyard could see that this was so, for between rear wall and courtyard lay the intervening rooms of the house. Through the windows of these rooms the first drifts of smoke were beginning to seep, and Fossombroni had felt the ground beneath his feet tremble at the impact of cannon shot. Yet most of his men, sheep like, were still looking towards the front gate, since it was from this direction that they had been told to expect any attack that might come.

After a half minute of indecision, a pikeman whose wits were sharper than those of his fellows threw open a door at the back of the courtyard and, followed by three others, made for the source of the commotion. Racing down a corridor, they met Leonardo, Scudo, and Piccio Berignalli, all of whom had just stepped off the end of the mast which now formed a footbridge from their boat. Scudo was in the act of wedging its tip into a crack in the torn masonry at the foot of the breach, in order to keep it steady for the gunners who were making ready to follow. He straightened up at the sight of the defenders running toward him, gathered the first man into his arms, and smashed him into the side of the corridor, as he held him by the neck.

'Where is the woman?' he asked.

The pikeman, whose halberd had fallen from his nerveless hands clattering across the tiles, rolled terrified eyes and—since he could not speak—pointed upwards. Scudo shook him, tossed him through the gap in the wall into the canal, and grabbed Leonardo by the shoulder. The latter disengaged himself from swordplay; leaving Piccio Berignalli to face the remaining defenders in the corridor until reinforcements arrived, they made their way to the foot of the nearest staircase.

The small hallway around this was already a seething mass of bodies as more defenders and gunners joined the fray. The turmoil was largely purposeless, since few besides Leonardo and Scudo had any clear objective. The defenders, still disordered, had lost any advantage they might have had under normal circumstances. They ought by rights to have been fighting in a disciplined manner in the open courtyard, not brawling in a confined space at close quarters; they were shouting and ignoring commands in equal proportion. As for the gunners, they were in their element. They cared not where they might be going, so long as they could see opponents before them to kick, gouge, or beat senseless with axle spikes. Roaring happily, therefore, they fell upon the luckless Venetians, the foremost among whom were attempting to follow Leonardo and Scudo up the stairs. Scudo broke loose the entire lower section of the banister rail, and his pursuers fell among the waiting gunners below them as though among a pack of wolves. Scudo watched the heaving battle for a few seconds until he was sure that his companions had things well in hand, and then lumbered his massive way to the floors above.

In the boat at the far side of the canal, Rigo issued his orders; Guccio Berotti, Marco di Carona, Tesoro and Balestraccio were to stay and man the guns, a task which they accepted with sour grace.

'You cannot play the Muse again with a rapier slash across your face, infant,' he told Tesoro. 'Therefore, preserve your beauty. Load one more ball—and you, Guccio, charge with grape. And after I have whistled thus'—Rigo did so, placing the fingers of his left hand against his teeth and blowing a shrill blast—'cease fire altogether. I do not wish to be blown to fragments by my own guns.'

With that, he followed Cipriano across the mast-bridge, and joined the fray beyond the breach in the wall.

'Stay where you are,' Neri hissed. 'Stand *quite* still. Very good.'

Leonardo froze in the doorway of the upper floor suite. Scudo almost thrust past him into the room, but Leonardo shot out an arm and barred his way.

Neri was at the window. One of his arms held Bianca tightly around the waist, while his other hand held a dagger at her neck. Her face was white, but the sight of Leonardo had brought a smile to her lips that belied her situation.

'He does not dare,' she said. 'He knows that if he kills me, his own life is not worth a straw.'

'Well reasoned,' said Neri into her ear. 'But reason is not everything, as you will see.' From behind the mask of velvet, his eyes gleamed. 'Put down your sword,' he commanded.

Leonardo threw his rapier across the room.

'What do you hope for?' he asked.

'Time,' Neri replied. 'What else? Time for your men to lose whatever battle they imagine they are waging. When they are cornered we can begin anew. Nothing has changed.'

He was wrong. Footsteps sounded in the corridor outside.

'Disarm him, too,' said Neri quickly. 'Whoever it may be.'

'I am not armed,' Rigo said, stepping into the room. 'You might even say that I am less than armed.' He stretched his right arm, and the split halves of his hook snapped together with a click, like a lobster's claw. He had brought with him the stink of brimstone, as though it were a faint reek from the depths of hell.

For a fraction of an instant, at the sight of the gunner, Neri relaxed his grip on Bianca's body. It was nothing, it was less than a hint of opportunity. Bianca seized it at once. She wrenched sideways, pulled free of his arm, felt the swift burn of the dagger's edge across her neck; she threw herself not—as another woman might have done—towards Leonardo, but away from him and into a corner, so as not to impede any action he might take.

He took none. Indeed, when Scudo began to move, Leonardo stopped him again with a touch.

Rigo advanced on Uberto Neri, who raised the stiletto. The gunner looked at it with contempt, and disregarded it. He was two paces away from the Venetian when he began to swing his right arm, adding to its momentum that of his own body. The metal hook glinted in the sunlight, and the deadly thump of its impact seemed to fill the room as it drove through cloth, skin, flesh, and bone. Neri's breath whistled, and the stiletto fell from his hand. He stood in a posture of surprise, dying on his feet. The point of the hook had sunk deep into his chest, tearing open his lungs and piercing the very chambers of his heart, and a terrible pressure behind his breastbone was squeezing his life away. It appeared as though he were trying to say something, but no sound came from the black hole in his mask that served him for a mouth. Rigo twisted the hook out of his ribs, and he leaned sideways slowly, and fell.

'God rot his soul,' said Rigo.

'Amen to that,' Leonardo said. He was holding Bianca close, his hands in her hair. Blood from a long gash across her cheek crimsoned her bodice, but she paid it no heed. She was alive, and Leonardo was with her, and there was nothing else that mattered.

Seventeen

ON THE LOWER floors of the Casa Albano, chaos reigned.

Piero di Fossombroni, the luckless commander of the Venetian defenders, was unable to form any clear idea of what might be going on. His crossbowmen were already on the second floor gallery when the engagement started, while the attacking Florentine gunners were either fighting on the ground floor or else—in the case of Rigo, Scudo, and Leonardo—were cut off in the upper story. Fossombroni's arbalesters, therefore, could easily have occupied the rooms and landings in between and would thereby have put the Florentines at a tactical disadvantage.

But this they had not done.

Instead, and almost to a man, they had streamed down the stairways at either end of the gallery to join their leader in the courtyard, hoping for instructions. It was true that a body of them, bolder than the rest, had forced their way as far as the breach in the rear wall of the building. Seeing them, Guccio Berotti at once fired his charge of grapeshot in their direction, decimating them. Those who were able to do so retreated to the courtyard again in great haste, and gave Fossombroni a garbled account of what they had seen. The *squadretto* thereupon scratched his head, summoned eight of those who were clamouring around him, and sent them out through the front gate of the courtyard to summon help.

'Find Signor Orso Contarini,' he told them, 'and also the Roman Captain-General, Count Girolamo Riario. And in Christ's name, make haste! I need swordsmen and pikemen!'

This was true enough, in its way. Crossbowmen are highly effective for defence at long range, but serve no purpose whatever at close quarters. Whether he liked it or not, Fossombroni was already faced with close-quarter fighting. A dozen crossbows in the hallway at the foot of the stairs would have made not the slightest difference to the balance of power there, since any bolt discharged from them would have been as likely to kill one of his own men as a Florentine.

On the top floor of the house, Scudo opened a window in Bianca's prison by the simple means of grasping its bars and wrenching it bodily, frame and all, from the surrounding brickwork. With Rigo beside him, he peered out to see how matters stood.

Leonardo was in the passageway beyond the open door, holding Bianca's hand. They were standing, he thought, somewhere below the cargo loft whose gabled doors he had seen as they approached the building, and he had now found in the ceiling a trap which seemed as though it might give access to this loft. He reached up and pushed at it with the tip of his rapier. It gave slightly, and he summoned Scudo with a shout.

'Hoist me,' he said.

Scudo made a stance by linking his hands together at waist level, and Leonardo used it to clamber onto his shoulders. He heaved at the trap door, and it fell back, revealing a vast attic deep in dust and littered with forgotten debris. Bales of decayed cloth stood in dark corners, their wrappings gnawed away long since by generations of rats. But what drew his attention were the tangles of rope and the wooden tackles which, though unused for years, had once served to winch up goods from the holds of boats lying in the canal basin below.

He pulled himself up into the attic, and crossed its floor to the outer wall. Here he kicked open a pair of rotting doors beneath the central gable and found himself, as he had expected, gazing down at the black waters and swirling gun smoke some forty tâ fifty feet beneath him. Tesoro di Veluti caught sight of him, and cheered.

Leonardo came back to the trap door and called down through it.

'Scudo ?'

'Yes.'

'Tell Captain Leone to sound retreat. Bianca, how is your wound ?'

'I shall survive it,' his lady answered. 'What have you found up there ?'

'Cobwebs and grime,' said Leonardo. 'Scudo, lift her, if you will.'

He lay beside the trap and held his arms down towards her. Scudo raised her as though she were a child, and a moment later she was sitting beside Leonardo with her legs dangling. He kissed her.

'Five minutes more,' he promised, 'and you shall lie at your ease upon a silken couch. Think of that.'

'So soon ?'

'Why, yes. We have enough silk to clothe the whole of Venice.' He laid the palm of his hand gently against her neck. She was still bleeding, although less severely than he had feared. 'Come,' he said, as he rose and helped her to her feet. 'One last effort, and we are there.'

'You need not be so solicitous, Leonardo. I am no fragile and terrified maiden seeking for reassurance. Or, at least,' she added, 'I am not any more.'

Rigo Leone went to the head of the stairs, where he blew an ear-splitting whistle.

'Scudo,' he ordered, 'go down there and see that all is well. Find Cipriano, and hold the rear while they retreat.'

'And what about you ?' demanded the massive gunner.

'I'll find my own way. Do you suppose I am going to stay for ever in this flea-ridden Venetian hole ? Get the rest out.'

Scudo took steps down the stairway, and stopped.

'If you are thinking of jumping, Captain,' he said, 'you'll be sorry.'

'I intend to sprout wings and fly,' retorted Rigo with some

irritation. 'Get down there before I stuff my boot up your backside.'

On reaching the ground floor, Scudo found the gunners reluctant to end the fight with those few Venetians who remained to oppose them. He fought his way across the hall, cursing Florentines and Venetians impartially, and managed to reach Cipriano, who was fighting with a tall infantryman. Scudo picked the unfortunate Venetian up by his breeches, hurled him across the room, as he shouted Rigo's orders into Cipriano's ear. Their own casualties appeared to be only Tomasello Cennini, whose nose was gushing scarlet, and Piccio Berignalli who lay unconscious in a corner. Scudo promptly draped him over one shoulder, and followed Cipriano back to the boat.

'Put your arms around my neck,' Leonardo said.

He had strung together sufficient rope, he judged, for their descent, and now hitched one end of this to a rafter that spanned the central gable. Holding the rope in one hand and supporting Bianca with the other, he leaned perilously from the doorway and immediately saw Rigo, who was sitting on the broken window ledge eight feet below him. Down in the canal basin, Balestraccio and Giunta di Lenzo were already thrusting the boat clear of the mud at the opposite bank. The first gunners to come aboard helped some of their comrades from the water and then swung the mast back to its original position fore-and-aft.

'All accounted for,' said Rigo from his ledge. He shaded his eyes with his left hand and squinted up at Leonardo. 'Can you manage?'

'If they bring the boat a little closer to this side,' Leonardo said. 'We have no wish to get our feet wet.'

'Don't stand there for ever, then,' rejoined Rigo, and jumped. He hit the water with a resounding splash and found it, as Scudo had prophesied, shallower than he had bargained for. He lost one of his boots while kicking free from the muck, a performance which was greeted with derisive cheers from his subordinates.

The boat drifted across the pool almost directly beneath

Leonardo. He held Bianca more tightly, felt for the rope with the soles of his feet and his knees, and allowed himself to swing outwards. He looked down, and saw that Cipriano had caught the lower end of the rope and pulled it aboard. He slackened his knee grip to slide down the rope. Bianca closed her eyes. His descent was neither as graceful nor as nonchalant as he had hoped. They fell across Scudo and the reviving Piccio in a tangle of arms and legs.

'Welcome,' said Cipriano. He was about to add some frivolous comment in order to cheer Bianca. At the sight of her wound he checked himself. As Balestraccio and Giunta di Lenzo, backing hard their oars, drove the boat stern foremost out of the mouth of the pool and into its neighbouring waterway, he began to tear strips of muslin from the fabrics beside her. Together with Leonardo he gently washed her face with clean water from a flask.

'It was almost like flying,' said Bianca.

Five minutes later, they emerged into the Rio Marin.

Some semblance of order had been restored to the boat and its occupants, though their Pastoral Scene showed signs of damage from which it would never fully recover.

As Leonardo had promised her, Bianca reposed on a coverlet of orange silk. He had not told her that she would be concealed from the eyes of the world beneath the feet of Tesoro di Veluti with the still warm barrel of the bow-cannon a bare arm's length from the top of her head. She had no great objection to her situation, since she perceived the need for concealment, but she was far from comfortable.

Above her, Tesoro was having little difficulty in transforming himself once again into Clio, the Muse of Heroic Deeds. His face was streaked with grime and the crown of myrtle leaves was somewhat awry. He searched for the symbolic cannon ball to hold aloft and found it in the forepeak. He would pass.

Some distance behind him lay a Rustic who was clearly in the last stages of drunken stupor. This was the unfortunate Piccio Berignalli who had a lump the size of a goose egg on the back of his skull and a splitting headache. By his side, Tomasello Cennini appeared to find his companion's smell offensive, to judge from the square of silk he held firmly over his mouth and nostrils. Fortunately, perhaps, the silk was itself crimson, thus disguising the fact that it was slowly becoming soaked with his blood. Elsewhere in the boat the Satyrs and Shepherds gave the curious impression of having recently been engaged in some sort of small fracas. They were cut and bruised and some were dripping wet.

Toward the stern, only Cipriano, dressed as a Shepherd, and Leonardo himself—returned to his former illustrious rank as Homer—were tolerably clean and tidy. Leonardo, with a bemused look on his face, studied the clock that stood on the table in front of him.

Though it was true, he supposed, that the instrument might have suffered some damage during the cannonade it informed him that what had seemed like an hour or more of frantic conflict had, in fact, taken a bare fifteen minutes. Accordingly, they would be able to resume their place in the cavalcade of boats. The tail end of the procession would not yet have passed the point at which they hoped to enter the Grand Canal.

'We must hurry,' he said.

In the loggia of the Ca' d'Oro, Lorenzo de' Medici found himself beside the Steward of Festivities, and laid a hand on that worthy's arm.

'Tell me something,' he said.

'Yes, my lord?'

'The noon volley. The salute?'

'Yes, my lord?'

'It seems to me,' said Lorenzo, 'that you told us it would come from the *Palazzo Ducale* and from the Lido. And yet it also seemed to me that, while the first ten shots were indeed fired from our left, there were some five more that came from over there.' He pointed directly across the canal. 'They were about half a mile distant, if I am any judge,' the Ruler of Florence concluded.

'My lord,' said the Steward in some agitation, 'I confess to being a little puzzled by the matter myself. I heard them. They were...' he searched for a word that would convey the full extent of his disapproval, '... unscheduled, my lord. Yes, indeed. I conclude that some of the rougher elements in our city—who are somewhat excitable—were exploding fireworks.'

'Hm,' said Lorenzo, looking at him keenly. 'They were over loud for fireworks, in my opinion. But never mind.'

The Steward turned away and stared to the right along the Grand Canal, where the end of the procession of boats had now come within sight. After a moment he laid his scroll upon the rail of the balcony, and examined it with a frown.

'What is the matter?' asked Lorenzo, idly curious.

'I beg your pardon, my lord. It is nothing of importance.' As with all men, the Steward was secretly gratified to find somebody taking an apparent interest in his concerns. 'It is merely that I seem to have one boat too many,' he went on, and studied his list again with keen concentration. 'It is really most odd.'

'Is it?'

'*Most* odd, my lord. I do not quite understand...' here the Steward surveyed the ten or so boats that formed the last of the cavalcade, and once again consulted the check marks he had made against the margin of his schedule. 'We have the fish sellers,' he said. 'Then the glass blowers under Master Rafaello Lazzarini... and then... my lord?'

'What is it?'

'Your eyesight may be keener than mine. If your lordship would do me the favour... it is the sixth boat from the rear that concerns me, you see. I cannot tell whose it may be. It has a figure, my lord, in white and blue, standing in the prow.'

'My dear sir,' said Lorenzo indulgently, as the boat in question drew nearer, 'being a visitor in your excellent and most gracious city, I scarcely see how I can help you. I will certainly describe it for you, if you wish. It has, indeed, a figure such as you describe, wearing a robe and a crown of some sort on her head. She is holding a silver sphere. It is an allegory, I dare say. There—there is... there seems to be...'

215

'My lord?'

'*Good God in heaven*,' breathed Lorenzo de' Medici.

He had just recognised Rigo Leone, whose right hand lay concealed under his sodden doublet. Behind him was the unmistakable Scudo, and a little to their left in the stern——

'It is certainly an allegory,' Lorenzo said, clearing his throat briskly. 'With shepherds and satyrs and the like. The man at the table,' he went on with a touch of spleen in his voice, 'I take to represent a poet. Homer, possibly. Beyond that, I'm afraid . . .'

'Your lordship is most kind,' the Steward said. He was still uneasy.

His uneasiness was, however, nothing compared with that of Lorenzo de' Medici, whose mind was seething. He had no idea of course, why his gunners should be here. They ought to have been seven hundred miles away in Malta, or possibly on their way back from that island to Florence.

Nor had their battered appearance escaped Lorenzo's eye. Rapidly linking all this with the unscheduled cannon fire he had heard, Lorenzo de' Medici concluded—to put it in the mildest possible terms—that his damned gunners, under the leadership of the thrice blasted Leonardo da Vinci, had for reasons unknown declared war upon, and invaded, the Sovereign and Most Serene Republic of Venice. With whom, he further reminded himself, gritting his teeth, he was at that moment seeking desperately to conclude a treaty of non-aggression.

More questions rose to his mind at once. Where, for instance, was his ward, Bianca Visconti? And where, for the matter of that, was the clock? He had no need whatever to ask himself where his two cannon might be; the misbegotten wretches were undoubtedly standing on them.

Preserving a carefully neutral face, Lorenzo leaned over the balcony rail.

Almost immediately, Tesoro di Veluti caught sight of him. After an instant of surprise, the young gunner waved with his free hand and turned to draw the attention of Tomasello Cennini to the fact that their city's ruler was standing directly above the boat.

Tomasello, equally taken aback, lowered the crimson square from his face, disclosing a half congealed trickle of gore running down the side of his mouth and into his beard.

Lorenzo de' Medici closed his eyes, as though stricken by some brief internal agony.

When he opened them again, the boat had drifted some yards to his left, and was now beneath the balcony occupied by the Doge of Venice. Horrified Lorenzo watched as Cipriano di Lucca, deliberately and gravely lifted a finger in an obscene gesture. Lorenzo was scarcely able to believe his eyes at this crowning piece of impudence. He turned to see what reaction it might have provoked and found Girolamo Riario standing at the Doge's right hand.

The Count was staring downward with a terrible and malign expression on his face, when suddenly there sprang to Lorenzo's mind certain possibilities that he had hitherto overlooked. It could not be said that all was yet clear to him. But as his rage evaporated, he began to calculate and to consider.

At the far side of the Grand Canal, a harquebus was fired, and then a second. A group of men in uniform, gesticulating wildly, had gathered by the water's edge in the mouth of an alley, and a pair of skiffs were being launched.

Rome and Venice, thought Lorenzo.

Casually, and amid a rising hum of indignation from those around him, he began to drift his way across the loggia to the balcony where the Doge was sitting.

Some seven minutes after their show of effrontery, the gunners found themselves approaching the Rialto bridge. Its central wooden span, hinged after the fashion of a drawbridge, had been raised before dawn to prevent too great a throng of townspeople from seeking to cross it. It was the only means, other than by boat, of crossing the Grand Canal, and it had once collapsed during just such a procession as was now passing beneath it. At both ends cheerful spectators crowded the approaches leading to the centre of the bridge.

It became clear to Leonardo that the hunt for them had begun. A platoon of soldiers, reinforced by officers of the watch, was battling its way through the citizens packed together on the right-hand portion of the bridge and an attempt was being made to lower the bascule.

'Tesoro?' he called. 'Are any of them carrying crossbows?'

'I see none,' Tesoro replied.

Scudo glanced behind them. 'They will not use crossbows in any case, as we are but a handspan from our neighbours. They will try to board us.'

'Let them try,' said Rigo.

Scudo was quite correct in his judgment. As they glided beneath the bridge, several soldiers jumped from its parapet, to the loud cheers of the onlookers. The Venetian crowd assumed this was all a splendid piece of nonsense, designed for their amusement and to enliven the end of the procession. Two of the soldiers landed in the boat, and were promptly tossed overboard by Cipriano and Scudo. One clutched at Balestraccio's oar, and was soundly beaten over the head with it for his pains. The rest, who were leaping from a considerable height, missed their target entirely and were forced to swim for the boats behind.

The gunners rowed on, leaving the cavalcade and edging to their left. Marco di Caroni and Guccio Berotti, on the instructions of Leonardo, stepped the mast and secured its foot to the swivelling tabernacle he had built for it. The others, abandoning all pretence of the tableau, hauled it upright and tightened its stays. Tesoro di Veluti for the last time unwound himself gratefully from the copious layers of muslin that were draped about him, and prodded Piccio Berignalli with his foot.

'Up,' he said.

'My head,' protested his victim. 'I am a wounded man, Tesoro.'

'Your head is as solid as this cannon ball,' rejoined Tesoro unsympathetically, 'and contains as little sense. Get on your feet. Walk with the others, or sail with Agnolo and myself. It is all one to me.'

'I'll walk,' said Piccio.

The prow of the boat touched the quay by the Palazzo Loredan, a little way past the Rialto Bridge on the eastern shore of the canal. Here, Leonardo helped Bianca tenderly from her hiding place. The Florentines disembarked, except for Tesoro and Agnolo Fulvio who were to sail the boat onwards. Rigo, in his stockinged feet, cursed roundly at the cobbles, as they all set off through the streets of Venice.

'My lords,' said the Steward, in great distress. 'My lords! I implore your forgiveness and your understanding! A terrible affair but the responsibility is not mine!'

'Peace, in God's name,' said the Doge. 'There is no need for this display of ... well, in short, good Steward, what are we speaking of here ? No more than a discourteous gesture ?'

They had gathered on a private balcony in the Ca' d'Oro, the doors of which had been firmly closed against the clamour in the loggia. At the Doge's right stood Girolamo Riario and the First Secretary to the Council of Five, Orso Contarini; at his left, Lorenzo de' Medici. The unhappy Steward, whom the Doge privately wished would go to the devil, was pacing up and down, delicately wringing his hands.

'Who were they, in any case?' asked the Doge. 'And cease flapping your damned parchment in my face.'

'My lord, that is the difficulty,' cried the Steward. 'I do not know!'

'Do not know?' said Riario, between his teeth. 'And I say you lie.'

'Oh ?' said Lorenzo, staring at him.

There was a discreet knock at the door, and Piero di Fossombroni entered. It had taken him some time to cross the Grand Canal, and he was in any case in a dilemma. With Lorenzo de' Medici and the Count Riario present, he could not be sure of how much of Venetian affairs he should now disclose.

'Well, sir ?' demanded the Doge.

'My lord,' said Fossombroni, 'I must report that the Casa

Albano has been attacked and—ah—severely damaged. Those who did it seem to have escaped.'

'Yes,' said the Doge patiently. 'And who were these miscreants?'

Fossombroni looked from Riario to Contarini, and swallowed.

'I am afraid, my lord, that I do not know,' he said. 'Except that they were gunners.'

'Gunners?' put in Lorenzo de' Medici. 'How extraordinary.'

'Indeed,' the Doge said. 'And were they Venetians, these gunners, or were they strangers?'

'Sir, they were in costume,' replied Fossombroni, 'and therefore——'

At this Riario lost his temper, and swung on Lorenzo.

'They were Medici gunners, damn you,' he said bitterly. '*Florentines*. And led by your bastard engineer Leonardo da Vinci!' He turned to the Doge. 'This is an act of war,' he continued, 'a treacherous assault upon the City of Venice at a time of peace and goodwill. So much for Florence. You will, my lord, draw your own conclusions, or so I trust.'

Lorenzo coughed behind his hand.

'I hate to interrupt your fantasies, Count,' he said mildly, 'But although I have been called many things, I am not known as a fool. May I point out that I am a guest in Venice, and hence I am unlikely to commit acts of war, as you describe them. As for your manners, I find them distressing. Let us hope that Florence, in due course, finds time to correct them.'

The Doge held up his hand. 'My lord Lorenzo,' he said. 'No matter how things stand between Florence and Rome, you and I are at present neither friends nor foes. Answer me straightly, then. Were the men in that boat Florentines?'

'Why,' replied Lorenzo, 'it is my devout prayer that you will apprehend them and uncover the whole truth of this unfortunate affair. You will doubtless deal with them as you see fit.'

'We shall hang them,' said the Doge. 'What then?'

'Do so with my blessing,' Lorenzo said. 'And now, if your lordships will excuse me, I must leave you to your own devices.

If you have further need of me, I shall be at the Medici villa on Murano. Or do you propose to detain me?'

'No,' replied the Doge. 'No, I think not.'

'Now?' said Tesoro di Veluti.

'Not yet,' replied Agnolo Fulvio. They were perhaps two hundred paces offshore, in the middle of the inner lagoon of San Marco. The sail they had hoisted as they left the mouth of the Grand Canal filled and flapped alternately, since they were far from expert mariners. But they were drawing away from the Ducal Palace to their north and approaching the island of San Giorgio Maggiore, beyond which lay the broad expanse of the outer lagoon.

To the right of the palace they could see the flashing of a heliograph from the top of the Arsenal. They had no doubt of the message it signalled; it was calling the heavy shore batteries of the Lido to fire upon them as soon as they cleared the tip of the island and open water.

Their task was a straightforward one; to draw off pursuit from the rest of their party, and then to scuttle the boat and its cannon. These could not be allowed to fall into the hands of Venice, and would be better at the bottom of the lagoon.

They held their course steadily, and continued to watch the distant mirror wink in the sunlight.

North and west of the Arsenal, the gunners were launching a workboat which Leonardo had hired from a trader in leather and hides. If the merchant had felt any surprise at the sight of a party of battered foreigners escorting a young woman whose dress was soaked with blood from neck to waist, he gave no sign of it; though he did charge them twice what his vessel would have fetched on the open market.

Leonardo sat on the foredeck, his arm around Bianca's shoulders.

'Safe, I think,' he said. 'Except from the wrath of Lorenzo.'

'And why should he be angry?' asked Bianca. 'You have rescued me and therefore you have done him a service.'

221

'Very true, but that will not help us. For some reason,' said Leonardo innocently, 'the mere sight of me is enough to send him into a passion. It is like a fact of nature. One must accept it.'

'But,' objected Bianca, 'by the time we get back to Florence . . . surely . . .'

'Unless I miss the mark we shall meet Lorenzo before we reach Florence,' Leonardo said. 'Do not ask me how I know. You might say that it is inevitable, just as his fury will be inevitable.'

On the island of San Giorgio Maggiore, Tesoro and Agnolo stripped off their wet garments and set these to dry in the sun. Their boat, from which they had recently swum ashore, was sailing proudly across the lagoon, its tiller lashed to starboard and its sail curved and full. As they watched it, they saw the first plumes of smoke blossom from the fortifications at the eastern end of the Lido. A moment later the heavy boom of artillery reached their ears. Water spouted upwards some fifty paces ahead of the little vessel which forged on unheeding.

'Poor,' said Agnolo Fulvio. 'Very poor. It will take them all afternoon to sink her at this rate.'

'Let them take all afternoon, then,' Tesoro said. 'Are you in any hurry? We cannot move from here until nightfall.'

'Just so. And therefore, infant, I am going to sleep. Wake me if they score a hit.'

Eighteen

'NEVER MIND MY ward. What of my alliance?'

'With whom?'

'With Venice,' said Lorenzo de' Medici thinly. 'I realise how ungrateful it is of me to bring these small details to your notice, but Florence remains at war with Rome. Or perhaps you had forgotten?'

'Well,' said Leonardo, 'Venice will not trouble you.'

'Not trouble me? Venice will not trouble me?'

'Lower your voice, sir, if you please,' said Leonardo. 'Your ward is in the next cabin.'

'I know that. She is wounded, and you have gallantly rescued her from death, and you still hope for my permission to wed her. You are not likely to get it. You have invaded Venice with your cannon——'

'*Your* cannon, sir. I am always having to remind you of the fact. And Venice will be occupied with the Turks, this year or next. So, for the matter of that, will Rome. Perhaps the whole of Italy. It is time her duchies and republics stopped quarrelling among themselves like children and considered who their common enemies may be. France, the Turks, and Spain.'

'Thank you,' said Lorenzo with heavy irony. 'Italy will be indebted to you for your advice. Where is the clock you promised me?'

'It was delivered to your villa, sir, three hours ago.'

'Then send a man to bring it back,' said Lorenzo. 'Captain Leone?'

'Yes, sir?' said Rigo. He was sitting at the far side of the great stern cabin of the *Juno*, from whose forward deck the voices of the Medici Gunners could be heard, raucously uplifted in song.

'This ship sails with the tide tomorrow morning,' said Lorenzo. 'Are your two missing men on board yet?'

'They are, sir.'

'Then inform Captain Molfetta of my orders. Tell him, also, that I shall be sailing with you.'

'Ah ha!' said Leonardo.

The Ruler of Florence regarded him narrowly. 'Have you any objection?' he inquired.

'None whatever, sir,' replied Leonardo. 'We shall be greatly honoured by your presence. But it is a long voyage.'

'And you would like to know my reasons for making it. They are three. I have no wish to ride across Italy in high summer when I have a perfectly comfortable ship at my disposal. I prefer to keep both my ward, the lady Bianca Visconti, and my clock, where I can see them. And finally, with myself on board, *this ship will sail to Florence*. If I leave you in command, Leonardo,' said Lorenzo de' Medici, 'it is more likely that you will choose to explore Africa or possibly annex Sicily; God knows what! Am I unjust in this, or prudent?'

'Unjust,' said Leonardo.

'Prudent,' Rigo Leone said. 'Sir, may I fetch you some wine?'